Champagne Book Group

Presents

Smile and Walk Away
Shatter, Book 1

By

Danielle Riedel

This is a work of fiction. The characters, incidents and dialogues in this book are of the author's imagination and are not to be construed as real. Any resemblance to actual events or persons, living or dead, is completely coincidental.

No part of this book may be reproduced or transmitted in any form or by any means, electronic or mechanical, including photocopying, recording, or by any information storage and retrieval system, without permission in writing from the publisher.

Champagne Book Group
www.champagnebooks.com
Copyright 2017 by Danielle Riedel
ISBN 978-1548989767
July 2017
Cover Art by Shiela Stewart
Produced in the United States of America

Champagne Book Group
P.O. Box 467
Oregon City OR 97045
USA

Dedication

In loving memory of Adrienne Mira Jarrett.

Prologue

The agent sat in a comfortable chair facing a blank screen. He wore a cuff around his upper right arm and had plastic clips over the tips of his right index and ring fingers. Rubber tubes were wrapped around his chest and abdomen. His head was shaved, and his scalp was covered in small white sensors. Wires from everything attached to his body were connected to a tabletop machine.

The doctor situated himself behind the machine with a pencil, a notepad, and a cup of coffee. A third man stood off to the side next to a projector. The agent in the chair couldn't see either of them. Plastic panels extended eight inches out from each of his temples so that he could only see what was right in front of him.

"If you're ready, Agent Majors, we're going to show you a series of images."

"Ready when you are, doctor."

"Excellent," said the doctor. He nodded to the man at the projector. An image came up on the screen of a child on a swing set. "I'm using the same electroencephalograph as the last time you were here," he continued. "If the results today match your baseline electroencephalogram, within a small range of course, we can move on to the next phase of testing." The doctor fixed his eyes on the monitor screen in front of him. The image on the projector screen changed to one of a dog urinating on a tree.

The agent relaxed as he looked at pictures of dolphins swimming beside a fishing boat, butterflies flying over a meadow, and a puppy catching a Frisbee. Two minutes passed, and those images became interspersed with ones of car crashes, open-heart surgeries, and amputees. Each photograph lingered on the projector screen for about three or four seconds. The doctor remained focused on the screen of the electroencephalograph.

Agent Majors saw three seconds of a nude woman on horseback, then four seconds of a man attempting to crawl out of the wreckage of his home after an earthquake. He saw four seconds of a new mother nursing her baby, then three seconds of a lion tearing apart a dead gazelle. The man at the projector was silent as he performed his simple task, and the doctor periodically glanced away from the screen to make a note or to sip his coffee.

The images became more graphic, ranging from sexual to grotesque. Pleasant and relaxing pictures would show up in between, but the contrast became more dramatic. The doctor continued his notes and observations. He picked up his coffee mug as the image changed from two women caressing each other's breasts to a child sobbing as a man prepared to strike him. The coffee mug shattered in the doctor's hand before it reached his lips. He cursed, but gestured for the man at the projector to continue. With the tail of his lab coat, he managed to stop the coffee spill from reaching the machine.

"Everything okay, doctor?" Agent Majors asked.

"I just spilled my coffee, it's fine. Focus, please." The doctor sat down, ignoring the small brown puddle and mug shards at his feet. *It was a cheap mug.*

The agent focused as he was told. The doctor wrote notes without looking at his paper, determined not to take his eyes away from the monitor.

An image came up of three kittens nestled together in a basket. The doctor signaled to the man at the projector that he should pause on this. He signaled again for him to proceed, but only after almost ten seconds had passed. Next, a picture appeared of those same three kittens screaming in agony as two adolescent boys set them on fire.

The doctor made no move to write anything. Then his pencil snapped in half with a distinct, high-pitched crack. The doctor laid down his notepad and the two halves of his pencil with shaking hands. His eyes widened as he looked from his monitor to the now kaleidoscopic image on the agent's screen.

"Stop the test."

The lens of the projector had shattered.

One

Velma Bloom's car was not at the bottom of the Hudson River.

Velma was on a plane flying east out of New York. It was 12:32 a.m. on her twenty-fifth birthday. In New York, it had been her birthday for thirty-two minutes. Where she was going, it had already been her birthday for several hours.

Velma waited for the stewardess with the beverage cart to reach her seat. She was going to be on the plane for seven hours. She would be safe for those seven hours, but she still wanted a drink.

She changed the time on her watch to coincide with the clocks she would see when the plane landed. Though the flight would last seven hours, those clocks would say it had been twelve. Her car would still not be at the bottom of the Hudson River.

Velma loved her car. She wished she could be in her driver's seat right now instead of on this plane. Finally, the stewardess made it up to her row with the beverage cart. At least on the plane, she could drink. Velma asked the stewardess for two mini bottles of spiced rum and a cup of ice. The stewardess asked for ID and Velma presented her passport.

"Thank you, Miss Kelly." The stewardess put the bottles and ice on Velma's tray table, then pushed her cart up to the next row. Velma poured the contents of both bottles into her cup, watching the swirls as the rum melted the ice. She took her first sip, enjoying the sensation of the liquor landing in her empty stomach. She was too distracted to be hungry, but it had been far too long since she'd eaten. She swallowed most of her drink in one gulp. She would have to remember to ask for a snack with her next one.

Velma reclined in her seat and closed her eyes. She let the calming effect of the rum and the white noise of the plane engine make everything that had happened in the last three hours go away. The sound veiled her thoughts of blood and panic, and of information she wished she didn't have. She tried to stop seeing the red outline around the gun behind her eyelids. She hushed the memory of the screams that had commanded her, begged her, to get to the airport, and to get on this plane.

She had done what she was told. She made it to the airport, and she made it onto the plane. She was where she was supposed to be. That much brought her some relief. But she had left an uncovered track. There was one thought she couldn't quiet, even as her mind replayed the sound of the evening's final gunshot in a way that almost sounded like music. Ugly discoveries and mass confusion would soon plague everyone who knew her, all because her car was not at the bottom of the Hudson River.

~ * ~

Thursday, June 2, 2005

The engine of a vibrant classic roared into the driveway of Velma Bloom's childhood home. The intensity of the car's yellow exterior matched that of the driver's vibrant red tresses. The fiery combination had turned many heads as she cruised down the New York highways. Velma was making her triumphant return to West Chester County after four years at Vassar College in Poughkeepsie. Two hours earlier, just before she left her college apartment for the last time, she sent her mother an email saying that she was on her way home, and explaining why her trust fund was empty.

Velma was used to attracting attention. She had large breasts for her five-foot three-inch frame, and a shape that called to mind the pin-up models of the 1950s. She kept her red hair dyed a brighter shade of red, and took a few minutes every morning to curl it. The curls disguised how damaged her hair was from years of chemical treatments, and the volume they added made her appear even more top heavy than she already did.

She had grown up in a semi-affluent neighborhood in White Plains, New York, the only child of two college professors. She was strong-willed, but always polite and even-tempered thanks to her upbringing and her natural good sense. She had a 4.0 grade point average in high school, and kept up with Vassar College's academic rigor with ease. She performed well at Vassar, dabbled in a variety of areas of study, and earned her degree. After that, it was time for her to rock the boat.

"Velma Annalise Bloom. What have you done?" Elizabeth Bloom could hardly get through saying her daughter's name, and her face looked as though she were about to projectile vomit. "Franklin!"

she called to her husband, "bring me a glass of wine!"

"It's three p.m.!" Franklin Bloom called back from inside the house.

"I don't care what time it is, bring me a glass of wine!" Elizabeth yelled to him over her shoulder as if he would see her face, though he was seated watching television and facing the opposite direction. She may as well have been shouting to the sky, but part of her thought that at least facing in the direction of her husband while conversing was a bit more civilized.

"We don't have an open bottle!"

"So open one!"

"All right, all right!" Franklin could be heard moving from the couch to the dining room. He opened the cabinet in which the Blooms kept their less important bottles of wine. "Red or white?"

"White! The Chardonnay, not the Pinot. Then come see what your daughter has done!"

What Velma Bloom had done was spend the contents of her trust fund, just over one hundred thousand dollars, on a restored 1970 Dodge Challenger.

Velma wore a smug expression as she watched her mother's face lose its color. She leaned against the car. It was beautiful. The paint glistened in the sun as though the car itself were bragging, and it had a lot to brag about. The color of both the body of the vehicle and the wheels was Dodge's original Top Banana Yellow, and it had a black racing stripe. She named it Smiley, for the black stripe on the bright yellow called to mind the smiley face stickers Velma remembered seeing everywhere when she was a kid. Smiley was out of place in the Blooms' White Plains neighborhood.

Franklin came out of the house carrying a glass of white wine, and dropped it the moment he saw the car. Velma smirked and Elizabeth looked at the ground. Franklin walked back in the house and returned carrying a new glass for his wife and a bottle of Brooklyn Lager for himself. He gave the pile of broken glass a thoughtful look, then stepped over it and stood next to his wife.

"Thanks, Dad, but I'm driving," Velma joked. Her mother yanked the wine glass from her husband's hand and drained a third of it with one swallow.

"That's quite a car, Velma."

"Isn't it? It's been restored inside and out, and it only has seventy-thousand miles on it." She patted the car with pride, and then used the bottom of her T-shirt to wipe off her fingerprints.

"Only seventy…" Franklin moved his eyes over the exterior of the car, just now taking in how old it was.

"What Velma hasn't told you," her mother chimed in, "is that she purchased this monstrosity with the entire remaining contents of her trust fund. With the money she was supposed to use for graduate school!" Franklin's eyes widened when he heard this and he almost choked on his beer. The conversation paused as his near-choke turned into a coughing fit. Elizabeth sipped her wine and her face changed from white to red. Velma just watched them, trying hard not to smile.

"This car cost a hundred thousand dollars?" Franklin pushed the words through his final cough.

"A hundred and twelve thousand dollars including taxes and title transfer. I chipped in some of my own savings."

"What the hell were you thinking, Velma? This is the stupidest thing you've ever done! This is right up there with sending in those incomplete graduate school applications."

"I didn't purposely send them incomplete, I just didn't check them for completeness before I sent them."

Her father shook his head and her mother began to cry. "We tried so hard to instill good sense in you," he said. "We put all that money aside for your education. You got an almost perfect score on your SATs and your GREs. You spent four years at Vassar. I didn't think you were capable of something this idiotic. And it's a Dodge, an American car! You'll be spending money on constant upkeep, and just look at this thing! It's going to be a crime magnet. For that money you could have bought two and a half Audis, and now you have no trust fund, and not a penny to your name!"

Velma stood up straight and admired her car, then turned to her parents. Their reaction had been what she'd expected, and she was prepared with a response. "Mom, Dad, it means the world to me that you brought me up how you did. I'm very grateful for my education and all the opportunities you gave me. I'm grateful I had the trust fund money to live off in college. I admit I spent some of it on stupid things over the years. The time I tried cocaine, for example, that was pretty stupid. It was expensive and not even that much fun." Velma paused to look at her parents. Their faces showed less shock than she'd expected, making her wonder what drugs they'd done when they were in college.

"This car," she continued, "is not on the list of stupid purchases for a number of reasons. First, consider the cost-to-enjoyment ratio. The cocaine cost a certain amount of money, and was enjoyable, but not, in my opinion, so enjoyable that it justified the expense. The Challenger, however, promises to provide me with a level of enjoyment commensurate with its cost. In addition, it's in excellent condition and is not without function. Concerning money, I will get a job. Without the security blanket of my trust fund, I'll be forced to develop a much better work ethic than I've had up to this point in life. This, you must concede, will have inherent value whether or not I decide to continue my education. As far as the car being a so-called crime magnet, despite what you may think, most criminals are not so stupid as to attempt to steal or vandalize something so conspicuous. The extreme likelihood of someone getting caught targeting something this color or this rare, or victimizing me in it actually makes this car a crime deterrent."

Velma opened the Challenger's door and paused a moment before getting inside. "All things considered, Mom and Dad, you have, indeed, instilled me with uncommonly good sense."

Velma took her place in the driver's seat and buckled her seatbelt. She started the engine and rolled down her window. Lowering her sunglasses, she peered over them to make sure both the Professors Bloom saw her victorious smile before she drove away.

Two

Friday, April 25, 2008

Detective Jackson Duran of the Yonkers Police Department woke up delirious at seven a.m. He saw a white blur when he opened his eyes. It took him a few moments to realize he had fallen asleep at his desk and constructed a makeshift pillow out of his paperwork. He laughed at himself.

Duran had been a Yonkers police officer for close to seven years, ever since he finished college and chose the police academy over graduate school. His plan had always been to become a detective. After pounding the beat and paying his dues, passing out at his desk while doing paperwork after hours had not been part of his plan.

It was Duran's fifth day as a detective. He had an active imagination, but tried to be a realistic man. He began his new position with no suppositions that he would immediately be thrown into the thick of a fascinating, high profile case and show off his untapped capacity for heroics, and yet, he was disappointed when that didn't happen. Over half of all crimes committed in Yonkers were non-violent thefts, and all of what Detective Duran had done in the last four days was paperwork.

He lifted his head and realized he was still intoxicated from the night before. He laughed at himself again, thinking about how many of his mornings in college had been just like this one. He would often wake up with his face in a book or a term paper and find it covered in whisky-scented drool, but his work was always done. He looked through the stack of papers that had been his pillow. Sure enough, sometime between when he decided to work late while having bourbon for dinner and when he passed out, everything in the pile had been read, reviewed, and sorted. Impressed with himself, he decided he'd earned some coffee and Advil.

Duran reminded himself this was the last day of his first week as a detective. He would get to do the more exciting parts of his job in time. For now, he only needed to get through the next eight or nine hours before he could go home and drink himself to sleep again, but this time with the reading materials of his choosing. Tonight, he decided, it would be red wine and James Joyce.

Two hours later, his plans changed.

"Guess what, Duran? You get to have some fun today." Duran's former beat partner, now fellow detective, Jeremy Stevens, handed him a thin folder. He sat down across the desk from Duran and wrinkled his nose. "Jackson, I've always been a little jealous that you still live like you're in college, but right now you're at work, and you still smell like whisky."

"Hey, I'm doing my job. I'll grow up on my own time." Duran patted the large stack of papers that had been his pillow. "Regardless of what I smell like, I get things done."

"Spoken like a classic high-functioning alcoholic."

"That's just a fancy term for someone who can hold their liquor. You know who was…"

"Sherlock Holmes. Yes, Jackson, I know. You've told me before. You know I'm just busting your balls. Listen, we've gotten two reports of this woman going missing. I thought you'd be the right one to be the liaison on this case."

"Velma Bloom?" Duran pulled a picture out of the stack Stevens had handed him. "I've met this girl. She works at Lonnie's Pub where that break-in was last week. I got a statement from her."

Stevens nodded. "Is this the girl who disarmed the perp?"

"Sure is. She was a bad ass little number. Classy though. I couldn't stop wondering what she was doing working there."

"Maybe you'll find out. We got reports from her parents in White Plains and from Lonnie, her boss. Head out and talk to them and we'll go from there."

"I'm on it."

Duran perused what little information Stevens had given him on Velma Bloom. He decided to pay a visit to her parents in White Plains first. Lonnie's Pub wouldn't be open yet. He could stop there on his way back. He wasn't expecting much to come of those visits. Everything he had in front of him indicated that a twenty-five-year-old woman had just decided to skip town. Then he remembered the night he met this woman, and some distressing possibilities hit him.

After Duran reviewed the few documents he had on the missing woman, he prepared for his trip to White Plains by chewing four breath mints. He hoped it would mask the residual smell of alcohol that would taint his breath as he spoke. When he got up to leave, grateful to get away from his desk, the phone rang.

"Detective Duran," he answered.

"Duran, this is Detective Woods, Mount Vernon PD."

"What can I do for you, Detective Woods?"

"I'm working on a double homicide case. Two men, both Russian nationals, were found in the basement of a house on Forester Avenue. We're waiting on an official ballistics report. It looks like they shot each other, but there's a lot we're trying to make sense of."

"Um, Detective Woods, is it possible you meant to call someone else here?"

"No, I called the station and was transferred to you."

"I don't know if there's anything I can help you make sense of." Duran marveled at the turn his day had taken. Not long ago, he'd been waking up half drunk, and now a detective from another jurisdiction calling him about two dead Russians.

"Well, I'm not sure either, but you and I will need to keep in touch. I have some information that might be helpful to you."

"Oh?"

"There's a very distinctive car parked in front of the house where we found the bodies. The neighbors all say they've never seen it before. A bright yellow Dodge Challenger. I ran the plates. It's registered to a Yonkers woman who was reported missing this week."

"Velma Bloom?"

"Velma Bloom."

Three

After Velma Bloom bought her Challenger, unburdening herself of her trust fund, she became a waitress. She wanted a job that would give her mind a much-needed break from academics, and enough hours to give her that break from her parents. She found herself at Lonnie's Pub, a small restaurant and bar in Yonkers with a diverse clientele, above average food, and a quirky, sarcastic owner. Lonnie McCarthy was thirty-seven years old but carried himself with what seemed like purposeful immaturity. He had grown up in Brooklyn with an Italian mother and an Irish father. As a result, he had a great fondness for pasta and whisky, a strong Brooklyn accent, and a healthy disdain for Catholicism.

When Velma first came into his pub, Lonnie took one look at her chest and declared, "You're hired."

"Do you want me to fill out an application?"

"Have you waitressed before?" Lonnie asked her.

"No, but I went to Vassar."

"Uh huh. Hang on, I'll get you your application and a W4. And a uniform, tank top and an apron. What size top do you want?"

"I guess a medium?" Velma looked at the very tight, low cut tank tops worn by the waitresses. "Maybe a large." The two women working made no effort to hide their bra straps or the tops of their bras, which the tank tops refused to cover. She thought about her bra collection and wondered which ones she could wear to preserve some degree of class. Then she remembered where she was. Whatever vestiges of modesty she had from her upbringing didn't belong in this world. "Fuck it. Give me a small."

Lonnie smiled. "You're gonna do just fine here," he said.

Velma's parents were less than thrilled when she announced to them that she would be working at Lonnie's.

"A waitress? You're going to be a waitress?" Her father smiled as though trying to suppress a laugh.

Velma had always had a good relationship with her parents, until responses to Velma's graduate school applications began to arrive in the mail. Each was a rejection on the basis that the application had been missing one key component or another. Some were short a letter of recommendation, some were missing the application fee, others her transcripts from Vassar. This was all intentional. She did not want to go to graduate school. Not only had Vassar left her exhausted, she had no clear idea of what she wanted to study. The applications were sent out only at the insistence of her parents, and were to master's degree programs in a variety of disciplines including English literature, guidance counseling, secondary education, and medieval Spanish art. Velma had done what she needed to do to make sure she was not admitted to any of them.

"Yes, Dad, I'm going to be a waitress."

"What's this?" Elizabeth emerged from the kitchen with a glass of wine in one hand and an organic granola bar in the other. She was taller than her daughter by a few inches and had much darker hair, though it was starting to gray, but they shared the same blue eyes and fair skin. Franklin looked quite a bit like his wife and the two were sometimes mistaken for brother and sister. Both of her parents wore glasses, but Velma did not. She wondered if they needed them or if they just wore them to look more professor-like.

"Velma got a job."

"I got a job, Mom," she echoed with a more upbeat inflection.

"As a waitress?"

"As a waitress. Want to see my uniform?" She pulled off her t-shirt to reveal the tank top Lonnie had given her.

"Oh, Velma," her mother sighed. "Go ahead, you'll just have to face the consequences of your bad decisions." She shook her head and walked out of the room.

"Sweetheart," her father said, "when you get tired of manual labor, I'll help you redo your grad school applications. Try not to take too long."

Velma rolled her eyes but smiled at him, knowing he meant well. "Sure, Dad."

"In the meantime, I'll talk to your mother. She just needs some time. She'll be fine."

"Okay. Thanks." Velma hugged her father and went upstairs to her room, anxious for the next day to come so she could begin her new life. She couldn't wait to face the consequences of her bad decisions.

That Friday, Velma drove Smiley to Lonnie's Pub for her first day of work. Despite her confidence that Smiley's conspicuity would deter potential vandals, she was hesitant to park on the street or too far from the restaurant. She drove around the block twice, investigating her new surroundings. Alongside the building, she noticed an entrance to a small parking lot at the rear of the pub. She pulled into it.

To her right, there was a large dumpster and an almost as large recycling bin. Beside them were five parking spots, all occupied. To her left was the back of the restaurant. A door leading into the kitchen was propped open, and the concrete stoop in front of it was strewn with ashtrays. Next to the door, a set of rickety steps led up to a small, rusty landing. There, beside the steps, was what she'd been looking for: the perfect parking spot. She gauged she could pull Smiley right into it and have plenty of space to back out when she left. While there was room enough for more than one vehicle along the side of the building, there were lines indicating only one actual parking spot. No one could park next to Smiley, so there was no risk of door dings. If she could get through her first day as a waitress without her one-hundred and twelve thousand-dollar car sustaining any cosmetic damage, she would count it as a win.

All Lonnie required her to wear was the undersized tank top and her choice of non-slip shoes. The rest was up to her. For day one, Velma decided to stay casual like the other women she had seen working there the day before. Still, it didn't hurt to abandon modesty. She wore tight blue jeans and Converse All-Stars, which she hoped would count as non-slip. Her breasts stretched out the tank top so much that a couple of cracks could be seen in the words printed on it. It was also too short. No matter how she adjusted it, it would roll up, leaving half an inch of exposed flesh between its hem and the waist of her low-rise jeans.

Velma entered the building through the propped-open back door, taking in the foul smell of stale ashes, and reveled in her new surroundings. She followed a narrow hallway to the main part of the kitchen. Ill-maintained, flickering fluorescent lights gave everything an eerie quality. There was a door with cracked paint leading to a dark storage room, and an exposed doorway with a hall beyond it that appeared to lead nowhere. The place would have been creepy if she hadn't just come inside from a gorgeous, sunny afternoon.

Velma ventured through the exposed doorway and found a tiny bathroom. The walls and ceiling were covered in cracking, mint-green paint, and the door looked like it could fall off its hinges at any moment. It did, however, have a full-length mirror hanging on it. Velma checked her reflection, making sure she saw what she wanted to see. Her curls were perfect and her breasts were evenly situated. Her "Lonnie's Pub" tank top and her apron were flattering.

"*Mami!*" She heard as she walked down the hallway into the kitchen. "*Ay, mami!*" A man holding a spatula leered at her chest. She was offended for the shortest of moments, and then she remembered where she was. She realized she liked it. The man with the spatula leaned over to a very short man who stood beside him in front of a deep fryer. "*Mira las tetas en esta pelirroja!*" Velma was used to hearing this phrase, "look at the tits on that redhead," and her usual response, "look at your own tits, jackass" was not hard to translate and deliver.

The man with the spatula looked horrified. "*Lo siento, mamacita.*"

"Velma. *Me llamo* Velma." She giggled, hoping he would realize he hadn't offended her.

"Luis." With his spatula, he indicated the short man at the fryer. "Jorge." The man at the fryer turned and smiled at her.

"*Mucho gusto.*"

The two men returned to their work. Velma enjoyed the sizzles as the man with the spatula flipped a burger on his flat grill and the short man lowered a metal basket containing something breaded and frozen into his deep fryer.

She didn't think her new job would be difficult. Having eaten at restaurants, she figured she knew the basics. Take a person's drink order, take their food order, and take their money. Still, she knew there would be some gaps between her observations as a restaurant patron and the actual actions of the workers. There had to be things going on behind the scenes, and these were the things she needed to learn. *This is its own version of graduate school.*

Infused with confidence, Velma entered the pub's dining area and scanned it for Lonnie McCarthy. Lonnie had told her to arrive for training between two and three p.m. It was now 2:07 p.m., so Velma expected that when she passed through the swinging door from the kitchen into the restaurant, he would be waiting for her. There was no sign of him. She looked around. All the customers seemed happy. No one had an empty glass and no one was at a loss for condiments.

Everyone at a table was conversing, and the three people at the bar appeared to be content drinking their drinks and ignoring each other.

"Honey!" A man called to Velma from one of the tables. He had two male companions. They were all wearing double-breasted suits and looked to be in their early forties.

She approached him and smiled. "Hi there." All three men looked at her chest, then at her face.

"Oh, I'm sorry," said the first man. "You're not our waitress."

"Well, I can get you something if you need it," she said. "I'm not sure if there's anyone else here."

The men laughed.

"We just need coffee, doll. Three cups of black coffee."

"Sure, I'll be right back." Velma had no idea where the coffee was. She went into the kitchen and called through the window between her and the cooks. "*Papi!* Luis!"

Spatula man looked alarmed, yet somehow pleased. "Haha, *mami!*"

"Sure, whatever. I need your help." He cocked his head and blinked at her. She figured he spoke English but was now getting back at her for knowing more Spanish than he'd thought she did. "*Donde esta el café?*"

"*Que esta detrás de usted, al lado del microondas.*" It's right behind you, next to the microwave.

Velma turned, relieved to see a microwave and a pot of coffee on the counter behind her. "*Gracias.*"

"*¿De nada, señorita. Estoy a su servicio.*"

"*¿Por qué me hablas tan formalmente?*" Why do you address me so formally? She shot him a flirtatious look. She wanted to show him she was a coworker, not an INS agent.

"*Porque usted es realmente una señora, y usted merece ser tratado así.*" Because you are truly a lady, and you deserve to be treated as such. He smiled at her and she smiled back, impressed with his response.

"Are you fucking with me because you need a green card? *¿Estas jodiendo conmigo porque se necesita una tarjeta verde, amigo mío?*" His face went pale with shock until Velma started laughing.

The three of them laughed together, and Velma knew that everything here was going to be just fine. She laced the fingers of her right hand through the handles of two of the coffee cups and picked up the third with her left. She was grateful the men hadn't wanted cream. *It's going to be okay.* The ability to carry three cups on their saucers would come with time.

As she approached the men's table, she noticed a fourth person had joined them. It was a petite woman with breasts almost as large as Velma's, but with the tell-tale water balloon shape of saline implants. She wore the same Lonnie's Pub tank top that Velma wore, though in a size that better accommodated her chest. Her dark brown hair was highlighted and flat ironed to perfection; not a single strand was out of place. Her makeup was flawless. She appeared to be a few years older than Velma and a few years younger than the men around her.

"Oh! Thanks so much, babe!" she said to Velma with a huge smile, and took the mugs from her, passing them out to the men. She stood up. "You must be Daphne, I'm Nancy. I'm going to train you today." They shook hands. Velma was relieved she'd be getting guidance from a peer and didn't let it bother her that Nancy had gotten her name wrong.

"Nice to meet you," she said. "My name is Velma, actually."

The men at the table chuckled. Before she could stop herself, Velma jerked her head toward the table and, in a split second, reined in her anger before it could show.

Nancy took Velma's hand. "I'm sorry, honey, my fault. Lonnie just told me the new girl has the same name as the chick on *Scooby Doo* and I picked one."

"It's okay," Velma shook off the comment, forcing herself to stay calm. "It happens all the time."

"Come on, let me give you a quick tour." Nancy pulled Velma away from the table and led her around the pub.

She showed Velma the touchscreen computer system and how to send food orders to the kitchen, and explained how the tables were numbered. When the three men at what Velma learned was table number twelve were ready to pay their bill, Nancy explained how to run a credit card and close a tab. When the men departed, Velma expected Nancy would clear the table and clean it. Instead, she sat down and reclined against the wall, propping her feet up on an empty chair. Velma joined her.

"This job isn't too hard, so far."

"It's the easiest job I've ever had." Nancy pulled a pack of cigarettes and a lighter out of her apron pocket. She offered one to Velma, who accepted with hesitation.

"Thank you, but should we be smoking inside?"

"No one cares. The place is empty anyway." She let her ashes fall into a dirty coffee mug. "You know how I make my tips better?" Nancy laughed, dropping her cigarette into the mug. "I just tell people stories about how shitty my life is." She winked and began clearing the mess on the table.

Nancy regaled Velma with a brief story of her life and Velma listened with intrigue. Nancy was only twenty-nine years old, and in addition to having four children with three different boyfriends, she had worked in a dozen different restaurants.

It amazed Velma how responsible and well-adjusted this woman was. In Velma's world, women didn't have four children with three different men before the age of thirty. In her world, women had children when they had finished their educations, were employed, and *planned* to have children. They didn't have to be married. In fact, one of the children in her parents' neighborhood was the daughter of a sperm donor and an independently wealthy woman in her forties who had a PhD in Jewish Women's Studies. Velma herself had been the result of years of planning by her parents. Also in Velma's world, when a young woman, or young girl, got pregnant by accident, she would have an abortion no one ever knew about, or at least no one ever talked about. In Nancy's world, when you got pregnant by accident, you had a baby and you dealt with the consequences.

Velma appreciated how few of her actions had met any consequences up to this point. Velma had gotten in trouble before, but the results of careless behavior were much different for trust fund babies from White Plains than they were for most people.

When Velma was fifteen, she and her high school boyfriend, Brett Riley, were caught behind a tree in the schoolyard with their pants around their ankles. Velma was in tenth grade and Brett was in eleventh. They had the same study hall period and used it to meet in various locations on school property and mess around. A teacher sneaking out for a mid-day cigarette had stumbled upon them engaged in half-naked, urgent teenage sex. They were both suspended from school for three days for "aberrant behavior." Velma's parents also grounded her for two months, and her permission to see or speak with

Brett was revoked.

Ultimately, the only consequence of this for Velma was the embarrassment of having to explain the incident to an interviewer at Vassar, who, as it turned out, thought it was hilarious. Velma and Brett had continued to see each other behind her parents' backs. Unlike her new coworker, Velma had managed to avoid pregnancy in her teen years. As she listened to Nancy's tale, Velma felt a wave of guilt. She'd always known she had a privileged upbringing, but now she had a seed of fear inside her as this alternate version of the world came to life.

Nancy and Velma spent a few hours together, serving the light flow of customers who came in during the hours between lunch and happy hour. Velma followed Nancy and watched her. Around four-thirty, Nancy announced she'd be leaving soon and the evening waitress would be coming in.

"You're ready to be on your own, right?

"Um...I think so?"

"You'll be fine. Edie will be in at five or so, and Lonnie will be here."

"Will Edie help me if I get overwhelmed? I didn't think I'd be on my own on the first day."

"If you need anything, I'd ask Lonnie. Edie's great but she's...well, you'll meet her. I'm sure you'll do fine."

Velma didn't think it appropriate to ask how much tip money Nancy had made that day, but the wad of bills in her apron pocket looked substantial. She wondered how long it would take her to save up enough money to move out of her parents' house.

After Nancy left, Velma was alone for almost half an hour before Lonnie McCarthy arrived at his pub. He bolted through the front door and jerked his head back and forth, looking around the dining room as though expecting to find a chaotic scene requiring his immediate intervention. Velma snickered to herself. She had things under control. There was no one sitting at any tables, and she had only two customers at the bar. They were both nursing their beers and watching ESPN, seeming pleased with where they had situated themselves for the Yankees game that would air in just over two hours. Velma had already served one of them a basket of mozzarella sticks. Lonnie walked behind the bar, but before she could greet him, he turned to the two men.

"Which one of you guys drives a ridiculous yellow car?" The men both shook their heads, mouths full of either beer or fried cheese. "Come on, you're the only ones in here. Somebody move it. Old-ass Dodge Challenger. It's in my parking space and it don't belong there." The two men glanced at each other. Velma turned away from the bar and grabbed a towel. She picked up a beer glass out of the spinning dishwasher and proceeded to dry it as slow as she could.

"Sorry, buddy, it ain't mine," said one of them.

"I got a Dodge, but it's red, it ain't a Challenger, and my wife's picking up my kids in it right now, so not mine either," said the other.

Lonnie grunted. "Damn. If it's not you guys it could be any shithead who works on this block. Fuck."

"Calm down, buddy," said the man with the mozzarella sticks. "It could just be somebody running into a store or something and they'll be gone a couple minutes."

"Not with my luck." Lonnie made a sound that was half sigh and half grunt. "Could be worse. Just a parking spot." He walked over to the cash register and popped it open. He glanced over Nancy's sales report for the day before counting the money in the drawer. Velma turned to him, still pretending to dry the beer glass.

"Hey, Lonnie."

"Hey, Velma. Nancy train you okay?" He had started counting, making it apparent that he intended to converse without looking at her.

"Great."

"Good. So Edie's running late, you'll be on the floor by yourself for a few minutes." He leafed through the cash, mouthing numbers as he counted the bills.

Velma put the beer glass away and tucked the towel into the back of her apron. She looked at Lonnie's back and crossed her arms. "That's fine. Did you want me to move my ridiculous car though?" She flashed her sweetest smile to offset her defiant stance.

Lonnie stopped counting and turned to face her. "Ha! No shit, that's yours?" He smiled back at her and laughed, shaking his head as he put the money back in the register drawer.

"Yep. And by the way, it's a restored classic and it's in damn near mint condition, so I didn't want to park anywhere I could get door dings." The men at the bar joined in the laughter.

"Sweetheart, I'm sorry. I guess none of us took you for the muscle car type," said mozzarella stick man.

Velma was long over letting a comment like this anger her. Her head filled with all manner of clever retorts, but it was still her first day on the job, and these men would be tipping her, so she chose her words accordingly.

She uncrossed her arms and leaned on the bar in front of them. "Well, I guess I'm full of surprises then."

"Yes, you are," Lonnie said. "Park there for tonight. Don't park there tomorrow. Tell you what, you can park there on Mondays. Monday's my day off."

A man walked into the bar alone. He had gray hair and appeared to be in his late sixties, and Velma thought he looked sad.

"How are you, Sam?" Lonnie greeted him.

"I can't complain." Sam sat at the bar, leaving four empty stools between him and the other men. Lonnie poured a generous amount of Belvedere over two ice cubes.

"Can you put in an order of wings for me, honey?" said the man next to the mozzarella stick man. "Hot, with extra blue cheese?"

"Sure." Velma went to the touch screen computer on the other side of the bar instead of the one closer to her so she could listen to Lonnie's conversation with Sam. She entered the order for the wings as Nancy had taught her. Lonnie handed Sam a glass containing a massive portion of vodka, making it look more like a small glass of water.

"Did you get a new car?" Sam took a large swallow of his vodka. Velma smiled, remembering how wonderful that first gulp always felt after a full day of classes.

"No, I got a new waitress who's got a sense of entitlement." He winked at her and chuckled.

She was relieved to see he wasn't serious and smiled back. "I don't have a sense of entitlement, I just don't want door dings."

Lonnie smiled and shook his head. Sam laughed as he lowered his glass after his second and smaller mouthful of vodka.

"What's your name, sweetheart?"

"Sam, this is Velma. Velma, this is Sam. You'll be seeing a lot of him."

"Nice to meet you, Sam." She shook his hand. He had a kind face and a kind voice.

"Velma, huh? Like Velma from *Scooby Doo*?"

She felt a pinch of dread. She knew she'd be hearing this more often than she'd like.

Velma excused herself to go to the kitchen to check on her wings. They weren't ready yet, so she took the opportunity to use the employee bathroom behind the lockers. It was occupied. She waited for about a minute and then heard the sound of a toilet flushing, followed by running water. A petite, very pretty young girl with black hair emerged.

"I think I put my tampon in sideways," said the girl.

Velma couldn't remember the last time she truly did not know what to say to someone. She proceeded as though the girl had not spoken. "Hi, are you Edie? I'm Velma, I started working here today."

"Oh. Yeah, I'm Edie. Hey, watch this." Edie kicked off her right shoe. She lifted her right leg and then grabbed the top of her foot, bringing it all the way to the back of her head. She stayed balanced in that position for a few seconds before dropping her leg.

"Wow, that's impressive," said Velma.

"Thanks. I'm a dancer. I mean I'm going to be a dancer. Not a stripper, like, an actual dancer. So I'm working here until I get a job."

"And um, how is that going?"

"I have an audition in the city next week. I'm going to show them that. God, I hope I'm not still having my stupid period."

"I hope not, too." Velma smiled at Edie, filled with a combination of awkwardness and wonder. Edie smiled back but didn't move, she only batted her eyelashes and continued to block Velma's path to the bathroom door. "Will you excuse me?" Velma said, "I need to get to the bathroom."

"Okay! I'm going to go clock in. Then I'll be bored. Come hang out with me." Edie bounced out of Velma's path.

"Okay." Velma went inside the small bathroom and locked the door. Edie walked into the kitchen and Velma could hear her singing the wrong words to a Disney song, then addressing the cooks in rudimentary but still very broken Spanish. Edie must have switched to English at some points, because Velma heard the words "tampon" and "vagina."

Shit. I work here too.

Four

Velma's first weekend working at Lonnie's, she felt like she'd stepped through a portal to another realm. She was intrigued by the set of characters she met. Some people were nicer than others, but all of them, her coworkers and her customers, were like pieces in a museum to her. She even liked Edie.

Edie, she learned, was eighteen years old. She had dropped out of high school six months ago, not long before she would have graduated, to pursue her thus far non-existent dancing career. She lived in a kind of fantasy world, having fashioned herself the stage name Edie Wind. Velma thought this would be an excellent name for a stripper. Her real name was Edith Weinberg. She had a Jewish father, a Puerto Rican mother, and a typical suburban upbringing. She also exhibited an absolute lack of awareness or caring regarding what came out of her mouth. No filter existed between her thoughts and her words. Declaring that she had put her tampon in sideways was just the beginning.

"I just realized something. When Homer Simpson's mouth is closed, it looks just like my vagina," Edie had declared in the middle of their Saturday dinner rush. Velma just smiled at her, enjoying the color that the new people in her life brought into her world.

As she was cleaning up after the pub closed on her third night as a waitress, Lonnie made her an offer. "Hey, Velma. My tenant just got locked up for selling cocaine to an undercover cop. You wanna rent the apartment upstairs?"

Velma's heart leapt. Did she! She was always happiest when she felt in control of her life. Moving out of her parents' house would give her what she needed to seize that control: privacy, a little piece of the world in which no one could reach her. She had loved living on her own in college, but her independence was marred by the need to do school work and the annual interruption of her semi-adult lifestyle by the end of each school year's second semester.

The apartment upstairs had no such caveats. It was perfect. She didn't need much space, the neighborhood was reasonably safe, and everything she might want was within about a one-mile radius. The only place she went that she wouldn't be able to walk to in under fifteen minutes was her parents' house. Her smile broadened at the thought. She caught herself and tried not to sound too eager.

"For how much?"

"Well it's a studio, it's small but it's got everything you need and the appliances are new. Okay, they're not for real new but they're new for Yonkers. Well, they work. It's a grand a month."

"Okay, but I've only been working for three days so I don't have any money yet. Am I going to make that much working here?"

"Oh yeah, you've never waited tables before. Look, how much did you make in tips this weekend?"

"Two-hundred and fifty-three dollars."

"And that's just one weekend! You'll make plenty." Lonnie smiled like a salesman. "Tell you what, since you work for me, I'll do nine-fifty."

"Okay, but right now I don't have nine hundred and fifty dollars. I have two-fifty-three."

"You're telling me the only money you have in the world is what you made here this weekend? Mom and Dad didn't give you nothing? You got nothing stashed away?"

"I spent it all."

"You sp... Shit, Velma. How about this, why don't I make the rent due on the thirtieth instead of the first? That way you have time to save it up. I'll take just two-hundred for a security deposit."

It was a reasonable offer. Lonnie could put out an ad for that apartment and get a thousand dollars a month for it, plus a full month's security deposit, with no problem. But she realized that there was something else in it for Lonnie. If he rented the apartment to her, he would be getting more than just a tenant, he would have an employee would always be there. She'd never have an excuse to be late for work, she'd never be able to call out if the weather was bad, and she'd always be right upstairs if Lonnie was shorthanded. She was okay with that, and was going to make the most of her bargaining power.

"Okay. Rent is due on the thirtieth. Today is the fifth. I move in on the tenth after you've had time to get the place clean for a new tenant."

"All right, you got a deal." He extended a hand.

"Almost. Make it nine hundred a month and prorate it. I move in on the tenth and owe you six hundred on the thirtieth. No deposit;

my Challenger eats gas, and I'll have to drive here for the next five days."

"You're breaking my balls, Velma!"

"How about one hundred dollars for security? I'll give you that right now. Then six hundred prorated rent on the thirtieth. I get the reserved parking spot behind the building, and I'm allowed to have a cat."

Lonnie hung his head and rested his hands on the bar, barely avoiding the broken glass. "Fuck. Okay, fine. You can have a cat, and I'll prorate nine hundred dollars a month. But no parking spot, that's mine."

"I want the parking spot." She sighed, pretending very well that she didn't know what she was doing all along. "Can I have it if we up the rent to nine-twenty-five and I give you a two hundred-dollar deposit?"

"So if I throw in the parking spot, you give me an extra hundred dollars security and an extra twenty-five bucks a month?"

"Yeah," She pulled a wad of cash out of her apron pocket and started to count it, "but I still want it prorated from when I move in on the tenth."

"Fine."

"Great!" She placed two hundred dollars in mixed bills on the bar in front of him. "We prorate nine-twenty-five, due on the thirtieth. What do I owe you the end of this month?" She waited.

"Fuck. Okay kid, nine hundred." He folded up her two hundred dollars and put it in his back pocket. "You'll owe me six hundred. Deal?"

Velma beamed with triumph and shook Lonnie's hand. "You got a deal, boss. I'll see you tomorrow, and I'll be in my parking spot."

~ * ~

On the day Velma moved in, she brought all her things over from her parents' house, then went back out. When she returned, she entered the bar carrying a large-boned and slightly overweight tomcat with a shaggy ginger coat and white paws.

"What the hell is that thing?" Lonnie said when he saw her.

She extended the cat before him, supporting him under the armpits so his torso lengthened and his white feet dangled. "It's a cat. His name is Carrot." She beamed. "I just adopted him."

"Well, he looks like a giant, furry carrot." Lonnie examined

Carrot from across the bar as Velma pulled him back toward her again. She supported him from underneath, but his curiosity kept him somewhat upright and his front white feet stood out against the orange tufts on his belly.

"Congratulations, Velma, you've adopted a large, fluffy carrot that looks like it stepped in ranch dressing."

"Thank you." She kissed the cat on his head, and he rubbed his nose under her chin and purred.

"Adorable. Now will you please take him upstairs and get him the fuck out of my bar?" Carrot turned to face Lonnie and meowed at him. "Oh, and then can you please come down to work the night shift at some point before it gets busy?"

"I just spent the whole day moving!"

"I promise to let you out early, just please don't leave me alone with Edie all night. I asked Nancy but she can't get a goddamn babysitter."

"Fine. I'll get Carrot settled and be down in time for happy hour."

"That's a relief." She waited a few moments and stood rocking her enormous cat like a baby.

"Thank you," Lonnie said. "Now get that thing out of my bar. Just because it's named after food doesn't mean it's allowed in a place people eat."

Carrot purred.

Velma walked out of the bar into the foyer and took the cat up the front steps to their new home. She showed Carrot the litter-box, scratching post, and catnip mouse she had purchased earlier that day. The cat seemed so happy to be out of a shelter cage and getting so much attention that he gave little resistance when she put a blue safety collar with a bell around his neck. He followed her into the kitchen, jingling all the way, as she filled a bowl with water for him. He lapped at it, then continued to follow her as she explored.

The kitchen was to the immediate right of the front door and the living area was to the left. It was all one room, but the kitchen and living areas were separated. The left side was carpeted, while the kitchen side had a white plastic floor covering with a gray line pattern that made a poor attempt to mimic tile.

Against the right wall were a stove, a refrigerator, and a small counter space with dented wooden cabinets above it. The bathroom was scrubbed clean and smelled of bleach, though there were still black spots on much of the grout. The tub and tile floor showed vestiges of whiteness. The small closet was just right for the few clothes she'd brought with her. On the very back wall a small window and a door led out to the porch. The hinges were rusty and made an awful sound when she opened the door.

The porch was about six feet on each side. Velma realized with delight that the set of rickety metal steps next her parking spot led right up to her porch and back door. She had a private entrance. She briefly allowed Carrot to join her on the porch and take in their magnificent view of a small, fenced-in parking lot occupied mostly by a huge, green dumpster.

"Carrot," she said as they looked down at the open trashcan and the pile of broken-down cardboard boxes that lay outside the pub's back door, "life is going to be wonderful here."

She stroked his head, and he meowed up at her, then purred as he pushed his head into her hand. A cluster of flies teemed around the trash. She was grateful their buzzing was drowned out by the frustrated shouts of the cooks that echoed from the kitchen. Two mice scampered around the garbage, battling the flies for the best bits of it. One of the flies buzzed up toward them from the trash pile below, and Carrot swatted at it. Velma could smell a faint trail of rancid meat behind the fly as it zipped away back to its treasure trove of filth.

A bee flew up to the porch and approached Carrot. Velma thought the bee looked threatening, so she swooped up the cat to rescue him. Her rapid movement scared the bee away and it flew off toward the dumpster. Velma kept her eyes focused so as not to lose sight of it. One of the dumpster doors was open, and the bee landed on a mound of exposed garbage. It crept toward an empty beer bottle. The moment it placed a leg on the glass, the bottle shattered, sending the bee away in a buzzing panic.

She laughed. "That'll teach you to fuck with my cat, bee." She took Carrot inside, unable to contain her smile.

She tended to break things. Sometimes it was on purpose, sometimes it wasn't, but it was always without touching whatever she broke. When she was a child, it was dangerous to make her angry. She couldn't always control herself, and anger was her trigger. She would shatter something, usually glass. For as long as she could remember, she'd known this wasn't normal, and she kept it a secret. When she was very little, maybe four or five years old, she told her secret to her parents. A boy had been making fun of Velma for having the name of a Scooby Doo character.

"Daddy, Mommy, why do things break?" she had asked.

"Why do things break?" Franklin repeated.

"What kind of things, honey?" Elizabeth said.

"Like glass. My teacher had a glass of water today, and it broke. Why does glass break?"

"Because it's fragile," her mom said. "If I picked up my glass of wine and dropped it on the floor, it would break. If I dropped my fork on the floor, it wouldn't break because it's made of metal."

Velma was not satisfied with this answer.

"Well, Velma," her dad said, "if your mother were to drop her glass of wine on the floor, it would collect kinetic energy on the way down. The kinetic energy would be converted into oscillatory energy, which would disturb the particles that make the glass solid."

He went on to explain, in no simple words for a small child, that impact following energy conversion was what caused the glass to break.

Velma barely remembered this conversation, but she remembered what she took from it: oscillatory energy. "But the water glass didn't fall. It broke."

Her parents humored her and then told her not to make up stories. Then they told her two things rather firmly that, for the rest of her life, made her wonder if they had taken her seriously. Did they know about her strange ability but refused to accept something they couldn't explain? Or did they always find another explanation for every broken glass and every snapped pencil they encountered around their daughter? The two things they told her were: don't ever talk about this nonsense again, and it's incredibly important to learn how to control your anger.

"It's okay to be angry sometimes, Velma," Franklin had said, "but try to think of it as going to the bathroom. Everyone needs to go to bathroom sometimes. When you're around other people, just hold it in until you're alone. Smile and walk away."

That advice allowed her to go through her childhood and most of her adolescence without ever revealing her secret. When children bothered her on the playground, she would hold in her anger until she was alone. It felt, in a way, as if she was holding in something physical. She would go to the edge of the playground where there was a metal fence and a few small trees and let herself feel the anger. It felt as though her whole body was a lung, and she'd been holding her breath. When she was alone to let the anger surface, there was relief as if she was exhaling through her skin. A small tree branch would snap, and Velma could rejoin the other children.

At that age, she couldn't pronounce the word "oscillatory" even in her head, but the understanding was there. She was producing vibratory energy, she told herself. She understood that this didn't happen to other kids. It seemed normal to her, but she could comprehend it wasn't something she should ever talk about. She never experienced shame, but on rare occasions she wished she could be like everyone else. Those thoughts were always fleeting.

She often fantasized about what she would do if she could use the energy when she wanted to, if she could find a way to make things break when she willed them to and not just when she felt bad feelings. She wondered if she could turn this ability, which often felt like a curse, into a super power. But as a child, she didn't have the freedom to experiment with it. She was afraid of what she could do, and her main objective was to avoid having it discovered.

She discovered ways to hide it, control it, or direct it. If she couldn't hold on to a feeling of anger or get anywhere private, she would focus on something specific, something that might break on its own. If she was in a classroom for example, she could focus on a pencil in someone's hand or the teacher's chalk. After all, chalk breaks all the time, and children snap their pencils all the time. Her secret remained a secret, but Velma spent much of her childhood isolating herself for fear someone might find out. She lived among people, she interacted with people, but she never forgot she had something to hide.

When she left for college, she discovered that alcohol and smoking helped suppress her odd, oscillatory power and helped give her more control. She had some theories about this, and sometimes searched the school library and the internet for information, or for someone else who had the same experiences. She never found a thing.

At Vassar, she took advantage of her lack of supervision. In addition to her academics, she had another course of study. She kept every empty beer bottle and every empty liquor bottle she could and practiced. She taught herself to use her power without having it triggered by anger. Over the course of her four years at Vassar, she learned to shatter the bottles with ease, and from farther and farther away. By the time she graduated, she could make a crack in a bottle almost a hundred feet away as long as she had a clear view of it.

The only person she ever trusted enough to share her secret with was Brett Riley. They were teenagers when she told him, and it had been over a decade since she last spoke of it. That day, Velma and Brett snuck off into the woods during study hall, as they often did in high school.

After they fooled around, he found a telling grass stain on the back of her skirt. He gave her the plaid flannel shirt he had on over his T-shirt to tie around her waist and cover it. Something about the gesture made her feel safe telling him, and his reaction was one of intrigue and delight, but with an understanding of how difficult it was for her to share something so far-fetched.

"You believe me?" she asked.

"Of course I believe you. Why would you make that up?"

"Thank you, Brett. Thank you for not thinking I'm crazy."

"I don't think you're crazy. I think everyone else is crazy." He kissed her and stroked her hair. "I wish there was something glass out here so you could show me."

"Do you have a pencil?" she whispered, looking around to make sure no one was nearby. If anyone saw her using her power, it could have more dire consequences than being caught having sex.

He withdrew a pencil out of his back pocket.

"Lay it flat on your palm. Now tell me something that will make me really angry."

"Okay…um…the assholes in the Supreme Court just gave ninety-percent of Ellis Island to fucking New Jersey." The pencil snapped in Brett's hand.

He smiled broadly and looked like a little boy who just had his every science fiction fantasy fulfilled. He put the two halves of the pencil in his back pocket and took her hand to lead her back to school. She would never forget the joy and relief she felt after that conversation. Brett believed her, and he accepted her.

Velma ended their teen romance before she left for Vassar, but they never stopped being close. She'd missed him far more than she thought she would, and often had him visit her in Poughkeepsie. A couple months before she finished college, Brett asked her if they could be a couple again when she returned home. Despite her affection for him, she declined. She wanted him in her life, but she had embraced emotional independence and didn't want to give it up by labeling herself as someone's girlfriend.

"Let's get together when I come home," she said. "You know I'll always want you in my life, right?"

"Me too, Velma."

She hated hearing the disappointment in his voice. "When I get back, I'll call you as soon as I can. I promise."

The day she moved into her apartment, she called him just before she went into work. She was itching to see him, and knew this was the perfect day. She also knew it would be easy for him to spend time with her around her work schedule, because he didn't have one of his own. He had a pre-law degree, but no desire to use it. He'd gone through a year and a half of law school online before his interest and his energy disappeared. For now, he was living on a modest inheritance he planned to stretch out as long as he could and enjoy his unregulated, nocturnal lifestyle. She told him to come see her at work at the end of her shift.

Brett entered Lonnie's Pub long before he was expected. Her heart fluttered at the sight of him, and every part of her body tingled as they embraced.

Wishing her shift were over, she released him before the urgency of her desire became strong enough to distract her from work. She led him to a table so he could wait for her to close the pub. He ordered a glass of red wine, which was the only thing he ever drank despite her attempts at encouraging him to branch out, and ordered his favorite food: mozzarella sticks. She found something childishly endearing about this, but she sometimes she was annoyed at the juxtaposition between his general open-mindedness and his egregious lack of it regarding food.

Velma sat with him, waiting for closing time, while he ate his mozzarella sticks and drank the red mystery wine she poured for him out of a box. She couldn't wait to show him her new apartment, to be alone with him without the possibility of her parents walking in on them. When it was time for the pub to close, she led him to the front door and asked him to wait outside while she cleaned up.

"Who's that tall drink of water?" Lonnie asked after Brett made his exit.

"That's Brett Riley." She was going to make Lonnie work a

little bit before she told him anything he wanted to hear.

"And who, I pray tell, is Brett Riley?"

"He used to be my boyfriend."

"Oh yeah? What is he now, then?"

"A customer."

"Sure, whatever." Lonnie laughed. "You're banging that guy."

"Yeah, but he's not my boyfriend."

"Whatever you say, Velma. He seems like kind of a weirdo."

"Well, get used to him. He's going to be coming around here a lot."

Five

Detective Jackson Duran found Lonnie's Pub vacant. The door was unlocked and the lights were on, but there were no customers and there didn't appear to be anyone working there. Shouting came from behind the kitchen doors.

"Does that fryer look *limpia* to you? Seriously, just fucking clean it, please." Lonnie McCarthy stormed out of the kitchen, cursing under his breath.

"Excuse me, Mr. McCarthy?"

Lonnie's features were tense, and he wore a snarl He looked up at Duran. "Officer Duran, right? You were here a couple weeks ago." His face relaxed as if he realized Duran wasn't a customer.

"I was. Different outfit, though. I'm Detective Duran now, as of four days ago."

To anyone else, he would have been loath to confess how new he was to his position, but Lonnie McCarthy had seen him in uniform just over two weeks ago. He and another officer had answered a call about an armed robbery in progress at the pub. They found the culprit before they even reached the crime scene. A masked man had run screaming to the police car, making an almost incoherent confession. Through the holes in his ski mask, they could see small shards of glass in his eyes. Duran had been the one to visit the pub and talk to Lonnie and the second witness, Velma Bloom. The other officer stayed with the culprit in the ambulance to St. John's Riverside Hospital. As far as Duran knew, he was still there.

"Well, Detective, you're looking great in the uh, civilian attire, but I'm sorry you have to be back here again. Can I get you a drink?"

"I'd love some coffee if you have it. Just black."

"That's the one thing I did get around to brewing this morning." Lonnie went back to the kitchen and came out with two large mugs of coffee. "If you wanted iced tea you'd be waiting ten minutes. We're pretty shorthanded. I guess you know I'm missing a waitress."

"I do, and I guess you know that's why I'm here." They sat

down at the nearest table. "Can you tell me how you discovered Velma was missing?"

"She didn't come to work Wednesday night. I called, and she didn't answer, I went upstairs and knocked on her door, and she didn't answer. It was her birthday, so I figured she probably asked me for the night off a while back and I forgot about it. That's something I would do. But then she didn't come to work last night, either, and obviously, she didn't come to work today."

"Can you think of any reason she would want to leave town? Run away?"

"No. Is that what you think happened?"

"It's too soon to say, but it's a possibility. I spoke with her parents. Yesterday morning they discovered her cat had been left on their doorstep, but there was no note and no fingerprints or anything else to indicate it was Velma who put him there."

Lonnie's face changed, betraying his false calm. This information didn't sit right with him. "She loved that cat."

"How long have you known Velma? How long did she work for you?"

"Almost three years."

"Can you think of anyone who would have wanted to hurt her?"

"Is that guy you caught here still locked up?"

"He is, and as far as I know, he's still blind."

"Then no." Lonnie sipped his coffee, still wearing an expression of fear and confusion.

"Did she have any family or friends in Mount Vernon?"

"Mount Vernon? I don't think so. Her only family I know of arc hcr parents, in White Plains. Why?"

"The Mount Vernon Police found her car. It was left parked in a residential neighborhood. Can you think of any other reason she would have had to go there?"

Lonnie shook his head. "Fuck. She loved that car almost as much as she loved the cat."

"Her apartment is right upstairs? A couple other officers and I are going to take a look around. Check for signs of foul play or struggle, look for a note, see if it looks like she packed a suitcase, that sort of thing."

"I'll let you in. Let me know if you, you know, find any clues or anything."

"I'll tell you anything I can."

"Listen, Detective. I gotta tell you, I don't think there's any way Velma ran away."

"Why do you say that?"

"Look, I hope you're right and she did just take off. I hope she's safe, I really do, but I'm telling you, I know this girl. If she was going to run off, there are three things she'd take with her—her cat, her car, and Brett Riley."

"Who is Brett Riley?"

"Velma's... I don't know. Friend? Fuck buddy? Whatever you want to call him, they were close. And you're telling me the car is in Mount Vernon and the cat showed up in White Plains, so neither of those things are with Velma. Brett was in here last night looking for her and said he had no idea where she was."

"Do you think he was telling the truth? Is there a chance she's still in contact with him?"

"He might have been telling the truth that he didn't know where she is, but if she's alive and she was going to contact anyone, it would be him."

"Thank you. I'm going to look around the apartment. It sounds like there isn't anything suspicious, but I just have to rule out the chance it's a crime scene. Then I think I'll have a chat with Brett Riley."

"You can try. He's kind of an odd duck. I wouldn't count on getting much out of him. I'm sure he'd lie for her if she asked him to."

"Well, I guess I'll see what he has to say."

"Detective, how good are you at knowing when someone's lying to you?"

"Honestly, not great. But I *can* always tell when someone's hiding something."

"Good, because even if he doesn't know where Velma is, I'd be surprised if Riley wasn't hiding something or other."

Duran shook Lonnie's hand, thanked him, then left. He was anxious to find out what Brett Riley was hiding, and he knew how to do it.

Jackson Duran had his own way of thinking, and his own way of doing things. In his years spent waiting to become a detective, he did a lot of private studying. In between the time he spent reading for pleasure, he read about cryptography and coding, and taught himself some basic hacking skills. These were skills he might need as a detective, but they were not taught in the police academy.

He didn't remember a great deal of what he had been taught in the police academy, but the things he did remember, he remembered well. Among them was that a police officer would face three temptations in his career. They called them the three Bs: booze, bribes, and broads. So far, he had only succumbed to the first one, so far with no consequences to his career.

The second temptation had never been a danger. He had been offered small bribes before, usually by people trying to avoid speeding tickets and sometimes by people asking him to turn a blind eye to minor offenses. Sometimes he did let a speeding driver go with only a warning, and he would ignore a minor offense if it didn't violate his personal code of ethics. The local bar that served college students who were a few months underage had nothing to fear from him, but not because its owner had paid off a few Yonkers cops. Duran had never accepted a bribe, or even been tempted. He lived by a code, it just wasn't always the New York Crimes Code. It was his own.

The third of the temptations lost its appeal after the first two years of his career. With his youthful good looks and his ability to be charming when necessary, he had no trouble approaching a woman on the rare occasion he was so inclined. He would have had no trouble getting that woman to spend more than one night with him, either. But he never met a woman whose company he preferred to a cocktail and a novel. Five years ago, he gave up trying. He had never met a real person who could live up to an imagined one. He seldom felt lonely, and any time he did, the feeling disappeared after the first drink and the first chapter. No broad was a match for a bottle and a book.

He spent most of his free time alone, reading and drinking. He often had what he thought were great revelations while reading and drinking. He would write these thoughts down so he would remember them the next day. Most of the time, when he read it sober, what he wrote turned out to lack its original greatness.

One night about two years ago, while Duran was drinking Swedish spiced liqueur and reading *The Girl with the Dragon Tattoo*, he wrote something that stayed with him. In the days that followed, he finished the novel, but didn't pick up a new one. He took a break from reading fiction and dedicated his nights alone to drinking and teaching himself a new language, a language called C. He knew that one day, when he became a detective, he would need to remember what he had once written on a booze soaked post-it note. *To find a skeleton in someone's closet, look in their computer.*

Six

Friday, January 4, 2008

Velma got out of bed at one p.m., earlier than usual when she wasn't due at work until four-thirty. She had plans with Brett after her shift and spent extra time doing her hair and makeup, hoping she wouldn't need to touch anything up before they went out.

Caffeine was an integral part of her routine before going to work. She went to her refrigerator and got herself a can of Trigger Finger Energy Drink. Trigger Finger was the most economical caffeine source she could find. It cost just under a third of what Red Bull did, and though she preferred Red Bull, this was what she could afford. In her fridge at all times was a supply of Trigger Finger Pink, a too-sweet, supposedly strawberry flavored version. It was neon pink and stained anything it touched.

"I should just get a coffeemaker," she said to Carrot as she cracked open the can.

In five huge gulps, she drank two-thirds of the pint-sized can of caffeine, sugar, guarana, and pink dye. She enjoyed the surge she felt when she swallowed a lot of it at once. She took out a second can and put it in her apron pocket. She wanted that feeling again, and this was going to be a long night.

Lonnie's Pub was more crowded than usual. Around seven p.m., Velma and Edie were at their busiest point. They took turns, as usual, taking care of customers as they walked in the door. By seven-thirty, the pub was crowded enough that Velma was close to being overwhelmed. She was relieved when her next turn came and just one man entered by himself.

She greeted him with enthusiasm, and he nodded. She took him to one of her empty tables and handed him a menu.

"Do you know what you'd like to drink? The list of draft beers is right there and I can give you a minute to decide." She pointed to the printed beer list mounted in a plastic stand on the table.

The man shook his head and picked it up. He held up one finger indicating she should stay for the moment. After a brief look at the beer list, he gave it to her with his index finger on Budweiser and nodded.

"Sure, I'll be right back." She went to the bar and found Lonnie busy mixing drinks while Edie stood nearby with a tray waiting for him to finish and hand them off to her. She poured the quiet man's beer herself.

"That guy looks creepy," Edie said. "He looks like he could be a serial killer."

"Shh." She had wondered if the man was quiet because he was deaf, but indulging herself by listening to one of Edie's uncensored streams of consciousness wasn't worth the risk of insulting him. "Edie, careful, he might hear you. He doesn't look like a serial killer, he just looks like someone's weird grandpa."

The man appeared to be in his sixties. He had dark blond hair with a touch of gray around his temples and a neat dark blond beard. His gray eyes were sharp and alert, but the wrinkles on his face gave away his age. He wore a fedora and a khaki trench coat when he entered, and removed both when he sat down. His attire was old fashioned but well-coordinated. Under a dark gray wool sport coat was a maroon turtleneck. Pressed light gray slacks completed the picture.

She did not find his look creepy, as Edie did, but his continued silence made her uncomfortable. His air of mystery led her to refer to him with a formal title, the Quiet Man, to herself. When she delivered his beer, she thought she heard him say "thank you," but the words were fast and so soft as to be almost inaudible.

"You're welcome," she said. "Are you ready to order?"

The man picked up his menu, pointed to the cheeseburger deluxe and nodded. He smiled, indicating his intention of being polite.

"Okay, I'll get that started." She took his menu and returned his smile before she left the table.

Edie approached and stood alongside her at the computer as she entered the man's order. "Maybe he looks more like a rapist than a serial killer." She peered over Velma's shoulder at the man.

"I think those guys look like rapists," she replied, tilting her head toward a group of three men Edie was serving. They appeared to be in their mid-thirties and each wore some piece of clothing or another to indicate their sports team preference.

"Holy shit! You're right, they do!" Edie said, examining the men. They spoke in loud voices but couldn't be understood since their mouths were always full of chicken wings. "But they look like the kind of rapists who might, like, roofie you and tie you up then let you go in the morning. Your guy looks more like he'd make you stay awake and lock you in his basement."

"Edie, what the fuck?"

"I mean, I can just kinda tell. Remember last week when that semen fell out of me and was running down my leg?"

"Uh huh." Velma remembered the incident very well.

She and Edie were standing in the kitchen when it happened, and Edie announced it loud enough for the cooks to hear, as well as Velma. Lonnie had walked in through the door for the tail end of Edie's statement, then spun and walked back out all in one smooth motion. Moments like that were one of Velma's favorite things about her job.

Edie continued her tale, "I remembered what happened the night before, was that I went to this gay bar and..." She rambled on, but Velma processed very little of it as she attempted to monitor her tables and assess her customers' needs. "...and then about three o'clock I woke up and I was tied to the bed."

"Um, Edie, did you go to the police about this?"

"No, 'cause I was totally fine. The guy was so hot. I wonder if I still have his number."

"I'm going to get back to work." The rest of the dinner rush was smooth, and Velma was glad it had been her turn when the Quiet Man entered.

He was very low maintenance. He nursed his beer, never asked for another, and didn't linger after finishing his meal. When his glass and plate were empty, she gave him his bill in a black check folder. She did the same for two other tables, and a man at one of them handed her a credit card. She turned around to see if the Quiet Man had one as well or needed change, but he was already gone.

She took care of the payments from her final two tables and then picked up the folder left by the Quiet Man. His total bill, including tax, was fifteen dollars and ninety-three cents. In the folder was almost exact change to cover this: a ten, a five, and a one, in that order. Behind the sixteen dollars that covered the bill, she found her tip. It was a brand new, crisp hundred-dollar bill.

Her eyes widened in disbelief. She grabbed one of the counterfeit detector pens Lonnie kept next to the register. The bill was real.

She made a point not to tell Edie about the Quiet Man's

generosity. Edie would have a very imaginative theory about it. If he had been Edie's customer, Velma would have delighted in hearing the wild vociferation of Edie's thoughts. As he had been hers, Velma preferred to assume he was wealthy, lonely, and eccentric, and leave it at that.

The crowd died down, and she was grateful she would be able leave work on time, especially when Brett arrived at midnight to pick her up. She was wiping puddles of wing sauce off a table when Lonnie saw Brett's polished, white, mid 1990s Cadillac El Dorado pull up to the front of the pub.

"Velma!" Lonnie called to her without looking up from cleaning his own puddles of wing sauce off the bar. "Are you almost done? Your weirdo boyfriend is here."

"He's not my fucking boyfriend." For the sake of conversation at work, she often referred to Brett as her "not-boyfriend." Lonnie chided her like an annoying older brother, enjoying the rise he got out of her when he challenged this.

"Yeah, right. He's your fucking boyfriend."

"He's a boy, he's my friend, and we're fucking. He's not my fucking boyfriend."

"Yeah, yeah. Finish up, your 'not-fucking-boyfriend' is outside waiting for you."

After ridding the last table of its condiment stains, she untied her apron and dashed out the door to Brett's car. She greeted him with a kiss and slipped her hand between his legs. He never objected when she asserted her dominance, so she sometimes tried to push his boundaries, always to discover he didn't have any.

"I'm hungry," she declared.

He drove them to the Argonaut, their usual dinner destination. The Argonaut was a popular twenty-four-hour diner in Yonkers. It had a chrome exterior that called to mind every possible 1950s diner stereotype. She was always disappointed it didn't have waitresses with huge blonde beehives and too much eye shadow who called everyone "hon."

It had all the other staple features of a classic diner—a counter with a fountain beverage machine and a huge urn of coffee behind it, mildly unpleasant fluorescent lighting, and a dessert case featuring a wide selection of delicacies that all looked like they were made of plastic.

She was tired of the Argonaut, but they could afford it, it had a full bar, and it was always open. After dinner, they almost always went back to her apartment. Sometimes, if the Argonaut's parking lot was empty enough, they only went as far as the back seat of Brett's car. Tonight, as they drove away from the diner, she unzipped his pants and teased him.

She didn't notice right away they were not heading in the direction of her apartment. "Am I distracting you too much? You're going the wrong way."

"Actually, I'm not. I have a surprise for you."

"Really?"

"Well, it's a special occasion."

"It is?"

"You don't remember?" He smiled at her, his cheeks flushed with arousal. "You will."

A few minutes later, he entered a parking lot meant for a single row of cars. Behind them was a cluster of trees, and beyond that, she saw a large and familiar building: White Plains High School. "High school? My surprise is high school?"

"Velma, what's the date today?"

"Well it's after midnight, so it's January fifth. Oh my gosh! January fifth!"

"Today is the ten-year anniversary of the first time we had sex."

"In the middle of those trees! I remember we knew we'd be safe because it was foggy that day."

"It was, and it was warm for January. Tonight it's not, but I thought it might be fun to revisit our tree."

She dashed out of the car, and he ran after her. "Which one was it?" she asked when they reached the trees at the edge of the school grounds.

"This one." He pushed her against rough bark and kissed her.

"I can't believe how long we got away with this before we got caught."

"Months." He panted as he put his hand under her shirt. "And tonight, we don't have to rush to catch a school bus." He forced his hand under her bra and pinched her nipple, making her let out an involuntary gasp. "Try not to scream," he whispered.

"Try to make me."

He unbuttoned her jeans and pulled them down along with her panties in one smooth motion.

"Holy shit, it's cold!"

"Shh." He knelt before her. "In a minute you won't care."

He tilted his head upward. When he was in the perfect position to do what he wanted, he grabbed her thighs for leverage and extended his tongue. She gasped again, stopping herself before the gasp became a moan. His motions were perfect, and it was only seconds before she forgot the cold. Within minutes, she felt warmth from within, and the ripples of pleasure that preceding her impending climax.

The lights of a passing car washed over them. He pulled his head away and leapt to his feet.

"For fuck's sake," she panted. "Don't fucking stop! Why did you stop?"

He yanked up her jeans. "We need to finish this back at your place." He grabbed her hand and tugged her in the direction of the parking lot.

"What? Why?"

"When that car passed by, I saw someone's shadow next to the tree, and it wasn't yours."

Seven

Detective Duran checked his coat pockets for two critical things—a picture of a yellow Dodge Challenger that had been faxed to him by the Mount Vernon Police, and a flash drive. He fidgeted with the flash drive. As he made his way to the home of Brett Riley, he took the drive in and out of his pocket many times. It meant making his first move as a hacker, his first illegal move as a detective. It didn't feel right to have the drive in his pocket, and didn't feel right not to. When he parked his car on the street in front of the duplex that held Brett's apartment, it happened to be there.

Het answered Duran's knock at his door wearing a bathrobe and Chewbacca slippers. Under different circumstances, Duran would have laughed seeing those slippers on a twenty-seven-year-old man. Brett looked malnourished, and as though he hadn't shaved or gone outside in several days. His pallor spoke of a deep sadness. He led Duran into his tiny apartment and sat on a futon that appeared to serve as both his couch and his bed.

"Have a seat." Brett indicated an aged easy chair next to the futon.

"Thank you." Duran hesitated.

The chair looked as if it belonged in a nursing home's dumpster, and he wondered if that's where Brett had procured it. He sat, expecting the chair to exude the smell of mothballs. It exuded the smell of stale cigarettes instead. The aroma reminded Duran of one of the few nuggets of information he remembered from the academy. Always bring cigars to a crime scene if there might be a corpse. Something about the cigar smoke, the instructor had said, would keep one from being sick when faced with the smell of rotting flesh.

"I know this is hard, Brett. I can only imagine what you're going through."

"Thank you. Do you mind if I have a cigarette?" Brett was already bringing one to his lips.

"Of course not, we're in your home." Duran took a pencil and notepad out of his pocket. He surveyed the apartment, assessing how he might get a few seconds of unseen access to the computer. "May I have a glass of water, please?"

"Sure. I have coffee."

It took Duran a moment to realize this was Brett's way of offering him coffee. "I'd love some. Just black."

He hoped Brett would also pour a cup for himself. In an apartment this size, his only chance to act would be if Brett used the bathroom. As he hoped, Brett went to his tiny kitchen and poured coffee into two mismatched novelty mugs. He returned and handed one of them to Duran. The coffee was room temperature, and the mug had a chipped picture of Wolverine on it.

"Thank you so much. Now, can you please tell me how long you've known Velma Bloom?"

Brett lit his cigarette, took a long drag, and exhaled. "Almost eleven years."

"Do you know of any reason she might have run away?"

He coughed then took a sip of coffee. "No."

That purposeful pause before his response told Duran less than an honest answer would have, but much more than Brett meant it to. "Do you know any reason she might be in danger, or of anyone who might want to hurt her?"

Brett paused before speaking again, mid-drag when the moment came for him for him to answer. "No."

To Duran, this was the same as if he jumped up and down and shouted, "I'm hiding something!" at the top of his lungs.

"Can you tell me about your relationship with Velma?" He needed to stage simple questions until he got his chance to do what he had come here to do. Maybe he would get some honest answers in the process.

"What do you want to know?"

"Well, start at the beginning. Could you tell me how you met?"

"She was my girlfriend in high school."

"You were still together? Are still together?"

"No." Brett's demeanor sank, but his tone became more honest. "Not really." His tone was so sorrowful Duran began to wonder if whatever Brett Riley was hiding wasn't what he thought.

"What was the nature of your relationship with her at the time of her disappearance?"

"I love her," Brett answered without his previous hesitation.

"She was my best friend. *Is* my best friend? We were together, mostly, but she didn't want to be my girlfriend."

"So they two of you were…"

"Fucking."

"I was going to say 'involved,' but that answers my question."

"Sorry. Excuse me, I need to use the bathroom."

A rush rolled through Duran. This was his moment to act. He waited for Brett to close the bathroom door and made sure he heard a urine stream before he took the thumb drive out of his pocket and hurried over to the desk.

Duran was impressed with his computer set-up. It didn't belong with anything else in the room. Brett had a very recent iMac with a clean monitor, and what looked like an expensive wireless speaker system. Duran put himself in stealth mode then inserted his thumb drive into the USB port. He left it there until he heard the urine stream stop, then returned it to the safety of his pocket and made a dash back to the decaying chair.

Brett returned to his seat on the futon and lit a fresh cigarette, even though there was an inch left in his previous one. "What else do you need to ask me?"

"Just one more thing." Duran reached into his inside jacket pocket and withdrew the picture of the yellow Challenger parked in front of the Mount Vernon homicide scene. "Can you please confirm for me that this vehicle belongs to Velma Bloom?"

He nodded. "That's her car."

"Do you recognize the house behind it?"

He looked closer at the photo, as though he wanted to recognize it. "No. I've never seen it."

The times when his heartache came through in voice were the times when Duran felt closest to certain he was telling the truth. "Thank you, Mr. Riley. You've been very helpful." He stood. "I don't want to bother you any more today. You look like you should get something to eat."

"Probably." Brett walked him to the door.

"Listen, I'll let you know if we find out anything. We've determined that her apartment isn't a crime scene, so at this point we have no reason to believe she's been harmed."

"Thank you, Detective."

Duran walked outside feeling much of Brett's sadness

lingering around him. When he settled himself into his car, he patted the thumb drive in his pocket. The deed was done. Duran felt the specific sensation of a victorious smile taking over his face.

"All right, lover boy. Let's see what it is you're hiding, or if you're paranoid enough to wipe your hard drive."

Eight

The Quiet Man had been making regular appearances at Lonnie's. He came in around peak dinnertime two or three times a week, but never two nights in a row. Each time he was there, he did the same thing. He drank only one beer and very, very slowly. He never spoke. He ordered by pointing and thanked her by nodding. She wondered if the time he said, "thank you," had been imagined. He always paid in cash, and he always left as close to exact change as possible to cover his meal and behind it, a new and flawless hundred-dollar bill.

"Here comes your creepy grandpa," Edie would remark when he entered.

Velma dismissed her comments about the Quiet Man, knowing his brief visits resulted in more than doubling her income for the night.

After the Quiet Man, Sam was Velma's second best tipper. He paid for his afternoon vodka with a fifty-dollar bill and never asked for change. When Velma began her night shifts, the first face she saw was Sam's. He typically arrived before five p.m., just after she did. He always left before much of a crowd gathered. Today, he was already there when she entered the pub.

"Hi, Sam." Velma walked behind the bar to clock in for the evening. "You're here early."

"I needed some company."

"That works for me. I'm glad you're here." She smiled at him, and he smiled back for a fraction of a second, looking embarrassed before his face returned to its usual melancholic state. She scanned the dining room to see if there was anyone else she needed to attend to and to look for her boss. "Is Lonnie around?"

"He's in the back cleaning the fryer. It's a wonder he trusts me up here alone with his liquor."

"That's why I asked." She reached into the well and selected a bottle. "Although you're not the one he shouldn't trust." She winked as she poured herself a shot of vodka.

"You know Lonnie wouldn't mind."

"I know, but he'd still bust my balls about it." She downed the shot and poured herself another. "I wouldn't do it if I didn't know he'd say yes if I asked, but somehow it still feels a little wrong."

"Is that why you go for the cheap stuff?"

"It feels less wrong. Besides, I don't care that much. To me, cheap vodka is like black coffee. I don't drink it for taste; I drink it for effect."

"That I can relate to."

"I'd love to go to bars and have expensive stuff all the time, but I usually opt for the liquor store. My cocktails are DIY. It's the only financially sound thing I ever do." She chuckled, hoping Sam would join her. He didn't.

"I'm old, and I've done the math." His smile was friendly, but his voice was matter-of-fact. "I'm not going to run out of money before I die."

"I probably will." Velma tried harder to laugh. Sam's mood needed a lift, as it often did.

"I don't think so. You're young, you have many years ahead of you to surprise yourself." He finished his drink.

"Ready for round two?" She headed for the vodka on the top shelf.

"Actually, that was round two. Well, it was round two here. I got started pretty early today."

"Nothing wrong with that."

"Thank you, Velma." He stood and dropped a fifty onto the bar. "I think I should get home."

After his departure, Lonnie's had a very thin crowd. She was bored, so she was delighted when she saw the Quiet Man enter. After he sat, she brought him his beer at the same time she greeted him. His drink order never changed, so she figured she would save herself some time and spare him the effort of pointing.

His food order did change, but he most often ordered burgers. She observed him over the course of time and noticed he was more apt to finish his burger when it was somewhat pinker. The first time she'd served him a burger, she'd forgotten to ask him how he'd like it cooked, so the kitchen automatically sent it out medium-well.

For his subsequent burger orders, she didn't bother asking. "How would you like your burger cooked?" was not a yes or no question, so she watched. After having served him his first half of a dozen burgers, she thought she had enough evidence to tell Luis to make it *medio*.

It had been over a week since he ordered a burger, so Velma was not surprised when she brought him his beer and saw he held up the menu with his finger on cheeseburger deluxe. "Okay, I'll get it started."

He nodded as a way of saying thank you and, as always, broke eye contact with her and sipped his beer. She didn't return to the table again until she brought his food, but then decided she felt like checking on him sooner than she normally would.

"How's your burger?" He glanced up at her with his usual scant smile and nodded again. She wasn't sure what compelled her, but Velma lingered next to the table. "You know, I feel funny we've never talked."

He took a sip of his beer and looked up at her again, this time with a different kind of smile. It seemed sincere. She took it as permission to continue.

She sat at the table across from him. "The first time you came in here, I could have sworn I heard you say thank you at one point, so I'm pretty sure you *can* talk, but I think I might have hallucinated it."

The Quiet Man's face and body gave her every indication of a little bit of laughter, but he still didn't make a sound. His face was warm and attentive, so she went on. "I'm Velma, but I guess you've heard that at some point in the last three weeks. I have no idea what your name is. You're probably never going to tell me."

He cocked his head and shrugged. He still wore a smile, but now it was different again. This smile had a dual purpose. It had secrets hiding behind it, but also revealed there were secrets to hide. She didn't know whether to continue or what to say.

"Well." She stood. "I'm sorry if I bothered you. I'm going to get back to work. You can talk to me, or tell me your name if you ever want to. If not, that's okay too." She smiled and walked away, half expecting to hear him mutter an ominous sounding name in an eerily low voice behind her, but she heard nothing.

When he left, nothing was any different. He paid with exact change and added a brand new hundred-dollar bill.

After that night, the Quiet Man did not return to Lonnie's again that week, nor did he visit the week after, or the week after that.

Nine

Velma glared at her black TV screen. Her left hand stroked Carrot, while her right alternately fondled her TV remote and moved a cigarette from her lips to her glass ashtray. She growled in frustration, exhaling smoke in the direction of her barely open window. She'd had a long and tedious day of waitressing.

The New York January air blew in through the window, dissolving her puffs of smoke and bringing a biting chill into the room. Along with the chill came the sounds made by drops of freezing rain hitting the window and landing on different surfaces outside. It made Velma want bourbon. Everything about that night made her want bourbon.

"Fucking lot of good Vassar did me," she said to no one.

It never bothered her that her line of work was far from commensurate with her education. The cat meowed, expressing no desired end. She wished the ashtray on her right were a rocks glass, that the ashes were whisky. She imagined it reforming and filling with an inch and a half of bourbon and three ice cubes. She could see the swirl around the cubes created by the difference in the densities of melted ice and eighty proof brown liquid.

She shivered, and her teeth chattered. She craved the warming sensation the bourbon would provide. It was 8:47 p.m. on a Sunday. If she left now, she could get to the liquor store before it closed at nine. Carrot meowed again. They both turned to the window and listened to the freezing rain against the glass.

"You're right," Velma said. "Not worth it."

She considered going back downstairs and having a drink at Lonnie's, but it wasn't just bourbon she wanted. It was bourbon in the peace and solitude of her home. She took a long pull from her cigarette then smashed it into the ashtray. She felt the tacky residue of her lip-gloss on her fingers and looked at the pink lip prints on the butt of her cigarette.

"Fuck it." She waved the last bit of remaining smoke toward her window and then hastened to shut it.

It was 8:48. She could go to the liquor store in her slippers.

She wasn't wearing a bra, but she didn't care. Grabbing coat and purse from their hooks on the wall, she made for the door. Carrot started to follow her. He cocked his head. 8:49. His reflection in the glass door of her microwave captured his critical expression. Velma grunted and sighed with acceptance.

"No bourbon for me." She dropped her things and returned to the couch. Carrot joined her. She reached for the remote, pausing as she formed an idea.

She investigated the liquor in the cabinet she used as a TV-stand. She had no bourbon, no whisky of any kind. Not one type of brown liquid. She reached for a bottle of vodka, trying to shake off her disappointment when she saw something she'd forgotten was there: absinthe. In the back left corner, covered with dust, was a bottle of French absinthe she bought on a whim over a year ago. She snatched it up and blew off the dust. Carrot and Velma both sneezed. She took the bottle to her miniscule kitchen counter and got a rocks glass out of her cupboard. She needed sugar and ice.

"You know, Carrot, drinking this makes me feel rather like James Joyce or Marcel Proust." She thought of herself in a chateau in France, pouring the absinthe over a sugar cube through a slatted spoon.

That image made her snicker until she reflected on the fact that, had she made some different choices in the last few years, she could have been in Paris. Perhaps not in a chateau, but in a spacious, urban apartment and certainly in possession of sugar cubes and a slatted spoon.

As it was, she was in her five-hundred-square-foot studio apartment in Yonkers. She didn't have a slatted spoon, and she didn't have sugar cubes. She did have most of a one-pound bag of sugar. It had been so long since it had been touched it had become essentially one giant sugar cube. Carrot sat on the floor beside her and watched.

"Don't judge me," she said. "I really wanted bourbon."

She poured two ounces of absinthe into the glass and added some ice. She smiled at the beginning of the absinthe's clouding from the initial melting of the ice. She still needed sugar. She went to the refrigerator and pulled out a can of Trigger Finger. It was packed with sugar. It was also bright pink, and absinthe was green. Whisky was brown. Despite objections from Carrot, who seemed to disagree with her that creativity won out over class in this situation, she opened a can and poured the dreadful pink liquid over the absinthe until the mixture was akin to a shade of brown. She felt victorious and embraced it.

The absinthe clouded when touched by the sugar and water-based mixer. Though brown, the concoction lost any resemblance it might have had to whisky in any form. It looked like watered down chocolate milk. Tasted like rubbing alcohol infused with Twizzlers.

Content with her impromptu bourbon alternative, she returned to sit in front of her still blank TV. Carrot joined her on the couch and went to sleep, resigning himself to the fact class had officially gone by the wayside for the evening. Though naught had been accomplished aside from a warped version of a victory over her lack of access to bourbon, her mind was at ease. She had won this one tiny battle, and for a waitress who had a long and tedious day, this was no small thing.

When she finished her cloudy, vile drink, she put the empty glass on the floor beside her and reclined with her head on the cushioned arm of the couch. Carrot stirred and repositioned himself around her feet. His rhythmic purring soothed her until she was as comfortable as she could imagine being, all things considered. She closed her eyes and turned off her thoughts.

At 10:02 p.m., the phone rang and her peaceful, not-quite-sleep state was broken. Before noticing that the number on her caller ID was blocked, she answered it. "Hello?"

"Is this Velma? Is this Velma Bloom?" The voice had a faint accent she couldn't identify. It sounded like the voice of someone who had worked very hard to use an American accent to cover their natural intonation.

"Yes, who is this?"

"I am speaking with Velma Annalise Bloom?"

Velma sat up straight and wondered if one serving of absinthe was enough to give her auditory hallucinations. She never used her middle name. No one outside of her family even knew she had a middle name. "Yes, what is this about?"

"Your father is dead. We need to speak."

"What? My father's fine. I just talked to him. Who the hel—"

"This is not safe. I will contact you tomorrow evening." The caller disconnected.

She sat in silence and stared at the phone while she processed what transpired. An anonymous caller's detached voice had announced that her father was dead.

Her mind raced. Could her father be dead? She had spoken to him on the phone the day before. It must have been a prank, she thought, until she remembered the man on the phone had known her middle name. Could it have been Lonnie? Had she written her middle name down on some document or other for her employer?

She didn't think she had. She never signed an official lease for her apartment. No, Lonnie wouldn't have heard the name Annalise anywhere. Even if he had, a phone call like that was not his sense of humor. Or anyone's. It simply wasn't funny.

Velma called her parents. Her mother answered. "Hi Mom."

"Sweetheart, is everything okay?"

"Um, yeah. Are you and Dad okay?"

"Of course we are. What's wrong, Velma?"

"Nothing, I just, um, I wanted to say hello."

"You never just want to say hello. What happened? Is there someone there? Did someone hurt you? Should we call the police?"

"Fuck, Mom! No, really, I'm fine. Seriously."

Then her father picked up the phone. "Velma, what's the matter?"

Relief washed over her when she heard his voice. "Hi, Dad. Nothing's the matter. I told Mom I just called to say hello."

"That's not like you. Are you sure you're okay?"

"Is your boss bothering you?" Her mother was going to dig.

"No…"

"Velma, are you drunk?"

"Mom! I-Yes. Mom, Dad, I'm kinda drunk, and uh, I'm going to bed early. I love you."

"We love you, too, honey," said Franklin. "Get some sleep."

Ten

Monday, April 28, 2008

Detective Duran entered Lonnie's Pub, wishing he could be there for whisky instead of business. He found the proprietor behind the bar talking to one of his few scattered customers while polishing a glass.

"Welcome back, Detective." Lonnie flashed him the friendly, comforting smile unique to bartenders.

"Hello again." Duran approached the bar and sat on the stool beside the man who had been talking with Lonnie. The man had gray hair, a kind face, and a shroud of melancholy common among regular patrons of bars like this one. "Sorry to barge in on you, Lonnie. I hate to interrupt, but I just need a second of your time."

"What can I do for you? Hey, it's after four. Feel like having a real drink?" Lonnie chuckled and put an empty rocks glass on the bar in front of Duran, as though he had read his mind and already knew what that drink would be. He failed to suppress a smile.

"I'll make this real quick." He pulled out the picture. "Can you confirm that this is Velma's car?"

Both Lonnie and the gray-haired man looked at the picture. "Yep," Lonnie said, "I'd recognize that monstrosity anywhere." The gray-haired man nodded.

"Do you recognize the house behind it?" Both men glanced at the photo a second time and shook their heads.

Duran wasn't surprised. He hadn't expected either man to have information for him, at least none they'd be willing to share. He folded the picture and put it back in his inside jacket pocket.

"Okay then. Thank you, gentlemen. That concludes my work for today. Lonnie, I would love to have that drink now. A burger too, medium rare with Swiss cheese."

"Sure thing. Drink?"

"Johnny Walker Black. Neat."

Lonnie poured a generous helping into the empty rocks glass then turned to his computer to put in Duran's food order.

"Oh, Detective," Lonnie indicated the gray-haired man. "This is Sam. He knew Velma. Sam, this is the guy trying to find her."

Duran extended his hand, and Sam shook it. "Jackson Duran. Good to meet you, Sam."

"Likewise, Detective."

Duran swallowed a mouthful of his whisky and decided he would keep this visit short so he could head to the liquor store for a bottle of his own to take home. He would have to find just the right book to pair with it. "I've declared myself off duty for the day. Just call me Jackson."

Sam took a sip from what Duran thought was a small glass of water, but now realized was a large glass of vodka.

"Are you ever really off duty, Jackson?" Sam raised his eyebrows and smiled.

"Too soon to tell." Duran chuckled. "I've been a cop for seven years, but I've only been a detective for seven days."

"Well, I should say congratulations then." Sam lifted his glass, and Duran followed suit.

Both men brought their glasses to their lips. He realized how wonderful it was to be distracted from work, able to live in the moment, and feel like nothing more than a man at a bar.

"And I," Lonnie chimed in, "get to say that I knew you back your uniform days. Sam, this was the guy who was here after the break-in two weeks ago."

"Really? So you've met Velma?"

"Briefly." Duran's wonderful experience of being a carefree man in a bar disappeared in an instant. "I just took her statement. Sweet girl."

"She sure was. Is, I hope." Sam took another sip of vodka, and Duran regarded his eyes. They were sad, tired…and they were hiding something. "The man who broke in here is still in jail?"

Duran sipped his drink to give himself a moment to think about how to answer, but Lonnie answered for him. "Jail? He's still in the fucking hospital, right?"

"Um, yeah. As far as I know." Duran wished Lonnie had kept his mouth shut.

"Hospital?" Sam raised his eyebrows and looked from Duran to Lonnie.

"He was, uh, injured during…"

"Injured?" Lonnie interrupted with a smile. "Velma fucking blinded him!"

"She did what?" Sam looked alarmed.

Duran sank in his seat. She had asked him to keep her actions a secret, and he assured her he would. He didn't know what he could say now to stop this conversation. He couldn't break his promise to her by telling Sam the truth, but giving a vague, non-specific answer might make Sam assume something worse than the truth.

Lonnie poured himself a shot of Jameson and leaned over the bar. "The guy's got his pistol about two inches from my head. Velma's standing, like, twenty feet away and throws a bottle of Tabasco sauce, hits him right in the face."

Sam went from looking shocked to looking ill. "Are you telling me the bottle shattered?"

"Right in the motherfucker's eyes. He cried like a little bitch."

"Velma asked me not to make that story public," Duran said softly.

Neither of the other men paid him any mind. Everyone was quiet as a short man in a dirty white apron came out of the kitchen to deliver Duran's burger.

"*Gracias*, Jorge," Lonnie said.

The short man nodded and went back to the kitchen. Duran took a bite, grateful for a reason not to speak.

Sam broke the silence. "How is that possible?"

Lonnie poured himself another shot. "Velma's got her quirks, but damn if she's not the smartest person I ever met. She saw this Tabasco bottle with no lid and a crack in it, and made it into a weapon. Pretty fucking brilliant."

"Yeah. Brilliant." Sam looked as though he'd been punched in the stomach.

Duran watched him pour his remaining vodka down his throat.

Sam held out the glass. "Lonnie, one more, please. Just single is fine."

Lonnie poured him a double. "Sam, I've never seen you order a single."

"All this talk about Velma… I'm worried. I know it's silly." He swallowed half the vodka, and his mind seemed to drift. He looked down as though his words were meant for no one. "She was just a girl working in the bar where I go to forget things."

Lonnie poured even more vodka into Sam's glass. "It's not silly. I'm worried about her too."

Sam took a fifty out of his pocket and put it on the bar. "Thank you, Lonnie. I actually think I should head home." He stood and put another twenty dollars on the bar. "Get the detective a round on me."

"Sure thing, Sam." Lonnie pocketed the money.

"Thank you," said Duran. "I promise we're working hard to find her."

"I'm glad." Sam forced a tiny smile and walked away from the bar. "It was good meeting you, Detective."

They nodded at one another. Sam left wearing an expression Duran couldn't discern beyond that there was something behind it that needed discerning.

"Nice guy," he said after Sam was out the door.

"Yeah. He's been coming here for years. Always takes good care of me and the girls. He liked Velma best. She was the smart one."

"Looks like he's pretty upset about the whole thing. I don't blame him."

"I've been a wreck myself. I'm just hiding it."

"Listen, Lonnie, how well did Sam and Velma know each other?"

"I guess as well as they could for being an old man who lives on vodka and a girl working in a bar."

Duran looked around to make sure no one else was within earshot. "I think I'd like to talk to him again. Could you tell me his last name?"

"Sam...shit, I don't know his last name. It's never come up, and he only ever pays in cash. It's funny, now that I think about it. I've known the guy for at least five years and I have no idea what his last name is. Or anything else about him, actually. If he has a job, he's never talked about it. I always just assumed he was retired. He's old, and he drinks a lot. He's gotta live nearby, though. With as much as he drinks, he always either walks or takes a cab. You don't think he did anything, do you?"

"No, but Velma didn't seem to know a lot of people. Anyone who knew her as well as he did is someone I'd like to talk to."

"Well, if it helps, I can at least tell you he's here inhaling vodka about five times a week, usually comes in between four and five o'clock."

"That's good to know. Thank you, Lonnie. This burger is delicious, by the way. I'll be back."

Eleven

Velma failed to sleep for the next thirteen hours. Her father was fine, and she was safe, but the phone call she received last night continued to trouble her. It infiltrated her dreams. She dreamt of finding out her father had died in some kind of fiery explosion, that his voice on the phone had been some imposter hired to soothe and deceive her. She dreamt Brett had killed her father in an act of chivalry so they could be together without enduring his objections. She dreamt both of her parents were shot and killed while being mugged in a back alley of Yonkers, having taken an alternate route to visit her.

That was the dream she was having when her phone rang at a few minutes after eleven the next morning. She didn't wake immediately, and the sound of the ringtone became the part of a dream in which she was receiving the news of her parents' deaths. The phone continued to sound for several seconds before she woke. The caller was Lonnie. Velma was overdue at work.

"Hello?" She tried to speak using the voice of a sick or very hungover person.

She didn't know why she bothered, Lonnie wouldn't have been angry with her if she told him she overslept. In his world, sleeping late and not getting to work on time was a normal and forgivable thing. That was one of many ways in which their worlds differed. She chose to put on an act rather than swallowing her pride.

"Velma, where are you?"

"Where do you think I am?" She chuckled as she sat up, mentally preparing herself to wash and curl her hair. If nothing else, that had to be done.

"Sorry, I mean, you okay? I need you to be here. I just came in on my day off because Nancy called out 'cause her fuckin' kid's sick, and we already had a customer and the goddamn door was locked."

"I'm okay, Lonnie. Sorry. I guess I'm a little hungover. I'll be down in twenty minutes. Will you set up for me please?"

"Yeah, Velma, I got it. Just get here."

She slipped out of bed and downed what remained of the

energy drink she opened the night before. She took a moment in between doing her hair and getting dressed to laugh at the previous night's beverage ingenuity, but her amusement ended as soon as she remembered the mysterious phone call. She looked at Carrot and said to him what she needed to say to herself.

"Everything's okay. It was just a prank, or a mistake, or something. Dad's fine, Mom's fine. I'm fine, and you're fine. Time to go to work." She pulled on her loose sneakers, tied on her apron, and dashed downstairs.

"You don't look so hung over to me." Lonnie greeted her from behind the bar.

"Good morning, Lonnie."

"We're all set up. Can you just put some coffee on for me? I made a pot when I came, but I drank it all."

"Was there whisky in it?"

"You're funny. Anyway, we're fine. Sam had a meeting or something so he came in for his liquid lunch a little early."

"I got the coffee. Wish I could do a liquid lunch."

"Fuck it. It's cold out, starting to snow, probably going to be dead today. Make the coffee, bring us each a cup and I'll make liquid breakfast." He already had a bottle of Jameson out on the bar.

"You're the best, Lonnie."

Three Irish coffees later, Velma was energized, but still haunted by the memory of the phone call. *He knew my middle name.*

If it hadn't been for the caller saying "Annalise," she could have dismissed it as prank and not given it a second thought. She kept herself distracted by helping Lonnie dust off the little-used top shelf liquor bottles. It was the perfect activity for a slow workday, especially after three cups of alcohol and caffeine.

After the bar and all its bottles were spotless, Lonnie poured her Irish coffee number four. Velma had started to experience a sense of calm when Lonnie's Pub got an unexpected rush. This didn't often happen on days it snowed, because the men who flocked there for lunch to escape their jobs had already used the weather as an excuse not to go in to their jobs in the first place. It was an ideal scenario for her.

For the next two-and-a-half hours, she multitasked with such intensity, the haunting disappeared. She dashed to and fro, taking orders, helping Lonnie mix drinks, yelling at the cooks, clearing tables, and stuffing her apron with cash.

Around two-thirty, the rush ended, and a sobered-up Velma returned to dwelling on her thoughts while she and Lonnie counted money. The restaurant had grossed almost nine hundred dollars in the past two and a half hours alone, and she found herself with about two hundred dollars in tips, triple the amount she expected to make during a lunch shift on a snowy day.

"Well, it may not be a great day overall, but we hauled enough ass to make that rush pay off," Lonnie said.

"Yeah." She stared down at her money. She hoped repetitive counting would soothe her mind.

"I'm not gonna ask, but you're acting like something's wrong."

"I'm just tired, Lonnie. That many customers would have been great if they were spread out over five hours instead of two and a half."

"Well, you kicked ass, kid. Let me get you some more fuel for the rest of the shift." He pulled out a new bottle of Jameson. "You want it with coffee or no coffee?"

"Fuck it. No coffee. No ice either."

"Look at you!" He poured her an inch of whisky. "You're making me think of my father. That old shit loved whisky. Didn't matter what it was, scotch, bourbon, that Canadian crap, whatever. If it was brown and would get him sloshed, he fucking loved it. Must in be in my genes or something."

"I don't know about me, then. My parents almost never had liquor around. They're obnoxious fucking wine snobs."

"Hey, your taste ain't so bad." He gave himself almost two inches of whisky and lifted his glass toward her.

She moved to do the same, but stood suddenly as he planted an idea in her head. It was a crazy idea, but one she knew wasn't going anywhere. She had some investigating to do.

"Lonnie," she said, scrambling to think of what to say, "I gotta go."

He put his glass down and looked at her with concern. "You gotta go?"

"Um...I think I had too much earlier, and I didn't have breakfast. Edie's coming in in an hour? I mean, the place is empty for now. You okay until she gets here?"

"Well, yeah, but can't you hang out until then?"

"Lonnie, please, I really gotta go. I promise I'll be back for the night shift." She turned and headed to the kitchen to get her coat and go out the back door.

"Okay, Velma, but you call me if you need help. Or come downstairs." He added, just before she was out of earshot, "and later you better tell me what the hell is goin' on!"

"Thanks, Lonnie, you're the best!" She called back without turning her head, leaving the kitchen door swinging behind her.

She was on a mission and was out the back door before she even donned her coat. She jumped into Smiley and pulled out of her parking spot, letting the engine roar all the way to White Plains.

Franklin opened his front door. He hadn't responded to her initial knocks, and she stood waiting until she realized he likely assumed the knocks were from an unwelcome solicitor. She sent him a text message. "It's your daughter. Let me in the house. Now."

As soon as the door was open, she entered. She strode past her father, curls bouncing with each step. When she reached the living room, she tossed her car keys onto the sofa and took a seat beside them.

Her father joined her, perching on the edge of his easy chair so he could face her at an angle. "Velma, it's good to see you but what on earth is this about?"

"Is Mom home?"

"She went out for groceries and wine. I don't know how long she'll be."

She leaned toward him. "Am I adopted?" She looked him in the eyes. He said nothing. "Holy shit, I'm fucking adopted!"

"Velma, calm down, I didn't say you were—"

"You didn't say I wasn't, which is pretty much the same thing as saying I was. I can't believe this. I'm almost twenty-five years old, and you never thought you could tell me you're not my goddamn parents!"

"We…Velma, start over."

"Okay. Mr. Bloom? I'm sorry, Professor Bloom, are you or are you not my biological father?"

"Please call me Dad."

"Fine. So, are you my dad, Dad?" His reply was almost exactly what she imagined before confronting him.

"I'm not your biological father, but I've been your dad since you were three months old."

"Wow. Wow!" She and Franklin sat in silence for the better part of an awkward minute. "So, I've got some questions."

"You can ask me anything, but I might not have the answers. How did you find out?"

"You may not be able to answer, but at least let me ask the first questions."

"I'm sorry."

"Who are my parents? My biological parents?"

"Your mother's name was Annalise Miley."

"Annalise. Anna-fucking-lise, explained at last."

"She died giving birth to you."

"How medieval of her." Velma almost felt guilty for not having more of an emotional reaction to hearing of her biological mother's death, but until moments ago, she hadn't known Annalise Miley existed.

"When we adopted you, we thought it was a very pretty name."

Velma suddenly felt very warm toward the man who raised her. All her life, she had thought her middle name sounded very hoity-toity, and her parents had chosen it out of snobbery. Hearing that they simply found the name Annalise to be "pretty" was refreshing.

"What about my dad? I mean, my biological father? Is he dead too?"

"I don't know."

"What do you mean you don't know? You don't know if he's dead, or you don't know who he is?"

"I know neither who your biological father is, nor if he is living or dead. No one does. The only person who knew was your mother. Your biological mother."

"She was the *only* person who…?" Velma felt her heart jump, and her mouth open on its own. "Dad, I'm sorry. We'll talk about this later."

She grabbed her keys and rose from the couch. She kissed Franklin on the forehead and strode toward the door with even more intensity than when she entered.

"Don't tell Mom I was here."

Velma pulled the front door shut behind her on her way to her car. She drove home as fast as she could without attracting attention and parked her car with a screech when she arrived. She called Lonnie, though he was but a few feet away, as she dashed up the back steps of the building.

"Velma. You're out of breath, what's…?"

"Something just came up. I got kind of a family emergency. I'm sorry I can't work tonight. Please don't be mad, I'll explain later." She hung up the phone before he could reply.

She entered her apartment, locking the door behind her. She threw her phone onto the couch, sat down beside it, got comfortable, and waited.

The phone call she wanted didn't come for almost seven hours. Half of that time, she spent pacing and the other half planted on the couch, staring at the phone. She had the TV on in the background, but paid it no attention whatsoever, despite her attempts. She had two phone calls, grunting with frustration when she saw they were not the one she wanted. The first was Brett. He was probably downstairs wondering why she wasn't at work, and she wondered why he didn't just knock on her door. He didn't leave a message. The second was Elizabeth Bloom, who left a very long message, which Velma ignored.

She took an occasional swig from a handle of rum to try to calm herself down, but between pacing, smoking, and pouring her generic energy drinks down her throat, she forgot the bottle was even there.

By the time the phone call came, she had consumed five sixteen-ounce energy drinks and smoked forty-seven cigarettes. After number six, she opened her window. After number twelve, she closed it and took the battery out of her smoke alarm. She was making her eighth trip to the kitchen trashcan with her ashtray when she finally heard the phone. She stopped mid-step, carrying the full tray back with her. She dropped it with a clunk onto the coffee table. Her heart pounded as she looked at her phone to make sure it was the call she wanted: unknown number. She answered.

"I just smoked forty-seven cigarettes waiting to hear from you," she said to the mystery caller.

It wasn't, perhaps, the most ideal greeting. The caller was silent for a few moments before she heard a breath.

"Hello, Velma." The voice was male, and she still could not identify the faint accent. "Accept my apologies for the delay and for my abruptness last night."

"Okay." She didn't know what else to say. "Who is this? How do you know my middle name?"

"I am a friend. I must speak with you in person." The man began to speak fast. "There are things you need to know."

"Well as of today, I know I'm adopted."

"Please be quiet and listen to me." He spoke even faster. "I am sorry you had to make that discovery. You have questions, and I have answers for you."

"Okay."

"You are not working tomorrow evening?"

"No."

"You will meet me at seven o'clock tomorrow night at the Applebee's in the Cross County Center. You will not drive your car. You will take a taxi, and you will tell no one."

"Okay. I can do that. Who are you? How will I find you? How will I know you?"

"I will be at a table in the restaurant alone. You will know."

"Well, can you tell me what you look like, or what you'll be wearing? Something? Anything?"

"You do not need this. You will know." The call disconnected.

Twelve

Duran leaned back in his chair with his feet on his desk. He was drinking a gimlet and reading Mary Shelly's *Frankenstein*. He had chosen a book he had read many times before, because he would not be giving it his full attention. Though he was home and clad in pajama pants and a T-shirt, he was focused on detective work. This was a stake out; every few seconds, he glanced up at his computer screen, watching for any activity from Brett Riley.

Brett was watching old episodes of *The X-Files*. Every so often, the episodes would pause while, Duran assumed, Brett got up for a snack or to use the bathroom. This went on for hours. He wasn't even checking his email.

Impatient, Duran let *The X-Files* provide some background noise for his wandering thoughts. He was hung up on one thing. He thought Brett was the only person hiding information from him about Velma, but now he knew there was someone else: Sam.

Duran knew Sam would return to Lonnie's Pub. If he didn't realize Duran suspected him of hiding something, he would have no reason to change his routine. If he did, changing his routine would only increase Duran's suspicion. He wished he could have thirty seconds alone with Sam's computer and his flash drive, but that would require being inside the other man's home—a place he didn't think he'd be invited.

Duran didn't even know where Sam's home was, his last name, or if his first name really was Sam. Not counting his certainty that Sam had some secret, all Duran knew for sure was that he was an old man with an impressive alcohol tolerance. Alcohol, he thought, was a tried and true, albeit old-fashioned way for a man with secrets to calm his mind.

He didn't like doing things the old-fashioned way, save calming his thoughts with a cocktail. He thought about his own secrets and looked at the drink in his hand. It gave him an idea. An affinity for alcohol was the one thing he and Sam had in common, and with a little more information, maybe he could use it to learn the old man's secrets.

Duran put down his drink, muted his computer, and called Detective Stevens.

"Jackson, this better be important," Stevens said in lieu of a hello.

"It is. Why?"

"Because it's two o'clock in the fucking morning. Some people sleep."

"It's two a.m.?" Duran's computer screen confirmed the time. "Shit, Jeremy, I'm really sorry. I've been working, and I haven't looked at a clock in hours."

"Working? You mean you've been drinking alone with an old book."

He looked down and saw he still had *Frankenstein* open on his lap. Then he peered into his right hand, the one not holding the phone. His fingers were wrapped around a cold glass. He hadn't left the gimlet on his desk for more than a few seconds. "You know me well, Stevens."

"Let me guess, Johnny Walker and Stephen King? Captain Morgan and John Irving?"

"Gimlet and Mary Shelley."

"Gin and *Frankenstein*. Very old-fashioned."

"Interesting choice of words. Maybe I'll make one of those next." Stevens chuckled softly. "Listen, I need your help with some detective work."

Stevens groaned. "I'm listening."

"I met a guy at Lonnie's Pub who knew Velma. He's suspicious as hell. He drinks there almost every afternoon, and nobody knows his last name or anything else about him."

"And you think he's hiding something."

"Yes."

"Go to bed, Jackson. Give me some more specifics tomorrow, and I'll follow him home in an unmarked car. After we have an address, we can go from there. Okay?"

"Thank you, Jeremy." Duran hung up and once again found himself alone with his book, his drink, and his secrets.

His biggest secret was that, in his mind, what was right and what was legal didn't always align. What he saw on his computer screen made him a criminal, but if Brett's online activity gave him any information about the safety or whereabouts of Velma, the ends would justify the means. It would prove Duran's belief there was no mutual exclusivity between criminals and heroes.

He went to the kitchen and made himself another gimlet. When he returned to his desk, Brett had turned off *The X-Files* and was now watching what Duran thought to be very boring pornography. He rolled his eyes and paid a little more attention to *Frankenstein* for the next eight minutes. After that, for the first time in hours, Brett's screen was not displaying any kind of video. Where Duran had seen a woman's shaved genitals moments ago and Agent Scully before that, he now saw text and hoped Brett was finally checking his email.

Duran sat up straight and looked more closely at the screen. Brett wasn't checking his email.

"What the *fuck*?" Duran rose and ran to the kitchen. He made himself a back-up drink, a sandwich, and a pot of coffee. It was going to be a long night.

Brett was doing in-depth research on CIA mind control experiments. He spent the next three and a half hours downloading and collecting material on Project MKUltra. He had a desktop folder containing a wide variety of articles on human experimentation and on at least half a dozen other declassified CIA projects. There was a separate folder dedicated to MKUltra with over a hundred documents inside. This was an obsession.

Around five a.m., exhaustion and alcohol won out over intrigue and coffee. Duran fell asleep at his desk, desperately trying to convince himself that Brett's research had nothing to do with Velma Bloom.

Thirteen

Velma stepped into a cab the following evening. She had made her plans without hesitation. There was no question in her mind that whatever answers her mysterious caller had for her were ones she needed to seek, but the moment she sat in the back seat of the cab and reached for the door to pull it shut, her heartbeat quickened. The arm she extended toward the door was suddenly cold and trembling. She let her fingers linger on the handle of the open car door. For a moment, exiting the cab was as much of a possibility as pulling the door closed and buckling her seatbelt.

"Come on, honey, let's go," said the driver.

Velma's fear intensified as she made the decision to close the door, but she did it anyway.

Should she have asked Brett to follow her, or at least tell him where she was going? Should she have gone to the Blooms and asked for more information before obeying an unidentified, detached voice? Should she have armed herself?

She wished someone knew where she was. During the entire cab ride, she wondered if asking the driver to turn around and take her home would equate to wisdom or cowardice. She decided it would be both, but also that her aversion to cowardice was more powerful than her desire to be wise.

When she exited the cab and paid the driver, he drove away and left her standing in the parking lot, alone with her hindsight and uncertainties. People walked to and from their cars and in and out of stores and restaurants all around her. The shopping center was bustling with warm bodies, but Velma was alone. She had felt fear before, but never for her physical safety. She had been so consumed by excitement and curiosity that her good sense hadn't the slightest opportunity to chime in. Driven by her thirst for answers, she forced herself to act in spite of her terror and walk toward Applebee's.

She entered the restaurant foyer. It was filled with people talking and looking impatient as they held the plastic discs that would vibrate to alert them it was their turn for an open table. She made her way through the crowd to the main doorway. Before she could look around, the hostess greeted her.

"Hi, how many?" The girl rocked as she held a pen over a piece of paper with the large list of waiting patrons, and had a plastic pager at the ready.

Amazing how the servers and food runners dashed about without running into one another. Velma pitied the bartenders as they struggled to keep up. "Um, I'm meeting someone who might already be here. May I just look around?"

"Oh yeah, yeah, go ahead." The girl seemed relieved that she could relax her hand for a few seconds.

"Thanks." Velma circled the bar area.

She didn't expect to find her mystery companion there, but it was the logical place to start. The place was arranged in a big "U" shape with the bar at the center. She didn't recognize anyone at the bar or any of the high top tables around it.

As she worked her way to the next row of tables, she took care not to get in anyone's way. She scanned the tables row by row on one side of the bar, then the other. It wasn't until she looped around the restaurant that she saw a tall glass of beer and a familiar face at a booth near the front corner of the restaurant.

She paused and made sure her breathing was steady. The familiar face made her feel both more and less afraid. She strode up to the booth and tossed her purse onto the unoccupied side of it, then sat down and faced the Quiet Man. "So where have you been? I've been short on booze and cigarette money."

He scanned her face, looking very serious, as though he had all the cares of the world to bear. Then he laughed. "Velma, I am certain you have other questions you wish to ask me." He spoke softly, but now with no attempt to disguise his accent.

"Oh, you're Russian!" He was still and silent. "Well, I was wondering about that."

"Yes." He sipped his beer and took a deep breath. "I am sure you must have been. Perhaps we don't talk very loud, okay?"

Before she could respond, a waiter approached their table. From his hurried tone, it sounded as though the Quiet Man had been there for quite a while. "Oh good, you're both here. Hi miss, how you doin'?"

He was handsome and exotic with long wavy hair tied back into a ponytail, dark eyes, olive skin, and a neat goatee. In any other situation, she would have found him quite appealing, but with these circumstances, she could not have wished more powerfully for him to go away.

"Hi." She waited for him to continue, anxious to conclude the pleasantries.

"Hi… Okay, well, I'm Andy, and I'll be taking care of you this evening. I'd love to get you a drink. Here's a list of all our current specialties, I particularly recommend the Perfect Margarita…" he trailed off as Velma rolled her eyes. The Quiet Man raised an eyebrow at her.

"Thanks, Andy, but you can save the spiel." She eyed her companion across the table as she ordered her drink. "I'd like a double Stoli on the rocks, please."

"Sure thing, I just need to see your ID please." She got out her wallet and presented him with her license. "Hey, Velma, like from Scooby Doo, right?"

She was in no mood for that tonight. She snatched her license back from him. "Skip the rocks, Andy, and bring me an unopened can of Red Bull, please."

"Okay, you got it. I'll be right back and we can start you with some appetizers." He walked away and Velma rolled her eyes again. The Quiet Man chuckled.

"What?" she said. "I never BS people like that. It's stupid."

"He's doing his job. You made a very interesting drink choice."

"Well, what can I say? I heard your voice, and I thought of vodka."

"Oddly, I never cared for it myself." He chuckled again and smiled at her, sipping his yellow American beer.

"That is odd. Then again, I grew up in White Plains, and I don't like any wine that doesn't come out of a box."

The man laughed and sipped his beer again. They were silent for a moment as he refocused himself. His face remained kind but became very serious.

"So…?"

"I know you have questions, Velma. I promise I will answer as many as I can."

"Thank you, I think. Can you tell me your name?"

"My name is Alexei Novikov. Doctor Alexei Novikov. You

may call me Alex."

"It's nice to, um, officially meet you, Alex."

"Thank you, Velma."

"Are we related? Are you like my long-lost uncle or something?"

"No, I am not. We have no blood relation. Although that I am your uncle is an excellent cover for why we are here tonight."

"Which is…?"

"Again, I promise to explain to you everything I can. Listen to me first, before the waiter returns. When he returns, he will give you your drinks and begin rambling about the food. He will want us to order appetizers. You will choose two or three, whatever you would like. Do it now." He pointed to the menu, and she opened it, scanning her options. "Then you will tell him we have not decided on meals and not to return until he delivers whatever you order, because, you will tell him, I am your uncle whom you have not seen in a long time and we have some catching up to do."

"Well, the last part of that is true."

The waiter returned and handed Velma her drinks. She did as Novikov instructed, ordering a quesadilla and spinach dip, adding to it an order of two more double Stolis, one for each of them.

"I told you I did not care for vodka," said Novikov.

"I know. They're both for me. I took a cab here like you said so I'm not driving. Plus, this way he doesn't have to make an extra trip and interrupt us."

"You're a smart girl."

She smiled and raised her glass, downing its contents in one gulp. "Okay, my friend. What can you tell me quickly before Mediterranean Fabio comes back with my vodka?"

"There is much to tell," Novikov said. "More than I can tell you tonight, and I need to emphasize caution."

"So why are we in an overcrowded Applebee's?"

"Simple." He peered around the dining room. "No one can hear us. Two people talking in a public place does not arouse suspicion. I arrived early and situated myself where we would not be overheard or seen through a window."

"Who is my father?"

He glanced behind him. Andy was at the bar picking up their two small glasses, a moment shy of making his way over to their table.

"His name, as I knew him, was Robert Drake," he said, anticipating the timing of waiter's arrival.

Velma cocked an eyebrow. "As you knew him…?"

Novikov looked at her sharply. "Shhh!"

Andy arrived at the table. She was so focused on Novikov she hadn't even noticed him approaching. They remained quiet until the drinks were delivered and the waiter departed.

"How did you know he was going to get here right at that moment?" she asked.

"Let's just say I've had many years to master judging the timing of a man's footsteps."

"Who are you?"

"Do you want to know about your father?" Novikov was calm, and he spoke softly.

Velma suddenly had ten times as many questions in her mind as she did moments ago. "Yeah, and about you. We can start with him. So… Robert Drake?"

"Yes."

"That wasn't his real name."

"No."

"You can't tell me his real name."

"Not here."

"Who was he? What… what did he do?"

"He was an agent for your government."

"What? Wow. Was he in the FBI, or…?"

"He was in the CIA."

"He was a spy?"

"That was part of what he did."

"Are you telling me my father was like…James Bond?" Dr. Alexei Novikov laughed his hearty laugh again. "That's actually kind of awesome." She kept a straight face, and Novikov chuckled.

"I am sorry to say, Velma, he was very little like James Bond."

"Hey, 'very little like James Bond' is way more similar to James Bond than anyone else's father I know."

He laughed again, this time letting his smile linger a bit. "Robert, your father, he had a sense of humor, and he was a good man." He choked on his words and wiped a tear off his cheek with his sleeve.

A pinch of guilt winged through her. She hadn't thought about the fact that her enigmatic companion was grieving. Her own shock and curiosity had eclipsed the fact her father had died. She couldn't force herself to feel any sort of grief. She had never met Robert Drake. She had just lost a father, but she hadn't known she had him to lose. Dr. Alexei Novikov, she realized, had just lost a friend.

"You two were close?" she asked.

"Yes."

"I'm sorry you lost him."

"Thank you, Velma." He took a sip of his beer and collected himself.

"What happened to him? How did he die?"

"You may be expecting a more exciting answer, but he died from lung cancer. He smoked too many cigarettes." He paused and looked at her with a hint of a smile. "You smoke too many cigarettes, Velma. You should stop."

"Okay, Doctor." She had no plans to stop smoking. "How old was my father? When he died?"

"He was fifty-nine years old."

"What was he like? I mean, what did he like to do? Besides smoke cigarettes. Where did he live?"

"One question at a time."

"The questions I want to ask you the most are the ones I'm afraid to."

"Are you afraid of the answers or just of asking the questions?"

"Well, until you said that, just of asking the questions. But now both."

"If the questions you are referring to are what I suspect they are, then the answers to them will leave you with new questions. I warn you those new questions will be ones to which I may not have answers."

"You mean you may not have answers, or you'll have answers that you can't give?"

"Both."

A food runner arrived with their appetizers.

"Now I… really have no idea what to ask." She picked up a wedge of their quesadilla. "Alex, why now? Why am I learning about all of this only after he died?"

"I suppose I must explain that. Then, please allow me to

answer the first of your previous list of questions."

"Shit, I don't even remember what that was."

"You wanted to know about your father. Who he was as a man?"

"Yes. I do. Very much."

"That is something I am very happy to tell you." He put a tortilla chip in his mouth and chewed, anticipating Andy's approach from behind him.

"I hope I'm not interrupting, but how is everything for you two so far?"

"We're fine," Velma smiled at him, hoping he would go away, but he did not. She took in the well-cut jawline underneath the wavy locks that had come loose from his ponytail.

"If you're ready, I can take your dinner order." There was a note of impatience in his voice, but it was masked by the smoldering charm in his expression.

"Oh, ha. I kinda forgot about that." Velma opened her menu and scanned it. "I'll have the Oriental chicken salad. Can the chicken be grilled instead of fried, please?"

"Of course," Andy said. The impatience in his voice changed to relief. "And for you, sir?"

"The same please." Novikov looked up at Andy only as he spoke and spoke quickly.

"Great, I'll get that started for you."

Velma noticed something odd about the waiter's voice. He sounded very much like a native New Yorker, but there was some other accent underneath. She started thinking out loud. "What's funny about his voice?"

"He is Greek."

"How can you tell?"

"On the surface, he speaks like anyone else from this region. From the top layer of his voice I can tell you he has spent most of his life here, likely in a lower income area of a Yonkers or a nearby suburb. But one can hear another layer, if one listens for it. He is Greek, southern. Probably Spartan. It is subtle. I imagine he came to this country as a very young child."

"Wow. I guess I shouldn't ask how you can tell all of that."

"There is much that can be learned about a man from his voice, if you know what you are listening for."

Velma was becoming more and more curious about Dr. Alexei Novikov. "Wow."

"I am digressing. I want to tell you about my friend, Robert Drake, your father. First, I should tell you why you are learning of this only now. Before I do, please know that I am telling you more than I should. I should only be telling you that which you need to know. It is because you are your father's daughter, because of the affection I have for him, that I am telling you that which I think you deserve to know."

"Thank you."

"What you are about to hear is the information I told you would answer much, but leave you with more questions. I need you to promise me you will take what I tell you for what it is and not ask the questions I cannot answer."

"If I say I can't promise that, will you still tell me?"

"I am now committed to telling you, and I suppose it is unfair of me to ask you to make that promise. I don't have to ask you to understand why I can't answer the new questions. You're a smart woman, you will know why."

"Okay." She nodded.

"You are learning of your father's existence only after his death because I now no longer need to protect his safety. I came to know him over the past twenty-five years, which he spent living in my country."

"Why was he living in…? That's one I shouldn't ask, huh?"

"May I continue? He spent the last twenty-five years of his life in my country because he was under our protection, the protection of the Russian government. His work, as you can imagine, had its dangers. His life was in danger, so we protected him."

Velma began to piece things together. Her mind kept churning out more questions, and she answered some of them for herself.

"If I may read between the lines," she said, "I think you may be telling me more about yourself than you intend to."

"I am counting on your reasoning skills. I am telling you no more than I intend to, but more than I am saying out loud."

"For all the things this makes me wonder, I guess I'm glad to sort of know why he didn't raise me."

For the next hour, Novikov regaled her with tales about her father. He was an avid, though not competitive, chess player. The two of them spent many nights drinking and laughing together. Her father was the best man at Novikov's wedding in 1987. When, in 1995, his wife was killed in a terrible car crash, Drake was at his friend's side, keeping him afloat when he would have drowned in his grief.

The man known as Drake was well liked by all who met him. He never mastered all the nuances of the language, but spoke remarkable Russian. He loved children and spent a large portion of his free time visiting local orphanages. He read the younger children stories and taught the older ones to play chess. Anticipating some of them might be adopted by American families, he taught non-vulgar American slang to those who wanted to learn. He had hair almost as red as his daughter's.

Drake was diagnosed with lung cancer just over two years ago. He lived longer than expected by more than a year. He continued to live his life as well as he could until the sickness took over.

She was entranced. She loved Robert Drake. The image in her head of her dead biological father had been one of a shadow; a silhouette of a man shrouded in secrets, detached and not quite human. Now she had been shown the man casting that shadow, and he was more human to her than any of the living, breathing bodies in the crowd around her.

She and Novikov finished their dinner and declined Andy's offer of dessert. Velma nursed the last of her third drink. She ordered one more, a single this time, and one more unopened Red Bull to take home. Andy dropped off their check, and Novikov barely glanced at it before placing a hundred dollar bill and a twenty-dollar bill into the black folder.

"That's much less than you tip me," she said.

"Velma." He lowered his voice. "I am not tipping you."

"What do you mean you're not tipping me?"

"Can you think of a better way to pass a wanted agent's estate to his daughter?"

Her jaw dropped. "He knew about me," she said softly. "My dad knew about me."

"Of course."

"And I never knew about him."

"He thought about you every day."

Her eyes swelled. "I'm sorry," she said. "I didn't realize I would...care this much."

"I know." They both looked around and saw the Applebee's

79

crowd had significantly thinned.

"I have so much more I want to ask you."

"I think it's time for us to part for tonight. You should call your taxi."

"But I thought of some questions it's probably okay for you to answer."

"We can speak again another night."

"Okay." Velma called her cab. "They'll be here in five minutes."

"Good. I will come to Lonnie's this week. It will be like it always has been, and we will behave as though we never had this meeting."

"Okay. But we can talk again?"

"We can talk again. There will be things I still cannot tell you, but yes. For now, I have something to give you, and it will answer some of the questions I know you are thinking about the most right now." He reached into a small satchel he had been concealing on the seat beside him then withdrew a small package wrapped in brown paper and packaging tape and handed it to her. "You will put this in your purse. Now." She did as she was told. "You will not take it out until you get home. You will not open it until you are in your apartment and you have locked the door behind you, and you will open it very carefully."

"Okay," she said, "thank you. I should go wait for my cab."

"Yes, and thank you. Tonight has been a great pleasure for me, Velma."

She put on her coat, picked up her purse, and stood to leave. "It was great to see you, Uncle Alex."

She considered drinking one of her Red Bulls on the cab ride home, but she dared not open her purse. She clutched it against her body, caring only about whatever answers might be found inside that small brown package.

The eight-minute cab ride felt like an hour. She paid the driver and, in case he or anyone else was watching her, forced herself to walk at a normal pace to the outside door. Once she let herself in, she dashed up the steps to the door to her apartment. Her hands shook as she flipped through her keys to find the right one. Her heart pounded as her trembling fingers fumbled with the lock, and Velma was awash with excitement when she got to the other side of the door. She slammed it shut, locking it with both the bolt and the chain.

Carrot greeted her with a long, loud meow. She breezed by him to the couch. He jumped up beside her and meowed again.

"Sorry. Hi."

He just sat. With a shaky hand, she unzipped her purse. She withdrew the brown package and the two Red Bulls, placing it all on the coffee table in front of her. She opened one of the Red Bulls and took two large gulps of it.

Her focus heightened as she picked up the package and considered it. It weighed about two pounds and was approximately half the size of a shoebox. As it was covered in clear tape, she was going to need a knife to open it. She thought about stabbing a hole in it with one of her keys, but then remembered what Novikov had said about opening it carefully.

With anticipation both torturing and delighting her, Velma got up and searched her kitchen drawer for the right knife. She needed something sharp enough to make a clean cut through the paper but not harm the contents. Her silverware drawer proved to be lacking. She could go downstairs to the pub and borrow a knife, but that would mean leaving the apartment, which would mean leaving the package. Then she realized the answer was in the liquor cabinet.

She moved the bottles around until she found what she needed. There was a flip-out knife on the back of her corkscrew. She snatched it the second she saw it, along with the bottle containing two inches of vodka. She sat back down.

Afraid to reach for it, she stared at the package. After she consumed about a quarter of her first can of Red Bull, she filled it to the brim with vodka and lit herself a cigarette. She was surprised she hadn't already torn the package open with her teeth, but something was stopping her. Maybe it was fear, or maybe just the desire to delay gratification. Maybe it was both, but curiosity took over.

The corkscrew knife was duller than she thought it would be. She took great care in puncturing the outer seal of the tape around the package. Beneath the tape, there were several layers of brown paper protecting the contents. She held her cigarette between her lips and cut away the remaining shell of tape.

When all that remained was paper, she put her lit cigarette in the ashtray and began to unwrap. At her first glance of what was inside, she gasped and snuffed out the cigarette with a smash.

Before all the paper was even stripped away, five bundles of wrapped hundred-dollar bills fell out onto her lap. She scrambled to gather them up and pile them on the table. She tore away the remaining brown paper on the table surface and removed the rest of the contents. Before her were nine bundles of hundred-dollar bills. The bank wrapper on each said ten thousand dollars.

"Holy shit." She had never seen so much cash. When she emptied her savings and her trust fund, she'd gotten cashier's checks to pay for Smiley. "Carrot, I think my dad just gave us ninety grand."

The cat leaned over and smelled the money. Before she could stop him, the curious cat took a step and placed his front paws on the table. She moved to pull him away, but not before he stuck out a paw and knocked over the second, neater stack of bill bundles, the stack of four she had removed all together.

She wrapped her arms around the cat's torso and pulled him onto her lap. "Look at the mess you've made."

Then she saw something she hadn't before. Ignoring his protests, she lifted the cat off her lap and placed him next to her. What she saw was a folded plastic bag containing a piece of paper.

She turned to the cat. "I'm not going to ask how you knew that was there."

With the utmost care, she opened the bag and unfolded the very old, well-preserved piece of paper. On it was a hand-written letter. The penmanship was gorgeous. She read it slowly, making sure she could decipher every word of the fading cursive.

My dear friend,

As promised, I have left behind the name by which I was once known and take care not to put in print the name by which I know you. All the same, I trust this piece of paper will encounter no eyes but your own.

Accepting that this will read as cliché, I must tell you that I owe you my life. Because of you, I am able to stay alive and do what good I can with the years I have left. I feel it is wretched of me to ask anything more of you, but I am desperate and can think of no option but to implore you to do an incredible favor for me.

I left my former life behind with an immeasurable regret. My love, my Annalise, is now six months pregnant with our child. It pains me deeply that I left her with no explanation. I have a sensation of claws in my chest as I imagine her pain, her confusion, and her anger toward me. Beyond that, I suffer the ever-present sting of knowing I will never meet my child.

I know I can never return to my country, I know I can never take my place in the small family I made and then abandoned. What I ask of you, my friend, is to find Annalise Miley, the mother of my unborn child. Please get this money to her, any safe way you can.

The last thing I wish is to have you put yourself at risk, but I know I cannot reach out to her myself. The only way I can ever have peace in my heart is if she knows I never wanted to leave her, that I had no choice. I know this is not possible if I wish to remain alive. The closest I might get to a measure of that peace is if I can at least provide her with whatever resources I can to help care for our baby, to give our baby an education and a future. You are the only person I trust to do this.

My friend, you owe me nothing, and I owe you everything. I beg this favor of you because two innocent people, one so innocent as to not yet have taken a breath, have so much emotional agony ahead of them, and so I might become the new man you have helped me forge and take less of their agony with me on my journey.

A man can muster no thanks sufficient for what you have done for me already. I hope in my heart that when I hand you this letter, it is not our final parting. You are a good man and a friend I truly hope I continue to have in my new life. Among my dearest hopes is that I might ever begin to repay you.

-R.D.

Fourteen

Detective Jackson Duran opened the bottom drawer of his desk and pulled out a bottle of scotch. That was all he kept in that drawer except for the stack of books he used to hide it.

"Duran," a voice called from behind him. He laid the bottle on its side and covered it with the case folder he had in front of him. Then he realized whose voice he'd heard.

"Stevens, you scared me." Duran had spent his day reading some disturbing selections from Brett Riley's collection of documents on Project MKUltra. He was looking forward to getting drunk and falling asleep at his desk

"Sorry. Now uncover that bottle and share it, please. I've got something to show you." Stevens pulled a chair over from a nearby desk and sat down. Duran moved the folder off the scotch and stood it upright. Stevens opened it and took a swig, then continued, "I followed that guy you asked me to. The guy from the bar."

"And?" Duran's attention shifted to Stevens and the answers he might have found. Drinking and sleep were forgotten in an instant.

Stevens handed him a folder and took another swig of the scotch. "I watched him go into a house then checked the address. The owner's name is Sam Ferguson."

"This is all you have?" The folder was thin. Duran had been hoping for more information than could possibly be on the few pieces of paper inside.

"The guy is like a ghost. He has no criminal record, no employment history, and no living family. He was born in Pennsylvania sixty-five years ago and now he lives in Yonkers. In between, all we know is he attended the Perelman School of Medicine."

"So we know he has a medical degree, but no idea what he's done with it."

"Listen, it's something. I got you a list of past addresses. I don't know if it's going to help, but look it over. He's been living in his house in Yonkers for almost ten years. Before that he lived in a swanky building near Central Park."

"No employment records. How was he affording that?"

"No clue. He's had a few different apartments in New York over the past twenty-three years. Now look at the second page of addresses. Most of them have him listed as 'Doctor Sam Ferguson.' He must have been doing something. But when he came to New York in 1985, the doctor title disappeared."

"Shit. This creates more questions than it answers."

"I know. Now I'm wondering if we should be after this guy for anything besides information on a missing girl."

"We'll probably never find out." Duran hoped Stevens would leave. He wanted to be alone with his scotch and his disappointment.

"Probably not, but what's interesting is *why* we won't. It could just be a coincidence, but check out the fourth address down."

Duran sat bolt upright with shock. He knew it wasn't a coincidence. Before 1985, the town Dr. Sam Ferguson called home was Langley, Virginia.

"Who the hell *is* this guy?"

Fifteen

Wednesday, February 13, 2008

Velma was awake most of the night. For hours she read and reread her father's letter, trying to fill in the gaps. She also counted and recounted her stacks of money several times over. She got the same total every time. She even went downstairs to Lonnie's and took one of the counterfeit detector pens from behind the bar. She used it on each and every one of her nine hundred bills. Eventually, she fell asleep on the couch in the middle of reading the letter for what felt like the eightieth time.

She opened her eyes at around ten o'clock in the morning. The events of the past twelve hours must have been a fantasy, or a dream. But Velma was clutching a twenty-five-year-old letter, and on the coffee table beside her rested ninety thousand legitimate American dollars.

She had a plan for the day. She had thought of it the previous evening during her conversation with Novikov. There were so many possible stories behind what little she knew. She needed to investigate one small thing.

She went about her usual primping routine and drank her remaining can of Red Bull. She donned her go-to jeans, a low cut black sweater, and her standard winter boots and leather jacket. It was bright outside, so she added her sunglasses to the flattering but practical ensemble. When she checked herself in the bathroom mirror before leaving, she thought the black sunglasses, black jacket, and black scarf made her look very secret agent-like. Just as she was ready to leave the apartment, she remembered there was ninety thousand dollars in cash on her coffee table.

It wasn't in any real danger. She would lock her apartment, and no one could see in the window from the street. The biggest risk was Carrot scattering it about. Still, it would be reckless not to tuck it away. She considered places she could hide it, ways she could disguise it, things a criminal would do with ninety thousand dollars. She could unzip a couch cushion and stash it in there, or sew it into her mattress. What she couldn't do was put it in the bank, or have it lying loose on her coffee table.

She chose two hiding places: one for the cash, and one for her father's letter. She organized the bundles in the compartments of an old travel makeup case and slid it into the back corner of her closet. She carefully folded the letter and put it back in its original plastic bag before tucking it out of sight on her bookshelf. Finally, she took one last look in the mirror and checked that her curls were still intact before locking up her apartment and driving Smiley to the Cross County Applebee's.

It was eleven-thirty, and she was surprised to see a small lunch crowd already gathering. She peered inside from the foyer and saw Andy attending to the high top tables that surrounded the bar. Most of them were empty. He busied himself wiping them clean and replacing empty ketchup bottles. She could tell from his expression that whomever had this section the night before was supposed to have done these things and didn't.

Velma waited for the hostess to begin escorting two other people to their booth before she walked inside. She went to Andy's section with three empty high tops in a row on the right side of the bar. She sat herself at the one farthest back, the one with another table on only one side of it. He looked up from the table he was cleaning on the other side of the bar. He dropped his towel and smiled as he made his way over to her.

"Hi there," he said, "Velma, right?"

"Impressive memory." She gave him a flirtatious smile.

"Not really, you're kinda hard to forget." He smiled back and winked at her. "But you look more like Daphne than Velma."

She fought not to roll her eyes. "You're sweet," she said. "Listen, Andy, I'm sorry my uncle tied up your table last night."

"Hey, no worries. You guys took good care of me."

"Thanks, but I know you could have turned that booth over at least three times if we hadn't been there."

"Sweetheart, if you hadn't been there, I'd have had an extra three tables, and they all would have run me around like crazy then left me five or six bucks on a forty-dollar check. Your uncle gave me a thirty-dollar tip on an eighty-seven dollar check. That's probably the highest percentage I've ever gotten in this place."

"Really?" She felt sympathy for the Applebee's servers, and a bit of guilt as she realized she rarely worked as hard as they did. She was also rarely under-tipped, and it sounded like Andy dealt with it frequently.

"Really. Plus you treated me like a human being. They make us act like robots here."

"I noticed."

"You wait tables too, huh?"

"Is it that obvious?"

"Well, today it was obvious. You'd have to be a server to know how to time tables. But I could tell last night."

"How's that?"

"You know how to order. I knew both of those Stolis were for you, and you knew I wouldn't be allowed to serve one person two doubles at once."

"I was trying to save you a trip."

"I know you were; it was sweet."

"How else could you tell?"

"Well," he chuckled, "you drink a lot. I mean no offense, of course, but you know how this business is. Most people here are going to get shitfaced as soon as they get off work. I'm sorry. I talk too much. I even forgot to ask you what you wanted. Double Stoli and a Red Bull?"

"Just the Red Bull. I'm driving today. You can put it in a glass, I'll drink it here this time."

"You got it. I'll be right back."

As he walked away, she let her eyes absorb him. He was just above average in height, but he had a striking, muscular stature. Velma reminded herself this was not the reason she'd come here. She wanted to take him out to her car and move to a far corner of the parking lot so she could tear off his Applebee's corporate polo and see what was underneath. She wanted to smell his long hair, tear down his pants, rip off her own, straddle him until she ruined her seat cover, and have him back before the lunch rush. But this wasn't the time for that. What she really needed from him was a specific piece of information.

He returned with her drink and handed her a menu. "So you're off today?"

"No, I'm just working night shift."

"I'm on a double myself. If I can ask, where do you work?"

"Well, you already identified my line of work by pinning me as a lush, so asking where I work is not out of line." She was smiling, but he looked guilty.

"I'm sorry, I'm so sorry. I shouldn't have run my mouth. I'm not judging, I promise."

"I work at Lonnie's Pub a few miles from here."

"Lonnie's... I know where that is. I don't live too far from there."

She ordered a wrap with a side salad. In between serving his other customers, he would come back to continue their conversation. They moved to talking about more pleasant, less serious things, and Andy told her how impressed he was with her background.

"I could tell you were a class act," he said.

She was glad he didn't pry about why a Vassar graduate was waiting tables. She found out bits and pieces about his family, his interests, his brief attempt to attend community college, and his taste in movies. She masterfully directed their small talk. Like a cat on the hunt, she waited for the perfect moment to leap and ask the questions that would lead her to what she needed.

"Did you always live in Yonkers?" she asked.

"For most of my life. My family moved here when I was four," he replied.

This was the information she sought. She forced herself to stop being distracted by his hair and his jawline. "Oh really? So where are you from originally?"

"Greece." It was the answer she thought she'd hear. "I was born in a city called Kalamata." His accent became pronounced when he said the name of the city.

"Kalamata? Like, where olives come from?"

"Yes." Andy chuckled. "Like where olives come from. I have an aunt and an uncle who still live there, but I haven't been back since I was a kid."

"You should visit them."

"One day when I can afford it."

"Oh, I'm sorry, but speaking of that, I should pay and get going."

"And here I am talking your ear off again." He had a genuine and unintentional charm.

"It's okay," she fluttered her eyes at him without meaning to, and considered asking him to come out to her car.

"It was really great to see you, sweetheart. I mean it was great getting to know you. You gotta get to work; I got your lunch taken care of."

"Stop it, no you don't." She reached for her wallet, and he put his hand gently on her arm.

"Velma, I got it. Listen, you made my day."

"Wow, well thank you." She stood up and put on her coat, stealthily taking a hundred dollar bill out of her pocket.

"You're very welcome," he said.

She picked up her purse and prepared to leave, then began to wonder why he hadn't asked to take her out or see her again. "So when you work a double shift here, do you get a break between lunch and dinner?"

"I'll get a break around two if it's not too busy, then I have to be back by four-thirty."

"That's when I go in too. Why don't you meet me at Lonnie's on your break, and we'll have a pre-night shift cocktail?"

"Oh, Velma, sweetheart, I don't really drink. My father died of liver failure, from drinking. That was about four years ago, and I haven't had a drink since."

"Well *I* didn't tell *you* that *my* father died of lung cancer—last week—and I smoke like a chimney. See you in a couple hours." She kissed him on the cheek, making sure he didn't see her put the bill on the table, and victoriously walked out the door. She doubted she would see him on his lunch break, but for now, he had at least satisfied her curiosity.

When Velma arrived home, she went straight to her computer. She looked up a map of Greece. Kalamata was near the southern tip of the country, less than twenty miles from Sparta.

"Holy shit." *Who the hell is Dr. Alexei Novikov?*

Sixteen

Friday, May 2, 2008

Detective Duran hadn't been expecting the cardboard box he found on his desk when he entered his cubicle. It was about a foot wide and over a foot long, but only about four inches high. He put his cup of coffee down on the right corner of his desk, the one area he kept uncluttered for this purpose.

He examined the package. It was addressed to "Officer Jackson Duran" and was covered in unfamiliar postal markings. Its corners were pushed in a bit as though it had been through a long journey.

He examined the postage and realized it had. "Who the fuck do I know in England?"

He searched for the return address and found it hiding under the markings made by a rubber stamp. The package was from Pemberton Booksellers in London. He dug out a pair of scissors, carefully cut open the box, and finally excavated the contents from what he thought to be a superfluous amount of packaging materials.

"Oh my fucking god!" He got up from his desk and moved his cup of coffee to the seat of a chair in the corner, as far away from the box as possible.

He stared agape at what was inside, petrified of touching it. Finally he reached out to pick it up. He made sure his grip was gentle, as though what he held could crumble and turn to dust. In his hands was a very rare, antique copy of what had long been his favorite book, *Ulysses* by James Joyce. He opened the front cover and gasped. The title page indicated the book had been printed in 1935, and it was signed by the author.

"Sounds like there's some excitement over here." Detective Jeremy Stevens leaned in the doorway of Duran's cubicle, sipping a cup of coffee.

"Don't come in here with coffee!" Duran barked. Stevens downed what was in his cup then showed Duran it was empty. "Do you know what this is?"

"A book. What cocktail pairs well with this one?"

"None. No liquid gets near this book, ever."

"Jackson, what's going on?" Stevens looked at the loose packing materials flowing out of the box.

"You don't know anything about this, do you?"

"I saw someone from the mail room bring it up here earlier, thought maybe someone sent you a 'congrats on the promotion' gift or something."

"If they did, this is a little extreme." He tilted the book so Stevens could see the signature inside.

"Who signed it?"

"James fucking Joyce."

"Who else?" Duran looked at him quizzically. "It has two signatures, look."

"Holy shit." Duran turned a few pages. "Henri Matisse. The illustrator. Stevens, this book is worth more than my car."

"And you don't know who sent it?"

"No clue. It's from an antique bookshop in London."

"Call them. Ask who bought it. I'm sure they'll remember selling a book that costs as much a car."

"That's a good idea."

"I'll be at my desk, let me know what you find out. And careful." Stevens pointed to the coffee mug on the chair across from Duran's desk. "There's liquid within ten feet of the most expensive thing you own."

As soon as he walked away, Duran looked up the long, strange looking, international number for Pemberton Booksellers. It was eleven a.m., so it would be four p.m. in London. The bookshop would still be open.

His phone rang before he could reach it to start dialing. Duran collected himself before picking it up. The bookshop wouldn't close for another couple of hours. He could take this call.

"Detective Duran."

"Duran, it's Woods from Mount Vernon." This was the third time Woods called him.

Their last conversation had been a dead end. Neither of them had been able to make any links between Woods' homicide case and the fact that Velma's car was parked in front of the scene. The day after she disappeared, the Mount Vernon Police got a call from a neighbor of one of the victims saying a strange car was parked outside of his house and the front door was hanging open. When police entered the house, they found two men in the basement, both dead from gunshot wounds. Woods and Duran were each hoping the other's investigation might yield some missing information on their own. Neither of them could find any connection between the shootings and the owner of the strange car.

"Woods, how are you? Any news?"

"Some. Any progress tracking down Velma Bloom?"

"I've got nothing." He looked at his book. "Her car is on a very long list of unsolved mysteries I have right now."

"If that woman ever turns up, I'd very much like to talk to her. She's not a suspect, but the circumstances are damn suspicious. We're considering her a person of interest, especially after we got a little surprise on our ballistics report."

"Really? What did the report show?"

"It was close to what we expected. *Close*. The owner of the house, Alexei Novikov, was shot first, in the stomach. But that wasn't the shot that killed him. He was also shot through the head. It looked like he finished himself off rather than waiting to bleed out. The bullet in his stomach came from the gun we found next to the other guy."

"Boris something?"

"Boris Ivanov. Apparently, that's the Russian version of John Smith. The report also showed his gun was used to shoot the lock off the front door. Ivanov was shot in the back of the head, and the bullet that got him came from the pistol we found next to Novikov's body. By the way, we found Ivanov's car parked a block away, and the keys were on him."

"Shit."

"I know." Woods and Duran had both been entertaining the idea that Boris Ivanov had stolen Velma's car. This would explain why it had been left there—Ivanov was expecting to drive away in it. While that theory did not make things look good for Velma in terms of her safety, it did reduce the likelihood of her being involved in the shootings, and simplified Woods' investigation.

"I'm afraid to ask, but what about the keys to Velma's car? I'm guessing they weren't on either of the victims?"

"No. But we found them, and it's another dead end. They were under the front seat of her car."

"Damn. That tells us nothing."

"Not only does it tell us nothing, it gives us one less way of figuring out whether or not she was in the house, which is a problem. Remember that little surprise I mentioned on the ballistics report? The bullet that killed Novikov, the one in his head, didn't come from his own gun. It came from Ivanov's."

"Holy shit. That means someone else was there. There was another shooter."

"Exactly."

"But Velma's not a suspect?"

"Like I said, the whole thing is damn suspicious, but there isn't enough evidence to make her anything but a person of interest. I'm telling you, we went through the place with a fine-toothed comb. We even brought in cadaver dogs. Velma Bloom isn't there, dead or alive, and it looks like she never was. There were no fingerprints other than Novikov's anywhere. There was no blood, no hair, no possible belongings, nothing to suggest Bloom was ever inside that house."

"That doesn't mean she wasn't."

"No, it doesn't. Maybe she was. If she wasn't, someone had to have been at some point to fire the second shot at Novikov. Everything up to that point makes perfect sense. Ivanov shot the lock off Novikov's house using a gun with a silencer so the neighbors wouldn't hear, then ran inside. He shot Novikov in the stomach from about a quarter of the way down the basement steps. The gun we found next to Novikov was on his right side and looks to have been in his right pocket. It seems Novikov drew the gun less than a second before he got shot, and fired it just as Ivanov had turned around to go upstairs. Ivanov was hit in the back of the head and killed instantly. He fell forward and landed on his stomach and slid part way down the stairs. He was lucky Novikov was a better shot than he was, and Novikov was lucky there was another shooter. Otherwise he could have taken hours to die."

"Do you know anything about these guys? Novikov was obviously targeted, but why?"

"We'll never know for sure. There's not a lot of information on either of them except they're Russian citizens. Ivanov was working in a restaurant in the Bronx, and Novikov was a doctor, but retired. We couldn't find any family, or anyone who claims to know either of them. Our guess, though we don't have firm evidence to support it, is that it was some kind of Russian Mafia hit."

"That makes sense." *Russian Mafia, my ass.* "And there's

nothing to indicate who else was in the house, whether or not it was Velma?"

"Nothing. We questioned some other persons of interest and got nothing. As far as Bloom is concerned, as suspicious as everything looks, I think she's less likely to have been the second shooter than some Bratva member. We also have no tangible reason to think her car being there is anything but a coincidence."

"So you think the presence of a missing person's car at a homicide scene is a *coincidence*? I don't know if I believe in coincidences anymore."

"I didn't say that's what I think, but we have nothing to prove otherwise. I hate to be the one to tell you this, but it is possible this really is just a fucked up coincidence. Sounds unlikely, but maybe Bloom wasn't even the one who drove the car there. Maybe, if your girl wanted to skip town and throw people off, she could have parked her car there and left it. Maybe she had someone with her and they drove away. Or she walked to the train station. Maybe she got a cab somewhere."

"Maybe. Or maybe there's something we're still missing."

"There are always going to be maybes. Sometimes we have to live with that. The fact is, none of the evidence we have can link the car or its owner to the shootings."

"One other thing doesn't make sense, Woods. You said Ivanov was using a silencer. But Novikov wasn't. He had his pistol on him, but that doesn't mean he was expecting the break-in, and I find it hard to believe he'd have a silencer on a gun he kept in his pocket. Didn't any of the neighbors hear the shot that came from Novikov's gun?"

"Look, Duran, I didn't want to go into this because it has nothing to do with the case, and I didn't want to give you any wild ideas. I know you're new, and you're excited, but this has *nothing* to do with your case."

"I'll decide that."

"Novikov's basement was locked. Ivanov shot that lock off, too, and the basement was lined with sound absorbent foam."

Duran's interest was piqued. "The hell you say?"

"Look, unless you find Bloom and she's in a condition to answer questions, you and I are done. I have other places I want to look for our second shooter. Don't get any wild ideas that have nothing to do with your missing girl."

"Don't worry about that. All the wild ideas I have are quite relevant to my missing girl, and I have several not so wild ideas about why a Russian national would have a locked basement lined in sound absorbent foam."

"Can I give you a piece of advice? Do this by the book, you'll be better off. But if you'd rather obsess over the Russian Mafia, I can't stop you."

"What I have in mind makes the Russian Mafia look like Robin Hood's Merry Men."

"Whatever's in your head, be careful with it. You're never going to find this girl if you keep chasing red herrings."

"*Red* herrings. Good one."

"I was being serious."

"So was I, and I'll chase whatever red herrings I please. You never know when a red herring is going to lead to a white whale. If I find anything pertinent to *your* case, I'll let you know." Duran hung up the phone, delighting in his choice of words.

He picked up *Ulysses* again, feeling an electric tingle in his fingertip as he gently ran it over James Joyce's signature. As he reached for the phone to call Pemberton Booksellers, he noticed the white blanket of paperwork covering his desk. He forced himself to put his personal mystery on hold.

Calling the bookshop would have to wait. If he discovered who sent the book, it would mean owing that person a thank you call. If, as he suspected, it had been his mother, that phone call would be a long one, and he couldn't spare the time. He needed to make sure he got his paperwork done before happy hour. He had a red herring to chase.

Seventeen

Lonnie's Pub never had much business on Valentine's Day since nothing about its atmosphere could be considered romantic. Velma was relieved no new customers entered the pub just before closing, and she had the luxury of leaving work on time. She expected to see Brett's car waiting for her outside. It wasn't there, so she decided to take an opportunity to go up to her apartment and change her clothes. He wouldn't expect her to be finish work this early and wouldn't arrive for another fifteen minutes, at least. This would even give her time to don a smaller pair of panties. But when she opened her front door, she found him sitting on her couch, sipping a glass of red wine.

"Happy Valentine's Day, Velma," he said.

"Thank you, I mean happy Valentine's Day. Sorry, you caught me off guard."

"Good, that was the idea."

"Should I regret giving you a key to my apartment?" She looked around. The coffee table was covered in red rose petals and votive candles. Brett had arranged the candles in the shape of a heart, and at the center of the heart sat a brushed steel travel mug and a bag of coffee grounds. "What's all this?"

"Don't worry, I gave Carrot some catnip so he wouldn't jump on the table. Look in the kitchen."

She flashed him a quizzical smile and walked over to her kitchen. She found a small, basic, black plastic coffee maker on the counter next to her stove. Its glass pot was only big enough to make two cups at once, so the whole device fit perfectly on her tiny counter. Next to it was a pack of miniature coffee filters designed to fit the undersized machine.

"Brett!" Velma ran back to the couch and embraced him, causing him to spill wine on his pants. "Sorry. I'm going to take those off soon, anyway." She crawled onto his wine-soaked lap and kissed him. "Thank you. This is wonderful."

"The mug is metal, so you can't break it." He picked it up and handed it to her. It had a plastic handle and a rubber grip over its insulated steel body. "And there's a lid in case Carrot knocks it over."

She was amazed by how well Brett had thought everything out, and how he had executed every detail. She felt an overwhelming tenderness toward him and started to feel tears forming, but stopped herself from crying.

"You know what the best part is?" she said. "I can't believe how great it feels to have someone know me this well."

She kissed him again, feeling his hand behind her head as he pulled her deeper into the kiss. She shivered as his fingers slid from her neck to her waist. She leaned onto his chest and felt his heart speed up just before he pulled his mouth away from hers.

"I want you to be my girlfriend again."

She slid off his lap and onto the couch beside him. "I…"

"You don't like labels and want to keep your independence?"

"Yeah… and I've had a lot on my mind. I'll fill you in. I'm sorry. You know I don't want to hurt you and I don't want you to go anywhere. It's just I think I'd be happiest if nothing changes. Is that okay?"

"It's okay." There was disappointment in his voice. "You make me happy; and it's okay with me if nothing changes."

"Thank you, Brett. You know you're my best friend, right?"

"And you're mine."

"Listen, I have something to tell you. I found out a few days ago…" She looked at the candles and the rose petals. "I wish it was a better time for this. I don't want to ruin the night, but it's important."

"What is it?"

She took his hand and looked into his worried eyes. "Don't freak out. I'm adopted."

"You're *adopted*?"

"Yeah, as in the Blooms aren't my biological parents. Two dead people are."

"Do you know who they are?"

"Not really. My real mom, I guess I mean my biological mother, was the only person who knew who my father was. All I know about him is he's dead, and she died giving birth to me."

"That's rather… old fashioned."

"I know, right? And get this. Her name was Annalise. Annalise Miley. That's where my parents, I mean the Blooms, got my middle name."

"Wow. How did you find out?"

"Mom and Dad—Elizabeth and Franklin—figured it was time to tell me, for some reason." She realized how suspect her cover story sounded after she said it out loud. She hated that she needed a cover story with Brett, but after what she learned, she wasn't sure how weighty the consequences might be of spreading the name Alexei Novikov.

"They just randomly decided to tell you?"

"Yeah." She considered Brett to see if he was showing any signs of knowing she was lying. He didn't, but he looked pensive.

"I didn't think women still died during childbirth."

"Neither did I. Leave it to me to kill my mother."

"Velma." He stroked her hair. "Don't think that way."

"I'm sorry, Brett. This is just a lot for me to take in. Can we fuck?" He put his hands around her waist and kissed her. She undid his belt buckle and bit his bottom lip. "You know you would have been a terrible lawyer, right?"

"I know."

She was relieved he didn't mention anything else about her becoming his girlfriend. He was the dearest person in the world to her, but she liked their friendship just as it was.

As he often did, he woke before Velma and left quietly so he wouldn't disturb her slumber. She opened her eyes naturally just before noon and was both disappointed and relieved to find Carrot where Brett had been when she'd fallen asleep seven hours earlier. She was well rested and refreshed, but then noticed the real reason she had awaken before her alarm told her to. She was naked and freezing. The night had been cold enough that, had Brett not been there, she would have slept on the couch to be farther from the window, and she wouldn't have fallen asleep naked.

She pulled her blankets tightly around herself and Carrot. She shivered, then decided to bite the bullet. She leapt out of bed and quickly donned the clothes she had worn the night before. She cracked the window and smoked a cigarette in record time so she could close it again. Then it was time to get ready to do something she'd been dreading.

She made herself a pot of coffee, turned on her space heater, and settled herself on the couch with two blankets. She wanted to make sure she was very comfortable before she undertook the very uncomfortable task of calling Elizabeth Bloom.

Velma dialed, and Elizabeth answered after the first ring.

"Velma!" She sounded as though she had been waiting by the phone, counting the seconds until her adopted daughter returned her call.

"Hi, Mom."

"Oh, Velma!" Elizabeth began to cry. "I'm so happy you... you still call me mom."

"Come on, Mom. I'm always going to call you Mom, unless you'd prefer Professor Bloom. But that wouldn't work because I'd get you confused with Dad." Velma maintained a lighthearted and affectionate tone.

Elizabeth laughed through her tears. "I love you so much, honey. So, so much."

"I know and I love you, too, Mom. And listen... Thank you for leaving me alone the past few days. I'm sorry I didn't call you sooner but I needed some time to process this whole thing." Neither woman spoke for several seconds. As far as she was concerned, it was Elizabeth's turn to talk, but she understood her adoptive mother's silence.

"How—" Elizabeth sniffled again, "—how did you find out?"

"Honestly, I figured it out. I had a suspicion and then, as I'm sure you know, I confirmed it with Dad." Velma wasn't sure if the story she planned was believable, but the Blooms knew nothing of their adopted daughter's paternity, so they would have no reason to challenge it. "I was just talking to Lonnie that day and he was telling me about his parents. We were having a slow day so he was showing me some of his family pictures and telling me how much his dad liked whisky. So it occurred to me that everything Lonnie's face had in common with the faces of his parents in the pictures were things that I didn't have in common with you guys. Lonnie made a joke about him loving whisky because his dad loved whisky."

"You always did hate chardonnay, Velma."

"And you hate whisky, Mom. So does Franklin—Dad. I know that sounds stupid but I just... made a connection. Intuition, I guess." She knew Elizabeth wasn't going to question her, but she still wished her story were a bit more solid. "Look," she changed the subject, "were you ever going to tell me?"

"We talked about it for years. When you were little, we

wondered if it was the right thing to do. As you grew up, we didn't know if there was a right time to do it."

"So you never would have told me."

"I'm not proud of this, honey, but no, we probably wouldn't have. In the beginning, we really didn't know if it was better for you to know or not know. Then we were afraid. Then you grew into such an independent woman, went off to school. You had the rest of your life to plan, and we didn't want to distract you. We didn't want to make you angry."

"I'm not angry, Mom. If you had told me at some random point, maybe it would have been different, but I promise I'm not angry."

"Thank you, Velma. I'm so sorry."

"Don't be sorry, really. We do have one big thing in common, and that's if I had been in your position, I probably wouldn't have told me either."

"I may not agree with all of your life choices, but I couldn't ask for a better daughter."

Elizabeth meant well, and Velma knew it. Well-meaning or not, she was still Professor Bloom and would have preferred to have raised another Professor Bloom. Trying be as good a person as Elizabeth hoped she'd raised her to be, Velma let the dig slide. She did, however, decide the conversation was over.

"Mom, I need to go. I'm glad we talked, and I love you. I just want to tell you that… I'm really glad it was you and Dad who adopted me and not anyone else."

They said their goodbyes. Velma was relieved knowing she would never have to have the same conversation ever again.

She had an uneventful weekend at work. Brett came in on Saturday night, which he rarely did because she was too busy to spend much time with him. He had his usual mozzarella sticks and red wine but didn't stay very long. The Blooms came in for lunch on Sunday. They went out of their way to act as they always had, until they both started to tear up when they hugged her before they left.

Just moments after the Blooms' departure, Dr. Alexei Novikov entered. He acted as he always had, except in addition to cash for the cost of his meal, he left her two sparkling clean hundred-dollar bills. His tips now felt like a tax return: less thrilling because she knew it was technically already her money.

The next day, she worked her usual double shift and returned to her apartment, as usual, just after midnight. She joined Carrot on the couch and was seconds away from turning on the TV when she received a phone call from an unknown number. Her heart leapt. She knew exactly who it would be.

"Hi!"

"Shh. Hello. You do not work tomorrow, correct?"

"No."

"Good. You will come see me at my home, in the evening."

"Really?"

"You understand the need for caution now. At my home, we can speak more freely."

"Okay. Where do you live? How do I get there?"

"Listen *very* carefully as I will not repeat myself. Remember *everything* I tell you and do *not* write it down."

"What if I forget it?"

"You will not. That is not an option."

Eighteen

Tuesday, February 19, 2008

Novikov's home was close by in Mount Vernon. But, he said, she couldn't travel there directly. He gave her instructions that involved short walks, two Bee-Line buses, and a cab ride. She was instructed to travel during evening rush hour and do her best to camouflage herself with the other commuters. She first had to walk a few blocks to a bus stop in Yonkers. The first bus took her to the Bronx, the second to Mount Vernon where she would get off at the Mount Vernon East train station. From there, she was to take a short cab ride to a residential neighborhood in an affluent section of Mount Vernon. After her cabdriver departed, she had an approximately three-and-a-half block walk to his house at 101 Forester Avenue.

He reiterated several times while giving the instructions that she not write anything down. As soon as he told her the address of her ultimate destination, he promptly disconnected the call.

Velma was annoyed when she heard the address because she realized, had she not been visiting a man whom she was almost certain was, or had been, a Soviet secret agent, she could take a bus directly to the Mount Vernon East train station in about twenty minutes, or even take a cab directly to his house in less than fifteen.

That would have been much less exciting.

She began her walk to the first bus stop a few minutes before four-thirty p.m., and followed every instruction she'd been given. It was nearly six-thirty when she finally arrived. Novikov's house was a huge Colonial with a grand exterior she thought befitting of someone involved in high profile espionage.

Her imagination went wild as she crossed the yard to reach the front door. She walked up six front steps to a landing accented by a black iron railing and two white cylindrical pillars on either side of it that were the entire height of the two-story house. She approached the door and it opened at the exact moment she was close enough to step inside.

Alexei Novikov stood before her. "I told you I was an excellent judge of footsteps."

He led her into the house. The rooms were huge. His living

room alone struck her as being larger than her entire apartment.

"You live here all by yourself?" she asked.

"Yes."

"This is a pretty massive house for one person."

"I suppose, but I chose it for the neighborhood. You know the expression, 'location, location, location.'"

"Which is why I live where I do."

"Walking down a flight of steps to get to work and driving only to and from the liquor store must keep the insurance cost down on your silly but magnificent car."

"How…?"

He shot her a look.

"Never mind." She followed him to the basement door.

Novikov pulled a small metal disk about the size of a nickel out of his shirt pocket then lifted a switch cover next to the door. Underneath it was a similar disk that was slightly recessed. As he aligned the two, a click was heard and he opened the basement door. There were walls on either side of the staircase covered in black foam. When the door shut behind him, another click indicated it had locked, and she saw the back of the door was also covered in foam.

"One thing Russia has in common with New York," he said as they descended, "is economic diversity. You will see houses like this, some much grander, as well as the most squalid of living spaces, and everything in between."

"No offense, but whenever I've imagined Russia, the squalid was all that came to mind."

"Ha! No offense taken. I have been in this country long enough I am not surprised."

"It also makes me think of vodka," she said as they reached the bottom of the steps.

"This also does not surprise me, nor is it inaccurate. If you ever visit Moscow, which I do *not* recommend, make sure you visit the Vodka Museum."

"Wait. You don't sound like you're joking. There's really a Vodka Museum?"

"Indeed. Please, have a seat."

Velma looked around the large, finished basement. The same black foam that covered the walls of the staircase and the back of the door also covered the ceiling.

"Is your basement soundproofed?"

"Proofed? There is no such thing. But sound-*protected*, yes." He indicated a modern, armless leather chair and gestured for her to sit.

The leather was soft, like nothing she'd ever felt before, but the chair was still less comfortable than it looked. In front of her was an oval shaped coffee table with chrome legs and a glass top. Across from her was a chair that matched the one she on which she sat. Against the back wall was a large desk with at least a dozen small drawers. To her left, two rocks glasses and a decanter of whisky rested on small counter. To her right was a mahogany upright piano. She could have been in the basement of a movie's wealthy super-villain.

"Do you play?" she asked indicating the piano.

"I do not."

"Oh, okay... but you own a piano?"

He chuckled. "Would you like a drink, Velma?"

"Yes, please. I just traveled two hours in the cold to get here. I'm surprised I haven't already started digging around for your booze supply."

"I do not drink watery, urine-colored American beer at home. I have several kinds of wine, though none of them are in a box. I believe you would prefer what I have in here." He picked up the decanter. "Smooth and well-aged bourbon. There is not much left, but you are welcome to it, as long as you are not one to commit the crime of diluting it with ice. I do not believe you are."

"You are correct." Velma almost giggled, suddenly feeling much more comfortable being in a basement alone with this man. "So... why the piano?"

He poured a small serving of bourbon for each of them and sat in the chair across from her. "Think that over. I am sure you will answer your own question."

"You have a sound-*protected* basement. And *why* would you have a sound-protected basement unless you played an instrument?"

"Good girl. I have a guitar and an amplifier stored under the steps as well. I also do not play the guitar."

"And yet, you *do* have a sound-protected basement." He raised his eyebrows at her, smiling as though he wished her to continue. "Once again, you're telling me a lot you're not saying out loud."

"You are a very smart girl."

"Are you expecting a visit from the Feds?"

"I am expecting nothing, but am prepared for anything."

"So, if I can speak freely in here, I'm guessing your real name isn't Alexei Novikov, and you're not a doctor. You know there was a CIA agent being protected by the Russian government, you probably work for the KGB. You drink gross American beer when you go out so you blend in. Besides getting my father's estate to me, you're probably here on some other spy mission, and you're probably a very dangerous person."

"You are a *very* smart girl." He looked at her proudly. "But you are only half correct. You are right, my name is not truly Alexei Novikov. My real name is Leonid Volkov. Your next assumption was not correct, because it is actually *Dr.* Leonid Volkov."

"What kind of doctor are you?"

"When I practiced medicine, from which I have retired, I was an anesthesiologist. Regarding my other work, you were close. I work for the GRU. I am bound to keep many secrets. I am telling you more than you are allowed to know, again, because I feel you deserve to know it. I am less watched than I would have been years ago when I was a more active agent, which is why we are speaking at all. Your next statement was also incorrect. I am on no other mission. I am sixty-eight years old and am not, at the moment, on any particular assignment involving espionage. Your last statement may be correct, or it may not be. Schroedinger's danger, you might say. Outside of this room, never speak of anything discussed within it, and you will never know if or not I am a dangerous person. Also, you may call me Leo."

"Wow." She sipped her bourbon. She loved how warm it made her feel after her recent time spent outside. "So um... Leo? That's the real one, right? I can get used to calling you that?" He nodded. "Leo. May I ask you questions?"

"You may. As before, I may not have answers."

"Or not answers you can give, I know."

"Correct. Although I can give you more answers here than I could at Applebee's."

"You were right about the waiter, by the way, about his accent."

"Does this surprise you?"

"I went in for lunch and talked to him. I kinda wanted to find out for sure. I guess it shouldn't surprise me, but you were right. He moved to New York—to Yonkers—when he was four years old. He's from Kalamata. You said Sparta, so I checked a map. They're seventeen miles apart. That's... pretty fucking impressive."

"I am well-traveled, you might say."

"I was almost positive you were a spy or a secret agent or whatever you want to call it halfway through our first conversation. After I saw the map of Greece, I was sure."

"You do your research. You would have made a good one yourself."

"Well, I guess I picked the wrong field. What was my father's real name?"

"Start with another question, please."

Velma raised her eyebrows. "Okay, why?"

"I will not tell you that right now. At the moment, it is inconsequential. Trust me also that it may be dangerous information to have."

"You said before that he was in some kind of danger. Can you tell me why? Why he needed protection?"

"I can answer that. But first, please let me assure you, despite what your initial reaction may be to what I am about to say, your father was among the most honorable of men. He never did anything that violated his personal code of ethics. Except...of course, for leaving you and your mother. You did read the letter?"

"Yes."

"Your father...was in danger from his own organization. He had secrets. It does not matter what they were. He had secrets that belonged to the CIA. The mission he had been involved with when he acquired those secrets was...exhausting for him. His superiors believed he needed time away from the agency. He was put on paid leave and told he would be called back when he was needed. In the meantime, some people in the CIA began to think there was a danger of him revealing certain secrets, and if he were to die, those secrets would die with him. This is where I came in. Based on the intelligence my organization had, I was able to locate your father and warn him of his peril. He had two choices: he could remain in the United States and stay on the run forever, or he could run to a place he could stay."

"Russia."

"Yes. Our intelligence had saved his life, so he defected. This only added to the reason he could never return home, much as he yearned for the family he might have had."

"My mother, Annalise, he met her when he was on leave from the CIA?"

"Yes. He began a relationship with her before he knew he was in danger, of course."

"Did you know her?"

"I… no. I did not know Annalise Miley."

"What did my dad do when he stopped working?"

"He moved to Coney Island in January of 1981, just after he was put on leave. He had been living in Maryland, not far outside of Washington DC. He did not have to move when he was put on leave, but he had his reasons. Mostly, I think he wanted a change of scenery. He wanted to forget about his recent work. And he loved the ocean. So, he rented an apartment by the shore."

"Is that where he met my mother?"

"They met only a week after your father had taken residence there. They met at a place I am sure you have been at least once or twice in your life: the New York Aquarium."

"Really?" Velma smiled. Something about them having met at the New York Aquarium increased her affection for her late parents.

"As he told it to me, they were looking at the same coral reef tank and saw each other's reflection in the glass."

She crossed her arms and snickered. "That's the most romantic thing I've ever heard. I may vomit."

"Please do not." Volkov chuckled in a way she found soothing. "Yes, their story, at first, was very romantic, but your father never felt at peace with the fact he had to lie to her about his history. He told her his personal truths, of course, but never about what he did for a living or for whom he had worked."

"So what did he tell her?"

"A very partial and warped version of the truth. He told her he had worked for the government, but downplayed the importance of his work. He never mentioned the CIA. He told her he had a clearance and could not speak of his previous work, which was, of course, true. But he did not tell her he was still employed.

"Your parents fell in love quickly. Within six months, your mother moved out of her small inland apartment and into your father's much larger beachside one. For a time, they lived together in bliss. He said the memories of his time with Annalise were the happiest ones he had."

Volkov relayed tales of her parents' early dates, as they had been described to him by her father. Her affection for these two people she would never meet deepened, as did her intrigue. In each story he told, every detail was carefully crafted. She thought about how meticulous he must be in his choices of words. He told her only what he wanted to, and would allow nothing of what he didn't to be unmasked.

"They were overjoyed when they found out early in the summer of 1982 that Annalise was pregnant," he continued. "Your father decided that if he were ever to be called back to work, he would find a way to keep you and Annalise with him. But that never came to pass, and their happiness was interrupted. When my organization's intelligence came through and I tracked your father down, he had to act quickly."

"When you told him he was in danger, he just believed you? What did you tell him?"

"Suffice to say that I had certain information I couldn't have had, were I not who I claimed to be. Everything had to be done with the utmost care. There was no doubt he was being monitored by those who wanted to kill him as well as those who wanted to protect him."

"What did he tell my mother?"

"Nothing. The risk was too high. Had he done anything but act normal around her and been seen, it would have looked as though he told her something he should not have, or told her where he was going. In either case, she and therefore you would have been in mortal peril as well.

"I told him the conditions of the asylum he was being offered: that he share certain things with the GRU. He made no objection. This was during the Cold War. He knew his safety would not be free. I arranged for his safe passage and a new identity. I flew, as Alexei Novikov, to Heathrow airport in London, and then to Domodedovo Moscow Airport in Russia. He flew, using the name Robert Drake and the passport with which the GRU had furnished him, to Paris. He spent a week there. Then he took a series of planes and trains—not unlike how I instructed you to get here—and arrived in Moscow."

"Could he speak *any* Russian? At all?"

"Only the most basic. He was fluent in French, Spanish, and

German, though none of these were of much help to him there. When he first arrived, I was there to meet him. I had a car ready for us and offered to escort him to his flat. I thought he would be exhausted as well as anxious to see the home he would have in his new country." Volkov stopped to laugh.

"He wasn't?"

"He wanted to go to a bar. He said his flat could wait, but it was urgent that he learn how to order his favorite cocktails." They both smiled.

Velma felt a pang of longing. "I would have had so much fun with my dad."

"Oh, Velma, more than you can imagine."

"So right away, you went out and drank together and became best secret agent friends?"

"I would not have used those words, but yes. We spent a lot of time together. I helped him learn the language, and I translated for him when he spoke to other members of the GRU if necessary. Most of them spoke English, some much better than others. I stayed two months in Russia from the time he arrived, and it was in that time our friendship began. He told me much about Annalise, but not the fact that she was carrying their child."

"When he gave you the letter, that was when you first knew she was pregnant?"

"Yes. I had my suspicions there was something important he was not sharing, but your father was smart enough during his first months in Moscow to keep quiet about certain things, even with me. Annalise could have already been in danger because of their relationship, and this would have only increased if the wrong people learned of her pregnancy, as would the danger to your father himself. For someone is his position, and mine, loving people is a liability, a weakness that can and will be exploited." Volkov paused and looked Velma in the eye. His voice became somber as he said, "To this day, I wonder if my own wife's death was a true accident."

Her eyes widened. She imagined the horror of going through life wondering something like that. She was relieved when he continued before she could think of a reply.

"That winter I was to be sent back to the United States so I could continue to act as a liaison between the GRU and an unscrupulous man in the CIA with whom we had an arrangement.

Robert gave me the letter, and the money, just before my departure. I settled myself in the United States and began practicing anesthesiology again. It was meant, originally, that I should stay in your country."

"But you never found my mother and you never gave her the money."

"I had the best of intentions, but you can see how dangerous the prospect was. In any case, my time here was cut short. About six months later, just after you were born, our CIA contact was arrested, and I fled back to Russia for fear of our connection being discovered."

"And it wasn't? He didn't give you away after he was arrested?"

"If he had, the CIA would have been after a man named Roman Gruzinsky."

"Huh?"

"When Leonid Volkov is in America, to the public he becomes Dr. Alexei Novikov. To anyone involved with espionage, he becomes Roman Gruzinsky. And *nowhere* in any office of the GRU is any record of Roman Gruzinsky, because Roman Gruzinsky never returns to Russia. Roman Gruzinsky only existed while he was gathering information. It was Leonid Volkov who brought the information home."

"Wow, you guys plan well."

"Indeed. If there had been hint that our purveyor of CIA intelligence had been a snitch, Roman Gruzinsky would have killed him. Yes, Velma. We are thorough."

She eyed her companion. "You don't look like a killer."

"The best killers are the ones who don't look like killers."

She couldn't take her eyes off him. "I'll do my best to remember that."

"Good."

"So what happened when you got back to Russia?"

"I took some time off for myself and then returned to work. At times, I would be sent back to the United States, or sometimes to another country, for short periods. During my time at home, I worked in a hospital, and it was there I met my wife. After she became my wife, I began to do less and less for the GRU, and my visits abroad were put on hold. Through everything, of course, I spent a great deal of time with my friend Robert."

"You said before that my dad knew about me?"

"Oh yes."

"Did he know about my mom? About how she died?"

"He did."

"I guess you were the one to tell him?"

"Your birth and your mother's death took place just before I left for Russia, so I knew what happened. Yes, it was I who had to deliver the news to Robert. In truth, I did not have to, but I felt he deserved to know. Otherwise he would have spent the rest of his days tormented by questions.

"He was heartbroken, as you would expect. Once he heard the circumstances of her passing, he asked me what had become of his daughter. I assured him that you were healthy and you were safe. He did not need me to tell him what this meant for you though, that you were in the hands of the state. I sat in his flat with him for hours and let him weep. I tried to return his money, but he would not accept it. 'Somehow, someday, I still want my daughter to have it,' he said. After he had calmed himself, he asked me for help once again.

"He became obsessed with what would become of you. At that time, we did not know if or when you would be adopted, or by whom. You were very lucky, Velma. Just as easily as an affluent, educated, and good-hearted couple adopted you and raised you as their own, you could have been another sad story to come out of a series of foster homes."

"I know. I'm so grateful the Blooms got me. I know what might have been if they weren't in the right place at the right time."

"So did your father, and this is where he asked me for help. He wanted to know, for better or for worse, what was to become of his only child. So in turn, one of four different agents, including myself, would bring updates on you back from their latest visit to the United States. This was not difficult or dangerous since you were a civilian, and most of what your father wanted to know was either public information or otherwise accessible.

"When you were three months old, as you know, you were adopted by Franklin and Elizabeth Bloom. This information was brought to me, and it was a great joy for me to convey it to Robert. Hearing you had a family, a permanent family, was the best thing he could have hoped for, short of raising you himself with Annalise.

"He grieved for her for a long time, but you were his greatest comfort. He delighted in the updates he received on you, even those that might have upset any other parent. For example, your high school indiscretion with a young man named Brett Riley."

"Holy shit! You knew about that? You told my *dad* about that?"

"I considered if or not I should, but yes, I told him. You must remember, by this time, I had known him longer than fifteen years, and I knew how he would react."

"Which was how?" Velma wasn't sure if she should be embarrassed or amused.

"He thought it was the funniest thing he'd heard in years. Now, had he been the one responsible for disciplining you, he might very well have felt differently, as the Blooms did. But Robert had no duty to ground you, so your... moxie, shall I say, made him proud."

"Wow." Velma laughed. She couldn't help feeling a little awkward finding out her dead father had known anything about her sex life as a teenager.

The man known as Robert Drake had many proud moments about the daughter he never met. Volkov told her how excited and then boastful Robert had been when she was admitted to Vassar, and even more so when she graduated. When Volkov told Robert his daughter had emptied her trust fund to buy a 1970 Dodge Challenger, he expected him to be concerned. Instead, Robert laughed.

"The Blooms must have been furious!" he had said. "Leo, you have to tell me, what color is it?"

"They call it Top-Banana Yellow," Volkov told his friend, "and it has a black racing stripe. It's ridiculous."

"That's my girl," was Robert's reply. "Moxie."

Velma had felt sorrowful when she first learned her father knew about her, but not she about him. Now, she felt joy and comfort. In his own way, her father got to keep her in his life.

"Does it make you happy, Velma," Volkov asked, "to know all of this?"

"Yes. Very."

"Your father did not, in truth, forget that learning the facts of your life was not a substitute for knowing you."

"No, but... was he happy?"

"He took the happiness he could from wherever he could get it. I don't know that his heart ever stopped aching over the loss of your mother, nor over losing the life that he might have had with her. He never said so out loud, but such as things were, I could tell his deepest hope was that there might someday be a way for him to meet you."

"Couldn't he have come back? I mean, after he knew he was sick?"

"No."

"But if he knew he was dying then…"

"No. Remember, after those years of hiding, and with him having a living daughter, he was not the only one who was in danger."

"Someone would have known you guys were hiding him… and about me."

"I know it is hard to accept. It was for him. I know he had many thoughts and fantasies about ways to make it happen, meeting you. But he never voiced them. He knew that each and every single thing he thought of had a way of putting you in danger."

"Yeah." Velma fantasized about what a meeting with her father might have been like and began to cry.

"Please, Velma," Volkov said, "take comfort in the way your father did. You know him now, as well as you can, in the way he knew you. Perhaps even a bit better. In essence, you and your father have met. You may never embrace and you may never converse, but for all the years he spent loving you, you can now love him back."

"Thank you, Leo." She nodded and thought over his words. She did find comfort in them, even more so knowing her father had found comfort in the same way. All the same, she wanted nothing more than to know the living man known as Robert Drake and embrace him in the flesh.

"I would like you to come see me again. Will you come back four weeks from today?"

"Of course. You know, I really feel like you're my uncle."

"I am happy you feel that way," he said, "as your father would have been." He smiled at her.

"I'm glad. But I don't think I'll ever stop wishing he was still here."

"Neither will I. I miss him every day. But I get to spend time with his daughter. In a way, this is keeping him alive."

Nineteen

Friday, May 2, 2008

Three days ago, Detective Jackson Duran learned a small piece of information about a sad old man he had met in Lonnie's Pub. For three days that information had been haunting him. He was afraid to confront Sam Ferguson. He didn't know what Sam was capable of. He didn't know if one of the things the other man could be hiding was a violent temper, or something worse. More than anything, he was afraid Sam would retreat inward, or even flee, and Duran would never get to have the conversation he wanted to have.

He would need to approach Sam like a cat approaching a mouse. Quietly, and exuding no hint of his intentions until he was close enough to let Sam know he was trapped, and it was too late to get away. Duran had no idea how to do this.

When the end of the week came and he still didn't have a plan for how to approach Sam, he walked into Lonnie's Pub without one. It was four-thirty p.m., so he knew Sam would be there in the middle of his first drink. He hoped he wouldn't catch Sam at the end of a drink, because at the end of a drink, Sam could find an unsuspicious reason to leave. He didn't think Sam would make himself look more suspicious by leaving in the middle of a drink for the second time.

When Duran entered the pub, two men were seated at the end of the bar closest to him, and one seated alone at the far end of it. Duran walked over and sat in the stool next to the man sitting alone.

"Hey, how are you Sam?" He tried to sound as friendly as possible and even feigned a little surprise at seeing him.

"Hello, Detective. Or is it Jackson today?"

"Well, I'm about to have a drink, so let's stick with first names."

"You may have to wait a minute. Lonnie's waiting tables *and* tending bar tonight."

"I guess Velma's hard to replace."

"Damn fucking right she is!" Lonnie walked behind them and around to the back of the bar. "Do you know how hard it is to find a waitress in New York who doesn't either have four kids or ridiculous

Broadway dreams?" Lonnie huffed. "Hello again, Jackson. Johnny Walker?"

"Black. Yes, please. Where are the other waitresses?"

"One's with her horde of unplanned spawn, and the other is downtown auditioning for some dancing gig she has no hope of getting. She'll make it back here in about two hours crying about it, but for now I'm stuck doing everyone's job."

Duran took two twenties out of his pocket and handed them to Lonnie. "You're swamped. Get the two of us our next round lined up and a round for those two guys down there. Maybe that'll let you catch up and take a breather."

"That works for me." Lonnie sounded relieved. "Thank you, Jackson, I owe you a burger next time there's a waitress here."

"Sounds great, Lonnie." He smiled and sipped his whisky until Lonnie had served a fresh drink to each of the four men. The two men at the other end of the bar looked over and raised their glasses in the way of a thank you. He returned the gesture.

"That was kind of you," Sam said after Lonnie was out of earshot.

"No it wasn't. I had an ulterior motive."

"Oh?"

"I needed Lonnie to go away so I can play detective for a few minutes."

"I thought you said you were off duty."

"I said first names. I didn't say I was off duty."

"Touché. So you drink on the job, Jackson?"

"I have my own way of doing things."

Sam chuckled. "You sound like Velma."

"Do I? How's that?"

"High functioning alcoholic with a rebellious streak."

"That about sums me up. Listen, I was hoping you wouldn't mind coming back to the station with me, just to talk for a few minutes. Velma didn't talk to very many people, but you were one of them."

"You make it sound like I'm in trouble."

"No! Not at all." He lowered his voice to a whisper. "I promise you're not suspected of anything. I'm looking for a missing person, and you knew her. I just want to talk to you for a few minutes."

Sam's face was red, and Duran saw him struggle to maintain his composure. "Why don't we talk here? I don't think I can help you, but I'll buy the next round."

He downed what remained of his first drink. Duran followed suit and swallowed the entire contents of his glass. For as much as he drank, this was more than he was used to swallowing at once, and he felt a burning sensation as the whisky traveled down his throat and through his body, landing in his stomach. Between the sudden internal deluge of whisky and his nervous excitement, he thought for a moment he was going to vomit on the bar. He let the sensation pass and focused on choosing his next words.

"Actually, I think you *can* help me, Sam. But I *really* don't think you want to talk to me here." He ignored the discomfort in his stomach.

Sam was beginning to sweat. "Jackson, I'm sorry, but I don't know anything that would help you find Velma."

"Let me be the judge of that, Doctor Ferguson."

Sam's calm mannerisms remained. "You're good, Jackson." He wiped the sweat from his brow. His tone stayed friendly but gained a business-like quality. "Very well. I'll talk to you at the station, Detective. But I must apologize in advance for wasting your time, because you're not going to hear what you want to hear."

Twenty

Lonnie's Pub was unusually slow for a Saturday night. Lonnie went home early and left Velma to tend bar while Edie took care of the customers in the dining room. Around ten, Velma was wiping down the empty and already clean bar when Sam came through the door. She was surprised to see him; he rarely came in on weekends and never this late in the evening. His visits were always late afternoon, just after, she assumed, his workday ended.

Sam sat at the bar. He always drank straight vodka and rarely ate, but he never seemed drunk, and was never inappropriate. She always assumed she would have a tolerance like his when she was his age, if she didn't already. She often thought she detected sadness in his mannerisms, even during upbeat conversations. Tonight, his demeanor was especially, and overtly, melancholy.

"Hi, Sam," she greeted him. "You look like you need a drink."

"Hi, Velma. Yes, please." He managed to smile at her. She poured him his usual water-glass-sized serving of vodka. He looked around the room. "Lonnie's not here?"

"We've been slow so I'm holding down the fort. In fact—" she looked around and made sure there were no tasks that required her attention— "I think I'll join you." She got out a rocks glass and poured herself a smaller serving of vodka before putting the bottle back on the shelf.

"You may as well keep that out," he said.

She chuckled. "Sure thing." She took a swig from her own glass and topped it off, then added a little more to Sam's larger one.

He looked from her glass to his own. "You must think I'm a horrible drunk."

"If you're a horrible drunk, then so am I." She laughed.

He smiled at her with affection and looked relieved. "You drink a lot?"

"*A lot* is an understatement." She had her reasons for drinking a lot and wasn't ashamed of it. Most people who drank as much as or more than she did couldn't possibly have as good a reason as needing help controlling their ability to shatter things with their brain waves.

"But I never drive or do anything stupid. So I guess no harm, no foul." She lifted her glass and took another sip.

Sam did the same. "You're smart, Velma. What are you doing here?"

"Tending bar." She knew what he meant.

"I apologize. I shouldn't have asked."

"It's okay, Sam."

"I never drink and drive either, for the record. I've got a car, but I don't drive it unless I have to."

"I hear you. I love my car, but I pretty much only drive it to and from the liquor store, and that's only if it's raining or too cold to walk."

"So why do you drink?"

"Me? Why do *you* drink?"

"Oh, Velma, I'm sorry. Again, I shouldn't have asked."

"Sam, we've known each other for almost three years, it's okay. I'll tell you if you tell me." She topped off both of their glasses and waited for him to reply. He was facing down, avoiding looking her in the eye. "Or not. That's okay, too."

"You'll tell me, first, huh?" He looked up at her.

"I like to turn my mind off. Alcohol keeps me from thinking too much—and cigarettes. They keep my brain calm."

"That's as good a reason as any I've ever heard."

"Okay, your turn. Why do you drink?" She waited for him to reply.

He opened and closed his mouth a few times, but no words came out of it before he finally said, "I suppose I also like to turn my mind off." He took a large gulp from his glass. "I have a lot of things I don't want to think about."

"That sounds like a good reason to me."

"I'm sorry. I didn't mean to come in here and be such a downer."

"No problem, Sam. We all have things we don't want to think about."

"I've done things I wish I could undo." His face was even sadder than when he'd walked in the door. "I shouldn't have said that." He downed his drink in a hurry.

She didn't have a response for him. She wondered what these things were that he'd done, but no good could come of asking him.

She changed the subject, and they passed time talking about movies and current events. When it came time to close the pub, she called a cab for him.

"Thank you, Velma. I needed a friend tonight." He stood up and reached into his pocket for his wallet.

"You're welcome, Sam. I'm glad I could be here for you. Drinks are on the house." Lonnie wouldn't mind and probably would have done the same.

Sam pulled out his wallet anyway and dropped a fifty onto the bar. "Don't be silly." He folded his wallet and put it back into his pocket then looked up at her face, smiling with affection. His eyes were blurry, though he spoke as clearly as ever. "I feel like I've known you longer than three years."

"Is that a good thing?" Before he could respond, they heard his cab pull up to the door. The driver honked, expecting his fare would have been outside waiting for him.

"Goodnight, Velma." He walked toward the door.

"Goodnight, Sam."

"Velma." He stopped as he opened the door to leave. "Your hair. I just realized you have red hair."

"I always have, Sam. Get some rest. I'll see you soon."

He gave her a pensive look with his blurry eyes. The cab driver honked again, and Sam walked out of the pub. She locked the door behind him and went about her final duties for the night. She wondered again what it was from his past that haunted Sam. Maybe one day he would tell her.

After Edie and the kitchen staff departed, she made sure everything was in order for the following day before locking up for the night. She replayed the adventure she had earlier that week in her head, as she had done many times over the past few days. Her thoughts turned inward. She wasn't paying attention when she turned to go upstairs to her apartment after locking Lonnie's front door behind her. She walked face first into the chest of the dark figure she hadn't seen waiting for her.

"Sorry, sweetheart. I didn't mean to scare you."

Velma stepped back in alarm. She looked up to see a familiar face she wasn't expecting. "Andy?"

"Hey, Velma."

"I never thought you'd show up; just thought I'd give it a

shot." She made sure her tone was just a little suggestive.

He was even more enticing to her when he wasn't dressed as a waiter. He was taller than she remembered. His wavy hair was down and fell just past his shoulders. It made her want to wrap her legs around his head.

"I'm sorry I didn't come to see you sooner. I've been thinking about you for the past three weeks."

"Have you?"

He nodded. "It's good to see you. Listen, I had a short night at work and figured you'd be closing up around now. I was hoping I could take you out for a bite to eat. It's the least I can do after you left me such a great tip. I'll drive you home, of course."

She thought she'd prefer to skip ahead to being driven home. "I can't stay out too late, but sure, why not?"

She followed Andy to his car, a black SUV that almost disappeared against the street. It was the visual opposite of Brett's bright white Cadillac. She experienced a rush from the newness of it and the newness of her companion. Though Brett wasn't her boyfriend, she didn't see other men; she didn't have enough desire to. She wanted to keep her independence, and forming a bond with another man was a laborious thought. But here she was, in another man's car, with a man she barely knew, and an unknown destination. It felt wonderful.

"So where are we going?" she finally asked. She enjoyed the excitement of not knowing where they were headed.

"The Raceway. Is that okay?"

She looked out the window and realized they were on Central Park Avenue. She tried to hide her disappointment. "Yeah, that's fine. They have a bar."

Andy ordered an ice cream soda, and she followed suit. It had been a long time since she'd had an ice cream soda, and she was reveling in deviance from her usual routine. She did not change her usual meal selection, though. Diners weren't always trustworthy, but a grilled cheese was always a safe bet. As always, she asked for a Bloody Mary to come with the sandwich. Their food was delivered quickly, along with the Bloody Mary. She had half of her ice cream soda left, but put it aside for dessert, opting for the drink that needed to be paired with grilled cheese.

"I get it." Andy chuckled. "Because they don't have tomato

soup."

"Exactly."

"You're a smart girl."

"I like to think so." She flashed him a seductive smirk.

He was pleasant company, but she was anxious for the meal and the conversation to end. She had no trouble admitting to herself that, after learning the origin of his accent, her only remaining interest in him was carnal.

"I'll be right back," she said when she finished her sandwich. "I'm just going to use the ladies' room. Then how about we get out of here?" She winked and brushed his leg with her foot under the table.

"You got it." He winked back.

Remembering the dangers of leaving a man alone with her drink, Velma slurped up the last of her Cherry Coke, rum, and melted ice cream mixture.

She checked herself in the bathroom mirror, making sure she was satisfied with the state of her curls and makeup. She ran her fingers through her hair and wiped away a smudge of stray eyeliner. She nodded at her reflection then opened the bathroom door.

Andy was hunched over in their booth, speaking in a whisper as he tried to conceal his cell phone with his hand. She stopped in her tracks, lurked in the doorway, and listened.

"She's good to go; it should be easy... Yeah, I have it on me just in case... I'll meet you when I'm done."

He hurried to put his phone back in his pocket. She stayed in the bathroom doorway trying to decide what to do. The rational thing to do would be to grab her coat, call a cab, and get the hell away from him. But she wasn't in the mood for rational.

She returned to the table and saw he had paid their check. He stood and took her hand. "Let's get you back home."

He flashed her what looked like a sexual smile, and she realized how disappointed she was that his plans to rob her interfered with her plans to have him in her bed. Then she absorbed his words. *Get me* back *home? I never told him where I live. The son-of-a-bitch cased me.* She smiled back and said nothing. She couldn't let him know he'd been caught.

As she climbed back into his SUV, she formulated ideas about how to handle the rest of the evening. She thought things out on the drive back. She was sitting next to a man who was planning to make her the victim of a crime, and from what she had heard him whisper on the phone, she was almost certain he was armed. Her intentions with him had been far from honorable, but would have ended well for them both. Now she knew the night could only end well for one of them, or for neither of them.

When they arrived at Lonnie's, she had Andy pull his car into the back parking lot and take the unmarked space right next to Smiley. Doubt and fear struck her as soon as the car stopped. The smart thing to do would be to run away and lock herself inside her apartment. What she was going to do instead was stupid and dangerous, but her fear and doubt didn't linger. *I got this. And I'm going to enjoy it.*

She unbuckled her seatbelt. "You're not just dropping me off, are you?"

"I was hoping I could come up to your apartment."

"Hmm. Maybe."

She leaned close to him, resting her hand on the top of his leg the slid it to the inside of his thigh, and he gasped. She lifted herself onto her knees in the car seat. She moved her hand from his thigh to his shoulder for leverage as she hoisted her right leg over his lap, avoiding the steering wheel. Pushing her left knee to rest on the center console, she positioned herself over him in a straddle.

"Mmm," she said, tightening her thighs around him. He pulsed and swelled beneath her. Then she felt the gun. "Oh!" She feigned surprise. "Andy, why don't you take that off for a few minutes?"

"We should go upstairs."

She put her hand between his legs again. She pinched and wiggled the pull of his zipper with the implied promise of opening it. "Please? Put it in the glove box. Just for a few minutes. I don't want it to go off while I'm down here."

"Okay," he conceded. He pulled the gun out of its holster and leaned to his right with her still on top of him, barely reaching the glove box. He tossed the gun inside and slammed it shut.

She lowered herself so the center of her jeans rested on his fly. He gasped again as she pressed herself against him. "You're a very dangerous man."

He leaned forward to kiss her. "Do you like dangerous men?" She pulled her head back but continued rocking her pelvis. "I like all kinds of danger."

She took off her coat and threw it onto the empty passenger seat. After hiking up her sweater over her head, she tossed it aside as well. His eyes widened as she lowered her bra straps one at a time over her shoulders, allowing the weight of her breasts to push down the last of what was covering them, exposing her swollen, pink nipples.

The chill in the air that had penetrated the car brushed over them as she ran the fingers of her right hand through his hair until they reached the back of his head. She pulled forward until her right breast came in contact with his parted lips. Grabbing his right hand, she brought it to rest on her left. With her left hand she situated his fingers around one aching nipple, and with her right pushed the back of his head toward the other until he responded.

He opened his mouth wider and extended his tongue, sweeping it back and forth. He moved the fingers of his right hand too softly, and she was ready to burst with impatience. After she pulled his head forward again, this time he wrapped his lips around her nipple completely. She moaned and tugged until finally she had him rolling one nipple in his thumb and index finger while he sucked the other.

"Harder," she said.

She relaxed her legs, allowing her full weight to rest upon him. She rocked her hips side to side until she aligned herself with exactly where he was throbbing beneath his zipper. She arched her pelvis forward and began rocking it in earnest, increasing her pressure on him until she unearthed the orgasm she had buried and begging to escape from inside her jeans.

She pushed his head away from her chest and let her own head fall forward on his shoulder as she caught her breath.

"Oh my god…" she heard him utter.

The words were more exhaled than spoken. As her breathing slowly approached normal, his quickened. She said nothing, taking her time to recover and let more blood return to her head. Still panting and feeling red heat behind her cheeks, she drew up her bra straps then slowly and carefully donned her sweater and her coat. She opened the driver's side door and lifted her left leg over his lap so she could slide out and land on her feet.

"Wow," he said, his eyes fixed upon her. She winked at him and reached into her coat pocket to find her apartment keys. He scrambled to unbuckle his seat belt as she began to make her way up the steps to the back door. He fumbled with the strap.

"What are you doing?" Before he had time to free himself from the belt and re-holster his gun, she had reached the landing. She looked down at him as he started to take his first step out of the car door. "Stop."

"Stop?" he called up. "What do you mean?"

"Where do you think you're going?"

Confusion twisted his face. "I'm coming up there with you." He hopped out of the car and she rushed to unlock her door.

"Oh no, Andy, don't be silly!" She bolted inside and stuck her head out the crack in her door. "You're a dangerous man, and I'm a smart girl. Smart girls don't let dangerous men come up to their apartments."

She shut her door and locked it. Outside, he cursed in frustration. Warmth filled her as she glowed in victory. Carrot walked up to her and meowed as though asking to be filled in.

"You know, I don't think I'll call the police. Technically there was no crime committed, and I punished him in my own way." She heard him start his car. "Or did I?"

She peeked out her window and opened it when she saw his car back up and begin moving out of the parking lot. She heard him curse again as a crack appeared in his back windshield.

Twenty-One

Friday, May 2, 2008

Sam and Detective Duran each finished half of their second drink before taking a cab to the Yonkers Police Station. Duran led Sam to the room that housed his desk and the desks of the other detectives. He looked around and listened before walking in. He couldn't see inside most of the cubicles, but as he hoped, he heard nothing.

"We're in luck, I don't think there's anyone else here."

"I wouldn't say we're in luck, Detective. I have nothing to say that would be worth overhearing." Sam followed Duran to his desk.

He sat behind it and gestured to the chair across from him. "Actually Sam, I disagree. I believe you have a lot of things to say that would be worth overhearing. What you meant is you're not willing to say any of them." He didn't reply. "Your silence tells me I'm correct, which I already knew. See, I know you're lying to me. I don't always know when someone is lying to me, but I *can* always tell when someone's hiding something from me. The reason I know *you're* lying is that I know you're hiding things, and that happens to be what you're lying about."

Duran wanted to be direct, but hadn't meant to be so forceful. He worried Sam would get up and leave, but he didn't. Forcefulness might get him further with this man than friendliness would.

"What do you want, Detective?"

"I have a theory. I've figured something out. My problem is that what I've figured out doesn't give me even a remote idea of how I should proceed with this case. This is where I hope you can help me."

"I'm sorry, but my being able to help you is very unlikely."

"That alone tells me my theory is correct."

"I take it you've done some research, and the 'something' you've figured out is what my former line of work might have been."

"You're right. But there's much more to it than that, isn't there?"

"Detective, *if* your theory about my past work is correct, I have a lifelong obligation to protect certain information. As an officer of the law, I hope you can understand that."

"I do. But I hope *you* can understand that my job, as an officer of the law, is to protect the safety of the people in my jurisdiction. Whether or not you can answer my questions, it would be irresponsible of me not to ask them. I suspect the answers would be pertinent to my investigation."

"Again, I'm sorry, but that's something you're never going to know. You have good intentions, Detective, but your job is to protect the safety of the people of Yonkers. Your jurisdiction does not extend to my former line of work."

"Here's where we're going to disagree again. See, it's my belief that your former line of work is related to the disappearance of a woman who, for the last three years, has had a Yonkers address. If my suspicions are correct, I would say that does indeed extend my jurisdiction to your former line of work. Or at the very least, to you." Duran leaned across his desk. "You live in Yonkers, don't you, Sam?"

"Please don't think I don't care about Velma, but my lifelong obligation stands." His demeanor was unwavering, and his constant politeness endured.

Duran's confidence vanished, replaced by frustration. He pounded his fist on his desk. "For fuck's sake, Sam, is your obligation to protect information really more important than Velma's life?"

He was quiet for the better part of a minute. Duran found it agonizing. "I will tell you *something*," Sam said after his silent reflection. "You should stop looking."

"Why? Am I not going to like what I find? Are you saying she's dead?"

"No. I have no idea if she is dead or alive. Regardless, you should stop looking. If Velma Bloom is alive, she is better off if she's never found."

The statement shocked Duran, and he couldn't accept it as truth. "I don't believe that."

"Detective, you are treading in the wrong waters. I know whatever I say is only going to fuel your pursuit. All I can do is warn you. You're dipping your toes into where they don't belong. The answers you're looking for would create a shit storm that, believe me, you don't want."

"That I do believe. But if those answers could help Velma, I think maybe the world needs a good shit storm. I'll be blunt. The same day she was reported missing, the Mount Vernon Police found two dead Russians in a house with her car parked outside it. In the past few days, I've discovered that someone very close to her has been doing obsessive research on Project MKUltra. Now, how the hell is my missing girl linked to a pair of dead Russians and a CIA experiment that took place years before she was born?" He couldn't believe how harsh his own voice had become.

Sam looked lightheaded. "I don't know anything about the Russians. As to the second part of your question, you have done your homework. I'm sure you have some more theories."

"That's true, but you haven't answered my question."

"Nor will I." He succeeded in maintaining his calm and his resolve.

"I didn't think so."

"I would appreciate it then, if you didn't push me to."

"I won't push you, Sam. I understand your position, and I know the rules. But the right thing to do and the legal thing to do aren't always going to align, and you have to make a choice. If Velma is in danger, and you choose not to tell me something that could get her out of it, you're going to have to live with that."

"I'm used to living with things, Detective."

"Fine then. If you change your mind, and I think you should, give me a call. I have a feeling the skeletons in your closet already have enough company."

Twenty-Two

Tuesday, March 18, 2008

Velma woke up at the early hour of seven a.m. Leo had suggested she leave during morning rush hour before this visit. Her desire to talk to him again, to learn more from him, was strong enough to make her get out of bed and onto a bus hours earlier than she would normally stir.

"Welcome," he said when she arrived. Once again, he opened the door at just the moment Velma reached it.

She'd forgotten he did this and was caught off guard. "Hi. Wow, you scared me. I forgot I wasn't going to have to knock."

"Come inside, please." They walked together to the entrance to his sound-protected basement. "If you ever have to knock," he said when the foam-covered door was closed behind them, "you will know I am dead."

"I'll remember that."

"Good. Please sit. I apologize for not offering you coffee or a drink, but I do not think you should stay too long today. I enjoy your company, and I would love for the two of us to spend more time together, but today, I'm afraid, needs to be about business. There is something important I am going to give you." He walked over to his basement steps. After opening the storage compartment beneath them, he removed a large duffel bag. He placed it next to Velma's feet and sat down across from her.

"What is it?"

"Your next eighteen and a half years in tips."

"What?" She was stunned.

"The remainder of your father's estate. I think you can do something better for yourself with it if you have it all at once. Besides, I am very tired of American pub food."

"Eighteen and a half years?"

"Even if I were not tired of the food at Lonnie's, I don't expect I would stay alive long enough to pass it to you at the rate I have been, and I hope you would not remain in his employ for that long."

"But you tip me, well, get my inheritance to me I mean, about two hundred dollars a week, sometimes three hundred a week. So this has got to be..."

"Two hundred and forty-thousand dollars."

"Holy shit. What am I supposed to do with two hundred and forty-thousand dollars?"

"I suppose you could go to graduate school."

"Very funny. I mean right now. What do I do with it? I have a duffel bag filled with two hundred and forty-thousand dollars, and I just carry it with me onto the bus like it's my gym gear?"

"That's exactly what you will do. Then tomorrow, you will go to work and you will go on as though you do not have it, until you decide how to use it."

"I'm a little scared, Leo."

"You would be a fool not to be. But you are a smart girl, and I trust your good sense. Will you come visit me again in another four weeks?"

"Sure."

"Good. I will come see you at work between now and then, but don't expect much over twenty percent." He winked.

"Speaking of work, morning rush hour is kind of like the middle of the night for me. Next time I come visit, can I come in the afternoon?"

"That will be fine. The afternoon, I find, is a much better time for drinking. So I will get us a very nice bottle of scotch."

"That sounds wonderful."

"For now, get yourself and that bag home safely. Don't spend it all in one place."

She took the afternoon in her apartment staring at her money. She opened the duffel bag and counted twenty-four wrapped stacks of ten thousand dollars, just like the ones he gave her before. She had only unwrapped one of them and spent very little of it. Not counting her recent tips and those loose bills, she had three hundred and twenty thousand dollars between her duffel bag and her makeup case.

"I could buy a Ferrari," she said to Carrot as he sniffed the money. He meowed at her with disapproval. "Yeah, I know. I could also buy a house. Or invest it. Or go to graduate school."

She zipped up the duffel bag and put it in her closet beside the makeup case. She had only had the money for a few hours. She had plenty of time to decide whether she should do something sensible with it or not.

Around seven p.m., she decided this was a night to do something frivolous and called Brett. "Hey. I want to go downtown tonight and drink seventeen-dollar martinis."

"Why?"

"I got a good tip this week."

"Okay. I guess I could handle a seventeen-dollar martini instead of a six-dollar glass of boxed wine for one night."

"Good. Come over, and we'll get a cab to the train station. Wear something nice." She hung up the phone smiling and went to her closet to find something for herself.

It had been years since she had needed to wear anything nicer than jeans. She rummaged through her closet until she found what she was looking for, the ultimate staple of versatility among women's clothing: a basic, little black dress. She had last worn it to a school sponsored graduation party at Vassar. She was delighted that it not only still fit, it was tighter, exaggerating her every curve.

Velma touched up her hair and makeup. She found a pair of sheer thigh highs in the very back corner of her sock drawer, and the red patent leather heels she'd worn with the dress almost three years ago. She made sure her breasts were situated under the strapless sweetheart neckline before covering them with her casual leather jacket.

"You know, we could just stay here all night," Brett said when he saw her. "You could teach me how to make martinis."

She had a strong temptation to tell him about the money, to tell him that, if she wanted to, she could afford never to make her own drinks again. Instead, she kissed him. "Don't worry. We're not going too far from home."

Velma and Brett traveled from Fleetwood Station to Grand Central and took a cab to 52nd Street's 21 Club, home of the seventeen-dollar martini.

"Velma." He put his arm around her as they entered. "I don't know how big your tip was, but I hope you can't afford too many drinks here, because all I really want to do is take you home and put my head between your legs."

"Even if I could afford it, there's no way I'm letting you get too drunk to do that."

"I'm glad to hear that. Now let's try to look like we belong here."

The bar area was full of well-dressed people who all gave off the air of having lifestyles constantly punctuated with over-priced martinis. There were intermittent empty seats at the bar and they managed to find two together. Velma ordered each of them the bar's standard Ketel One martini. They turned in their barstools to face one another. Her heart warmed as Brett looked into her eyes, and they clinked their glasses together, toasting something unspoken.

Over his shoulder, she caught a glimpse of a young woman who stuck out amongst the other Club 21 patrons. She had long, wavy blonde hair with a variety of colored stripes running through it. It reminded Velma of a watercolor painting. The woman had a youthful face. Was she even twenty-one? The girl was drinking a bright green appletini with a cherry at the bottom.

Velma chuckled to herself, thinking about how the color of the drink would have blended right into the color flow of her locks, and about how feminine and youthful the drink choice was.

The girl's companion was a man who appeared to be older and more conservative. Velma both admired and turned her nose up at his designer clothes and his forced charm. He stroked the girl's cheek and said something to make her giggle. He pointed to her appletini, picked it up to sniff it, and then laughed, likely for the same reasons Velma had.

The girl downed the remainder of the drink, and her companion snapped his fingers at the bartender for another. Velma snarled internally. It took a special kind of asshole to summon a bartender like that. As the girl's second appletini was being delivered, she stood and kissed her date, excusing herself to use the bathroom. She walked past Velma and Brett on her way there.

Velma looked over her shoulder and admired the girl's bold tresses as she walked away. She opened her mouth to ask Brett how he thought she'd look with turquoise stripes in her hair, but her words were halted as she saw something she wasn't supposed to see.

The charming, well-dressed man casually picked up the girl's appletini with both hands, pretending to smell it again. Only his right hand was actually holding the glass. His left rested on the side so his thumb and index finger could release a small amount of fine powder into it, which immediately disappeared as it touched the neon green concoction.

"Brett," she whispered. "Don't turn around. The couple

behind you—she's in the bathroom and he just drugged her drink."

"What? You should go warn her!"

"Shh. She'll be back any second. I have a better idea. Nod to me when she's about to walk past."

A few seconds later, the girl emerged from the bathroom and made her way back to her seat. Brett nodded.

"Excuse me!" Velma stopped the girl. She spoke at a volume the girl's date would be sure to hear. "I just wanted to tell you how much I love your hair."

She smiled. "Oh, thank you."

"I'm so sorry to interrupt you, but could you maybe tell me where you got that done?"

"I actually did it myself."

"Really? That's impressive. It looks so professional." Velma gave the girl her friendliest smile. "My name's Daphne. This is my friend Robert. Could we buy you a drink?"

"Thank you, but she already has one." The girl's companion walked over holding the tainted appletini.

As he was one step from handing it to her, the inverted-cone-shaped glass turned to razor sharp chips in his hand. The green fluid gushed out and mixed with the blood seeping from his sliced palm. "Fuck!"

The attention of the room turned to the young man with the bleeding hand and wet pants. Velma held in a smirk as she thought about how much those pants must have cost. The bartender rushed to hand the man a clean towel. He wrapped it around his bleeding hand and made a dash for the men's room.

She quickly swallowed what remained of her own drink and summoned the bartender. She took three of the crisp hundreds out of her purse, slipped them to him, and gestured with her index finger for him to lean over the bar. "Make that girl a fresh drink on me, please, and if her date makes it out of the bathroom, be sure he doesn't touch it. Either way, he won't be snapping his fingers at you again."

She turned around without waiting for a response, trusting the bartender to know what she meant. "Come on, Robert. Finish your drink, it's getting late." They donned their coats and made a quiet exit.

"That was brilliant!" Brett exclaimed. "Velma, that was a superhero move! Shouldn't we still have warned her? He's just going to buy her another drink and try again."

"No, he won't. I warned the bartender. I'm hoping whatever he put in that appletini goes right into his bloodstream and he passes out on the bathroom floor."

He took her hand and beamed at her. "Is there anywhere else you want to go? We could get some dessert. Or do you want to try another bar?"

"Actually, I was thinking we could head back home and have some sundaes at the Argonaut."

"Really?" He looked like a child who was about to get cotton candy at a carnival.

"But we're going back to my place first. I'm going to fuck your brains out and not even waste time getting undressed. Then we can have ice cream."

When they got back to her apartment, she unbuckled his belt and unzipped his pants before she even put down her purse. She pulled up her dress to the waist and dropped her coat and purse on the floor. Brett only had time to take his coat off before she pushed him backwards onto the couch, still clad in his jacket and tie. Such urgency rush through her that she didn't take off her thong, but simply moved it aside. She was on top of him before he could even get his pants down to his knees.

She felt charged. All of her base urges were intensified. She and Brett synched their pelvic movements. He kept up as she went faster and faster, until she stood and pulled him by the collar, leading him to the floor. She removed her thong and tossed it behind her, mounting him again and yanking down the top of her dress to free her breasts. The cold air around them refreshed her as she felt her body generating heat from the inside out. The fervency of her movements surprised him who, though supine and relatively still, was panting. She never stopped moving but leaned forward and repositioned herself, supporting her body with her hands on his chest. She climaxed much faster than either of them expected and let out a scream that she was sure could be heard in the pub downstairs.

Collapsing onto his torso, she rested her head near his neck as she caught her breath. Once she had recovered, he rolled her over onto her back. He kept his eyes on her face as he made just two final thrusts to achieve his own release.

He lay down on the floor beside her, both of them still panting. Velma looked over at him and saw he had sweated through his dress shirt. Then she glanced at her own remaining attire. She had rubbed holes into the knees of her thigh high stockings, which had also been pulled down and were resting loosely above her knees. She still had her shoes on.

She flipping onto her stomach and found the zipper on the back of her dress. Without getting up, she unzipped the dress and snaked her way out of it. Then, after kicking off her shoes, she removed her stockings and tossed them a few feet away. They landed next to her thong. Naked, she rolled over to Brett for warmth. He drew her close. She smelled him through his shirt, and the familiarity of his scent brought her mind back to where she really was.

"Brett, will you bring me some jeans and a sweater, please? I believe I promised you ice cream."

Twenty-Three

Sunday, May 4, 2008

Duran was drinking burgundy out of a thermos. Ridiculous, but his penchant for pairing his drinks and his reading material would not allow him to drink anything else while reading *Ulysses*. He hated that what he considered to be the only appropriate drink choice with his new prized possession would be the most detrimental to it if he spilled.

He still had no idea who was responsible for sending him his rare, grand, and expensive book. Had to be someone he knew well. Since it had been sent from a London bookshop, it was possible the buyer had instructed someone to include a note, and this had been forgotten or overlooked. It was also possible that whoever purchased it for him wanted to remain anonymous so he wouldn't know they had spent so much money, or so he wouldn't know they had so much money to spend.

He called the bookshop three times. The first time he called, he was told they had no record of the sale and knew nothing about it. The second time, the book had been ordered online, and they couldn't give out any information on the buyer. He tried a third time hoping to sweet-talk someone into telling him who purchased the book, but he was told what he had been told on the first call.

The only people who knew *Ulysses* was Duran's favorite book were Jeremy Stevens, his mother, and, at most, three of his college professors. Stevens behaved, believably so, as though he knew nothing about it, and Duran doubted he had the resources to afford it. He couldn't believe that after almost a decade his professors would remember him and certainly not with enough fondness to send him the book. His mother, however, was a retired librarian. They didn't speak much, and his mother's means were sufficient but modest. Still, she was the most likely suspect.

His mother never approved of his career choice. She had hoped her son would enter a safe and academic profession, marry, and provide her with grandchildren. He decided he was much more suited for indefinite bachelorhood and a career that promised at least the possibility of excitement and opportunities for heroism.

His father had been killed in the World Trade Center attacks, and this only strengthened his decision. His mother withdrew, angry that he didn't change paths to spare her the fear of losing her son. He was hurt, and their communication ever since had been scant. There was no animosity between them, but there wasn't enough love or money for her to have sent *Ulysses*.

He considered that his mother had sent him the book as a means of congratulating him on his promotion. She would be very happy he was no longer in a uniform patrolling the streets of Yonkers. Then he remembered he hadn't spoken to his mother in months and hadn't told her he was now a detective. It was possible she could have found out on her own, but there was only one way to know for sure.

He called her. "Mom, it's Jackson."

"Jackson! Oh, sweetheart, I'm so happy you called!"

"I know. It means I'm alive, right?"

"I can't tell if you're mocking me, but yes, it does."

"I'm only half mocking you, Mom. Listen, I have some news." He was surprised at how comforting it was to hear his mother's voice. She was, as he expected, thrilled to hear he'd become a detective. It was safer, as well as more befitting a young man with an education. As he expected, she asked him what he had been working on so far, and he told her what details he could.

What he couldn't tell his mother was that he suspected the missing person he was looking for had a connection to one or more secret government agencies, both Soviet and domestic. He also couldn't tell her that some of the evidence supporting this theory had been obtained through illicit means. He chose not to tell her about the car and the Mount Vernon homicide case. He knew what his mother would start thinking about if she learned of the shootings, and he wanted to protect her from those thoughts. While he kept the case details vague, he could tell his mother what he knew about Velma Bloom herself.

"Jackson, this girl sounds just like you."

"Just like me? How do you mean?"

"Well, you know. Independent. Strong-minded. Rebellious. You said she went to Vassar?"

"Yeah."

"And yet she was working as a waitress in a pub?"

"Yeah, not a very nice pub, either."

"I imagine Franklin was very unhappy about that."

"Yeah, her parents are…wait. Mom, I didn't tell you her parents' names."

"Sweetheart, I worked with Franklin Bloom. Well, not directly. It was when I first went back to work after you started kindergarten. You must have been too young to remember, but I had a part time job in his university's library. I remember, almost twenty-five years ago, he was so excited to tell everyone that he and his wife were adopting a baby girl. I'm so sorry to hear they're going through this."

"Did you work with him for long? Did you know him very well?"

"I was there for about a year and a half, I think. I didn't know him that well. We started talking one day, and I recommended some books for him on raising adopted children. Such a sweet man. He always took some time to chat when he came into the library."

"Mom, think back. Do you remember him talking much about his daughter?"

"Well, of course he doted on her. She was their only child. Does she have red hair?"

"She does."

"He mentioned that. He said something once about her showing quite a temper at an early age too. I remember a story he once told me. Velma was just a toddler. Franklin was trying to get her to take a nap, and she kept fussing. He read a book to her until she fell asleep, or pretended to. He left the bedroom and forgot his reading glasses on her nightstand. When he went back for them, she was wide awake and the glasses were broken."

"A toddler broke a pair of reading glasses?"

"That's what he told me. I don't remember him saying anything else unusual."

"Mom, this is great. You're actually helping me do detective work."

"That's wonderful. Oh, Jackson, I'm so relieved you're safe and off the streets."

"Uh huh." Duran was beginning to think he was further from safe than he'd ever been.

"I hope you find Franklin's daughter."

"Yeah, I do too."

"I know you've never had a temper, sweetheart, but she sounds *so* much like you. I bet she thinks like you."

"She *thinks* like I do?"

"Yes. You were so insistent on being a police officer no matter how much I begged you not to. Your father wasn't happy about it, either, he just didn't say so as much. Velma did the same thing, in a way. She didn't want the life her parents wanted for her, so she made herself a new one. That's the way you think. You're unrelentingly willful. You'll find her, Jackson."

"I hope so. Mom, listen, I need to get some work done, but it's been so great to talk to you."

"You too, sweetheart. I'm so glad you called, and I'm so happy to hear about your new job."

"Thanks, Mom. Oh, I forgot to ask you something. Did you by any chance send me something in the mail recently?"

"No, I didn't, but I think I should! I'm so proud of you, Jackson, really. I love you."

"I love you too, Mom. You don't need to send me anything. Just don't be a stranger."

At the end of the conversation, Duran still figured his mother was the most likely person to have sent *Ulysses*, but he wasn't thinking about that anymore. All he could think about was a red-haired baby breaking her father's reading glasses.

He picked up his thermos of wine and walked over to his computer. He had intermittently been watching Brett Riley's activity. It had been a couple of days since Brett had done any of his research on CIA experiments. Today, he spent most of his time watching old episodes of *Star Trek.*

When Duran returned to his desk after filling his thermos and calling his mother, Brett was reading about the CIA again, but this time, he was on the CIA's official website. He wasn't studying conspiracy theories and human experimentation anymore. He was looking for a job. Duran suddenly found his opinion of Brett evolving into something much different from what it had been on the day he planted his software on the other man's computer.

He brought his thermos to his lips and started to feel ridiculous again. He thought about getting up and pouring the remaining contents into a wine glass since he was no longer drinking next to his seventy-three-year-old book, the most expensive thing he owned. If he spilled wine all over his computer, it would cost him about twenty times less to replace it than the book would.

Before he could decide if getting up from his desk was worth transferring his burgundy into a more adult receptacle, the phone rang. "Hello?"

"Jackson? This is Sam."

"Sam! I didn't expect to hear from you."

"I wasn't expecting to call you, but I think this is important. I have to keep it brief. I'm sorry to say I'm not able to tell you anything now that I wasn't two days ago, but you're a man who can piece things together. I can't give you the information you want, but there is someone you should talk to."

"Who?"

"A man you arrested three weeks ago. The man who tried to rob Lonnie's Pub."

Twenty-Four

Monday, April 14, 2008

The night before she was to have her next visit with Volkov, Lonnie's had a busy night. Because Velma worked double shifts on Mondays, he would let her go home after the dinner rush and only have Edie stay until they closed at midnight. On a usual Monday, the dinner rush would subside by about eight, and Velma would be home upstairs and making herself a drink before nine. That night, however, the dinner rush itself went long past nine p.m. Edie wasn't feeling well, so Velma volunteered to stay until the end of the night.

As closing time approached, the steady flow of customers didn't stop. It was 12:04 a.m. before they had a chance to lock the front door and stop seating new arrivals. The people in the pub didn't linger for long, and by 12:45 a.m., Lonnie unlocked the door to allow the last of their guests to leave.

"Shit," he said. "Finally. I'm fucking spent."

"We're not done yet." She scanned the dining room. "I got a ton of cleaning up to do, and there's a bunch of dishes in the back. Jorge left before I finished clearing all the tables."

"Of course he did." Lonnie grunted. "Screw it. The dishes can wait until tomorrow. Let's just get this place in some kind of order and do a sales report so we can get the fuck out of here."

"That sounds good to me." She went to each table and worked on the necessary but annoying task of wiping up beer spills, dried ketchup, puddles of wing sauce, mystery stains, and countless unidentifiable crumbs.

Lonnie started to empty the dishwasher so he could reload it with the dozen or more dirty glasses that lined the bar. The pub was peaceful until they heard a boot being thrust into the door. The door flew open. A semi-automatic pistol entered the pub, quickly followed by the man who wielded it.

The man wore a ski mask and all black clothing. He strode up to Lonnie and reached his gun hand across the bar. Velma looked up to see the nine-millimeter pistol less than an inch away from Lonnie's face. He held up both hands to show he was unarmed.

"Open the register." Lonnie stood shaking. "Now! Do it!"

She moved to hide under the nearest table. If she managed to stay quiet and out of sight, she could take her phone out of her apron pocket and dial 9-1-1. She crouched and inched herself toward cover. The man turned to her but kept his gun pointed at Lonnie.

"Don't even think about it, sugar tits. I know you're there. You just face the other way and stay standing." She did as she was told. "I don't want to look around and see you with a phone in your hand, understood?" She remained facing away from him and nodded. He directed his next order to Lonnie. "Open the register, give me what's in it, then you and your porn-star-orphan-Annie-lookin' waitress over there can go home without getting your heads blown off."

Lonnie moved with trepidation toward the cash register. He kept his shaking hands up until he reached it and went to open the drawer. Velma turned her head to make sure the gunman wasn't watching her. He wasn't. He was watching Lonnie's trembling hands fumbling in the cash drawer. She reached over to a nearby table to pick up a bottle of Tabasco sauce and turned around.

"Hey, asshole!" She hurled the bottle at the man just before he rotated his head to face her. He had no time to react before the bottle shattered in the air three inches from his face.

The man screamed. The pistol fell from his hand and landed behind the bar within Lonnie's reach. He grabbed the gun and pointed it toward the screaming man while he dialed 9-1-1.

She rushed to the next closest table to grab another Tabasco bottle. She poured some sauce on the palm of her right hand, screwed the lid back on, and returned the bottle to its proper place.

The man in the mask panted and wailed as he stumbled out the door.

Lonnie put the gun down behind the bar as soon as the man was a few feet away from the building. He ran out from behind the bar over to Velma.

"Holy fucking hot sauce." He was still in shock and out of breath. His face was red and bordering on panicked. He leaned down, grabbed her upper arms and looked into her face. "Listen to me, Velma, are you okay? Are you hurt?"

"No. Are you hurt?"

"No, but son of a bitch. I can't believe I forgot to lock the door."

"We're fine now."

"I could have gotten both of our brains blown out."

"But you didn't. We're fine."

"Yeah, thanks to you. What the fuck happened? What the fuck did you do?"

"You, um… you didn't see?" She had a cover story ready for both Lonnie and the police, and it was going to be much easier to sell if he hadn't had a clear view of the bottle as it shattered.

"Not really. I was looking down at the register trying not to see the damn gun in my face."

"Well, I just… I was about to throw that bottle away because it was leaking. I grabbed it when I knew he wasn't looking at me and figured I was close enough I could hit him in the face."

"You're a fucking hero, Velma. That took some balls." He looked around at the shards of glass on the floor. "I just can't believe the bottle shattered like that."

"I hoped it would. I mean I figured it would. I saw it had a few cracks in it, and it was already open." She presented her Tabasco-covered right palm to back up her lie.

"You are fucking brilliant." He plopped himself onto a bar stool and put his head down to catch his breath.

Out of the corner of her eye, she saw the broken neck of the bottle on the floor. She scrambled to pick it up and put it in her apron pocket while he wasn't looking. The lid was still screwed securely around its threads.

The police didn't arrive for nearly ten minutes. A patrol car with its lights on stopped in front of the building and an officer entered the pub. "Lonnie McCarthy?" He had a pen and notepad already in his hands.

"Yeah, that's me."

"Is everyone in here okay? No one's hurt?"

"We're fine." Lonnie said. "Just shaken up. Are you fine, Velma?"

"I'm fine, Lonnie. I'm fine, Officer." She looked at the policeman. He had a kind face and looked very young, no more than a few years older than she was.

"Is it just the two of you here? Was anyone else present when the gunman entered?"

"No, just us," Velma said. "We were getting ready to close

and go home."

"What's your name, miss?"

"Velma Bloom." She looked at the officer's face. He appeared to be thinking. She knew what he was trying to remember, and prepared herself for him to mention Scooby Doo as soon as he remembered it.

"Bloom, huh? Like Leopold Bloom in *Ulysses*?"

"Huh? I mean, yes. Yes! Exactly like Leopold Bloom in *Ulysses*." She told herself that one day she would find a way to thank this man.

"That's my favorite book," he said. "I'm Officer Duran. Listen, I'm going to need to get a statement from each of you, but I think we already have your perp. White man about five foot ten, maybe a hundred and sixty-five pounds, wearing a ski mask?" Velma and Lonnie both nodded. "Yep. We found him on the street less than two blocks away. He confessed and begged us to take him to the hospital because, he said, in more colorful words, that a well-endowed redhead threw a broken bottle of Tabasco sauce in his face." Officer Duran failed to suppress a smile.

Lonnie and Velma both gave statements about what happened. She kept her story consistent—the bottle was open and cracked before she threw it. Officer Duran wrote down everything they said. He had a comforting way about him. She thought he was very good at his job, at least this part of it.

She was relieved when they were done talking to him. Her story was backed up by the Tabasco sauce on her palm and was never questioned. Even the gunman, it seemed, had reported it this way. It was likely that, in the split second he had to perceive what was happening, the man didn't see that the bottle had been intact for most of its flight. It was also possible he did see what really happened, but didn't want to sound crazy to the police. Maybe he refused to believe what he had seen and substituted it in his head with the most logical alternate explanation.

Either way, she had covered her tracks.

"Thank you both for your time," said Officer Duran. He put away his pen and notepad. "I'm so sorry you had to go through this tonight. We're just glad no one was hurt. Except for the perp. Thankfully this little lady can think on her feet. You're a hero, Ms. Bloom."

"Thanks," Velma said, "but I'd really like it if maybe you could keep my name private. I don't want this to be in any papers or online or anything. I'd rather be an anonymous hero, if that's okay."

"That's no problem. Robberies like this aren't uncommon, but if there happens to be any press, Yonkers PD will take care of it. If that's what you want, I'll make sure we keep your name out of it. You did an incredibly courageous thing, Miss Bloom, but I understand if you want your privacy."

"Thank you. That's exactly what I want." She just had to find a way to thank this man.

"Now you both get some rest. Once again, I'm very glad you're safe. You just be sure to call us anytime you need anything."

"We're very grateful, Officer," Lonnie said.

"We're here to help. You both take care." He nodded to them and opened the door to leave.

"Officer Duran?" Velma called to him. He was halfway out the door and turned back to her.

"Yes, ma'am?"

"May I ask what your first name is?"

"My first name? It's Jackson."

"Thank you, Officer Jackson Duran. Thank you so much for everything."

She didn't know if she would ever encounter Jackson Duran again, but she would remember the man who both kept her secret for her, and thought of James Joyce before Scooby Doo.

After Officer Duran departed, she tried to scrub the Tabasco sauce off her right hand. After washing it six times, she managed to reduce, but not entirely eliminate, the smell of it from her palm.

"Velma," said Lonnie, "you know, for all the times I act like an asshole, I really appreciate what you do around here."

"I know, Lonnie, but thank you for saying it."

"I guess having you save me from maybe getting a bullet in my skull made it easier to say."

"Listen, I'd really like it if we didn't talk about this anymore. I meant what I said to the cop about wanting privacy and all."

"Sure. I'm having a shot of something. Have one with me. I think we both need it. At least one."

"Thanks, really, but I just want to get home."

"I've never known you to turn down a free shot, but then again it's been one hell of a night. Go home, I'll take care of the glass on the floor. The rest can wait until tomorrow."

"Thanks. Are you okay?"

"I'm shook up, but yeah, I'm okay."

"Good. I'm going to go home, and I'm going to lock the door behind me. Make sure you lock it again after you leave."

"I'm not making that mistake again. Goodnight, Velma. I don't know what to say, but thank you."

"Goodnight, Lonnie."

She went upstairs to her apartment, making sure to lock her own door. Then she called Brett.

"Hello?" His voice sounded as though he hadn't been asleep, and she was relieved.

"Hi. Listen, can you come over like right now? I mean without taking a shower first or anything? Can you leave right away?"

"Is something wrong?"

"No. I mean yes. Something happened tonight and I need you. You're the only person who knows... you know. I just have to talk to you, and it's really important."

"I'll be there in eight minutes."

"Thank you, Brett." She hung up the phone, and eight minutes later, a bright white Eldorado pulled into the parking lot.

When she heard the car, she ran to her back door and tried to time his footsteps like Volkov did. She wanted to open the door at the exact second Brett was close enough to come inside. Her timing was off, and she found herself standing in the doorway when he was still a third of the way up the steps from the landing.

When he reached her, he embraced her immediately. "Oh, Velma." He stroked her hair. "Please, tell me what happened."

Carrot meowed from behind them.

"He's telling us to close the door," she said. Brett pulled her inside and onto the couch.

"What happened?" He grabbed her hands and laced his fingers through hers. "Can I make a drink for you? Can I bring you a cigarette?"

"Both please. I have ice in the freezer, just pick something from the cabinet and put ice in it."

"Sure. I'm going to bring you that and then open the window so we can smoke, okay?"

"Thank you. I'm really happy you're here."

He brought her a glass of Sailor Jerry on the rocks, and she was glad he chose it. He opened the window and lit a cigarette for her.

"You are okay, right?" He sat beside her and stroked her arm.

"Yes, but something happened. Lonnie's got robbed tonight."

"What?" He moved as though to put his arms around her.

She would have welcomed the embrace, but she had a drink in one hand and a cigarette in the other.

Brett put a hand on her knee and caressed her leg. "That's terrifying. You're not hurt?"

"I'm not hurt. Actually, we didn't get robbed. I mean no one took anything. Lonnie forgot to lock the door after we closed, and a guy just walked right in the door with a gun."

"Holy shit. What did you do?"

"I threw a bottle of Tabasco sauce at him. I threw it right at his face. It exploded in his eyes and he dropped the gun."

His eyes widened. "Velma, you made another superhero move."

"I guess I did." She recounted the events leading up to her attack on the gunman. Talking to him calmed her. Like the drink in her right hand and the cigarette in her left, he was a tonic. "I saw the bottle and then just did it. I didn't think it through. I just reacted. It was like I knew exactly what I was doing, but it was the first time I did it on instinct without any focus."

"Wow. Does anyone know…?"

"I hope not. I covered my tracks. We talked to the police. They caught the guy. He was in so much pain he couldn't even get away." A rush of adrenaline surged through her as she spoke. She told him her cover story and let him smell the Tabasco on her palm then showed him the bottleneck stashed in her apron pocket.

"Shit. If you hadn't found that…"

"I know. They'd know the bottle wasn't open, and I'd have a lot of questions to answer." She paused to sip her rum.

"Do you remember when you first told me about it? When we were kids?"

"Of course. I was so afraid you'd think I was nuts." She downed the rest of her drink and put the glass on the table with a clank. "I hated being a kid. I spent so much time just trying to hide it so I could live like a normal person. Until I met you, I almost completely isolated myself."

"We always did have that in common. I never liked talking to other kids, either." He stroked her back and held her. "You really could be a super hero, Velma."

"Maybe someday." She pulled herself out of his embrace.

She climbed on top of him, spreading her legs over his lap. She took off her own shirt and then his. She slammed it on the floor as though it were the pelt of a prey animal that stood between a starving lioness and the raw flesh beneath that would be her meal.

"You know," she said, "I could have gotten killed tonight, but somehow I feel really fucking good. I feel like I could go out and save the world."

"You should." He looked lovingly into her eyes.

She put her hand between his legs. "Fuck me first."

Twenty-Five

Gordon Casey, the man who tried to rob Lonnie's Pub three weeks ago, had been released from St. John's Riverside Hospital, but he wasn't in jail. Duran was unsettled but unsurprised when he found out where Casey was.

The black gate in front of Bellevue Hospital made it look like an elegant prison. Duran took in its brick exterior and immaculate shrubbery. Beyond the gate, Bellevue looked less like a psychiatric hospital and more like an apartment building whose rent he wouldn't be able to afford.

He walked past the shrubbery and paid it no additional mind; the reason he was there would be found inside the building. It hadn't been easy for him to arrange this visit. In order to speak with Casey, he had to be on Casey's list of approved visitors.

Duran made several phone calls before speaking with a nurse who said she would ask Mr. Casey if he was willing to speak with him. He was shocked when the nurse called him back and said Gordon not only approved Duran's visit, he wanted him to come as soon as possible and speak with him alone.

He showed his badge and ID to three separate people before he was escorted to the unit that housed Casey. A man who introduced himself as the head nurse greeted Duran and led him down a wide, well-lit hallway lined with open doors. The doors were to patient bedrooms, most of which were empty. The patients were in the common room where the nurse had been leading him.

Some were playing board games, some were seated on a couch watching television, and others were reading books or magazines. The atmosphere was peaceful, and he felt a bit of shame for having expected padded rooms with people rocking back and forth in straitjackets.

"He's not violent," the nurse whispered, "but he's excitable. You'll be able to talk in private, but there will be someone right outside the door in case he gets out of hand."

"Do you think he will?" The nurse ignored him and walked into the common room. Duran was left standing in the doorway. He knew which patient was Casey, even though he had never seen him without a ski mask. What gave him away was a pair of dark glasses and strips of white surgical tape that spanned his forehead to his cheek, holding a bandage in place over his right eye.

"Gordon?" The nurse touched his shoulder. Casey jumped in his seat and looked up. "Jackson Duran is here to see you."

"He's the cop, right?"

"The detective, yes." The nurse took Casey's arm and led him over to Duran. "Detective, this is Mr. Casey."

"Thank you for taking time to speak with me, Mr. Casey."

"I would shake your hand, Detective, but I can't see where it is, and I might grab your cock by accident."

"Gordon, I'm going to take the two of you to your room so you can speak in private. I'm trusting you to show Detective Duran the proper respect."

Duran followed as the nurse led them down the hall away from the common room.

"Don't worry, Detective," Casey said without looking at him. "I only grab my own cock, and that's if I'm lucky enough to find it."

In Casey's room, the nurse helped him sit on the edge of the bed. He had an aide bring in a chair for Duran.

"Remember," the nurse whispered again, "someone will be just outside the door."

"Thank you. I think we'll be fine." Duran sat. Both he and Casey stayed quiet until the door clicked shut.

"Detective, I'm not crazy." He took off his glasses.

His right eye was obscured by a white bandage. His left eye was grotesque. It was cloudy, and what was once the white of his eye was now pink and spattered with small red dots and lines. Viscous green puss seeped out from under his bottom eyelid.

"My god." Duran had seen a lot in his seven years as a police officer. He had seen corpses, blood pouring out of gunshot wounds, and junkies in alleyways passed out in their own vomit. Gordon Casey's eye was the first thing to ever turn his stomach. "Tabasco sauce did that?"

"No, glass did." Casey leaned toward Duran, giving him a closer look.

He remembered the eyes he'd seen through Casey's ski mask. He remembered the tiny shards of glass he saw in them. The red dots and lines on Casey's sickening, exposed eye matched Duran's memory of where those glass shards had been when they reflected the red light that flashed over them from atop the police car.

His stomach flipped again. "Mr. Casey, how much can you see?"

"I can see shapes and colors, but it's all a blur. I can see you're a white guy with brown hair, and you're wearing a blue shirt. But as far as I'm concerned, you don't have a face. Nothing has an outline. I have no depth perception. On a good day I can walk around without bumping into shit. On a great day I can feed myself and take a piss without someone helping me aim. Want to see my other eye?"

"Not especially, but I have a feeling you're going to show it to me."

"Actually, Detective, I'm not. Because I don't have it." Casey put his dark glasses back on. Duran was relieved to be spared the view of the eye that remained. "The doctors at St. John's said the infection was so bad they had to take it out before it spread. They said I shouldn't have rubbed my eyes because I just pushed the glass in deeper, but I didn't rub my eyes. I swear to fucking God I didn't rub my eyes. I told those doctors I *didn't* rub my eyes, I told them what happened, I told them the lid was on the bottle, and they sent me here."

"Why? What did you tell them happened?"

"What did that little ginger cunt with the giant tits tell you?"

"You had a gun in her boss's face. She threw the bottle at you to get you to drop it."

"What bullshit did she tell you about how the bottle broke?"

"She said the bottle was already broken. She said it was cracked, there was no lid on it, and it was leaking."

Casey laughed. "She lied to you."

"Tell me what happened, Mr. Casey."

"I may be fucking blind now, but I wasn't then. I know what I saw. The waitress did this." He took off his glasses again. "Look at my fucking eye, Detective. Look at it. If I could find your eyes with it, I'd look into them so you know I'm not lying. She threw the bottle, and I saw it flying toward me. There was no crack. It just…shattered. It shattered in the air in front of me. I need you to believe me. I need someone to believe me."

"I'm not saying I don't believe you, Mr. Casey, but listen to me. If you change your story, if you say the pain made you think crazy

152

things and you understand that now, then they'll let you out of here. You'll serve some time for the attempted robbery, but you'll get out. A class D felony will probably mean two years. It doesn't matter if I believe you, what matters is if the doctors here believe you. They don't, and there are mental health laws in New York that make it possible for them to keep you here forever. Do you understand that?"

"Yes, Detective. I do."

"I know how awful two years in Sing Sing sounds, but it's two years and then it's over. Maybe less, if you behave yourself. You're gambling here. If I were you, I wouldn't want to gamble with forever."

"I understand. Now I have a question for you. After I left that shit hole pub, what happened to the broken glass?"

"What do mean?"

"Did they clean it up? Throw it away? Did you look through it?"

"Why, Mr. Casey? What's important about the broken glass?"

"That glass would prove I'm telling the truth."

"How?"

"The lid. There was a lid on the bottle. I know I can't prove the bottle wasn't cracked before she threw it, but she lied about the lid." Casey dropped his glasses. He fell back onto the bed and began breathing heavily, his voice steadily rising until it reached the volume of a scream. "The lid *was* on the bottle. She lied about the lid. She's lying. She's lying. She's lying!"

Duran stood and slowly crept back to the door. Casey kept screaming, and the aide outside called for a nurse. They opened the door and bolted past Duran to Casey, who was now tossing and turning as he continued his chant.

The orderly held Casey still and his screams became sobs. "There was a lid was on the bottle. She's lying. You have to believe me. She's lying!"

Duran watched until the nurse took out a syringe and asked him to leave the room. He stood outside the door, still hearing Casey's words, unsure if he was still chanting, or if the phrase was just ringing in his head.

When Casey calmed, the nurse came out of the room, leaving the orderly to watch the sedated patient.

"I'm sorry, Detective," he said. "I shouldn't be telling you this, but he chants the same things every night. 'There was no crack,'

'She's lying,' 'The lid was on the bottle.' He repeats them over and over in his sleep. When he tells the story of what happened the night of his… injury, he tells it with consistency and conviction."

Duran shrugged. "He believes it to be true."

"Do you think so?"

"That it's true?"

"No, of course not, but do you think he *really* believes it is? When he first arrived here, I thought he was just another criminal feigning madness to avoid prison. Usually, people drop the act very quickly once they realize a jail sentence is finite, and here… well, you know."

"I do know. So does Mr. Casey."

"We're doing our best. He seems impossible to treat."

He looked at the nurse's anxious face. "Listen, I'm not a doctor," he said in a low voice, "but I would like to make a suggestion as an officer of the law. With what I know about what happened to him, I would advise you to keep him here for as long as you can, and keep him *quiet*."

He left the hospital with Casey's words echoing in his brain. *The lid was on the bottle. She lied about the lid. She's lying.* He alone knew Casey was a sane man telling the truth. It was a truth that needed to stay inside the hospital walls. For all that Duran had gone through to get it, this was a truth he had no idea what to do with.

When he arrived at home, he found a small package on his doorstep. It was from Amazon and was about the right weight and dimensions to be a book. Would this box contain a clue about who sent the box he received the previous week? It didn't, and it wasn't a book. It was a brand new Kindle.

He had mixed feelings about this device when it was released the year before. Part of him thought the idea of having one's entire book collection on something handheld was brilliant, but another part of him was fearful of the beginning of the end of the printed word.

By the time he decided it was something he had to own, Kindles had sold out. Now he had one in his hand, and he began to wish he could retire immediately and download everything onto it that he might ever want to read for the rest of his life. He checked the box, hoping to find something with the Kindle that had not been included with *Ulysses*, a note. He found one.

Dear Jackson,

*Congratulations! I'm so proud of you. I know this is
something you will enjoy. Please stay safe.*

Love, Mom

He wished he could have felt happy, but he was troubled. The
Kindle felt ominous. It took away the only logical theory he had about
the source of the last gift he received. It told him one thing for sure,
something he would have been happier not knowing: his mother
hadn't sent *Ulysses*.

Twenty-Six

Tuesday, April 15 2008

Velma slept for almost ten hours, but it was a restless sleep. She woke up around three p.m. and scurried to arrive at Volkov's on time. When she arrived, he was there, as always, to open it before she could knock.

"Velma," he said as she entered. "Welcome. I got us a fine bottle of scotch, but you look like you are either terribly hungover or have already been drinking for hours today." His voice sounded as though he were both joking and scolding.

"Hi, Leo."

"Apologies," he said, walking her to the basement door.

"I don't get hangovers," she began as they descended the creaky wooden stairs. "I'm immune. And I haven't been drinking for hours, because I haven't been awake for hours." She wished she had a drink before she left. "Actually, I didn't sleep well last night. Something happened at work," she admitted.

"I see. You would enjoy some scotch, then?"

"I would very much." She plopped into what had become her usual chair and let her purse and coat fall to the floor beside her. "I would also enjoy some coffee. If you have coffee." She sniffled. "Do you have coffee?"

"Milk or sugar? Black?"

"Black, please."

He nodded and went back upstairs, returning a few minutes later and presenting her with a large, very full mug. It was too hot to drink, but it felt good to hold onto and warm her hands.

After walking over to the counter, he set up two rocks glasses then showed her a bottle of eighteen-year-old Macallan. "I assume you will not take ice with this?"

"Do you think I'm some kind of savage?" Velma managed a laugh.

"Good girl," he said and filled the glasses. "Now tell me, what happened last night at work that disturbed your sleep?"

"We had a break-in." She sipped her coffee. It was still too hot.

"Oh?" He stopped short for a moment while pouring the second glass of scotch.

"It was only Lonnie and me, and neither of us got hurt." She put down the coffee mug with a clank, then moved it onto a coaster.

"I see." He handed her a glass and sat down across from her, taking a sip from his own.

Velma lifted her glass to do the same. It was the quintessence of comforting. She took a moment to savor the taste and the feeling of warmth it gave her from the inside out. She recounted the events of the night before, much as she had to Officer Duran. As Volkov listened to her story, his face had no discernible expression. His features appeared fixed with intent, but his focus seemed heightened. He was silent for several seconds after she finished her tale.

Then he said something she did not expect. "You were seen."

"Holy shit. You know about this."

"Do you trust me?" His voice was firm and steady, almost frightening.

"Why? Should I?"

"I am the only person you should trust." He leaned forward and caught her eyes. "Does anyone know the truth about the Tabasco sauce?"

She froze. "It sounds like *you* know it." She tried to read his face. All she could see was fear in his eyes. She stiffened. His fear was contagious.

"Velma," he said, "listen to me now more carefully than you ever have. I need you to leave here now. I need you to be very calm, as calm as you can be. Put on your coat and gather your things. You will leave through my front door and turn left. You will cross the street and walk one block to the house on the corner of Claremont and Primrose. Stand in front of the yard. I am going to call a taxi for you right now. It will pick you up there. Have the driver take you straight home. Do not get on any buses or make any other stops. Go home."

"You know about this. You know what this is. Leo, you have to tell me!"

"Stop. Be quiet." He crossed the room and pulled a phone out of a drawer. "Take out your phone please and look up the phone number of a taxi company you have never used before. Tell the number to me and do not call it yourself."

She wanted to demand information, but he had become

someone terrifying. She did as she was told. He made the call, disguising his accent as best as he could.

"Yes, hello, I need a taxi for my niece please, as soon as possible. Mount Vernon. The corner of Claremont and Primrose. She will be in front of the large house with the red roof. Excellent. Thank you very much." He disconnected the call, removed the memory card and battery from the phone, and put it back in the drawer. "They will be here for you in fifteen minutes. I trust you have cash to pay the driver?"

She nodded.

"Good."

"Thank you," she said, hearing her own voice shake. She put on her coat and picked up her purse.

"Listen to me. When you get home, go directly inside and speak to no one. Either turn off your phone or do not answer any calls. I do not care who it is, do not answer any calls."

"Okay."

"Good. Lock your door and stay inside for the rest of the night. Eat something. Smoke cigarettes and make some drinks, do whatever you have to do to relax because you will want to go to sleep early and set your alarm clock. You will come back here tomorrow during morning rush hour. Get on your first bus by seven a.m."

"But I..."

"You will, and you will arrive here before nine a.m. Yes?"

"Fine. I guess having a GRU agent scare the shit out of me is one way to keep life interesting."

"Velma, get out of my house. Wait for your taxi. Do not be late tomorrow. *Go.*"

Twenty-Seven

Friday, May 9, 2008

Duran was not expecting the phone call he received during his lunch break. The caller wanted to speak with him in person, but not at the police station. This excited him enough for him to rush home from work early and prepare for a visitor. Two hours later, he answered a faint knock at his door.

"Sam, please come in." Sam Ferguson's face had aged a decade in the week since Duran saw him. "I'm grateful to you for coming to see me. Have a seat anywhere you like, make yourself comfortable."

"Thank you, Jackson. Two things first."

"Okay."

"Number one, trusting you is against all my better instincts. You're a sneaky cop, but for some reason I think you're an honest man. On your honor, assure me there are no recording devices of any kind in this apartment."

"On my honor, there are not. I promise."

"Good. Number two, please get me a drink." Sam cracked a smile for a fraction of a second, and it disappeared before Duran could greet it with his own. "Or a bottle."

The gravity of the conversation they were about to have crushed any vestige of cheer out of the room. Duran figured Sam wouldn't be smiling anymore that day. "Vodka?"

"Honestly, Jackson, today I don't care. Anything."

"Well, you might as well enjoy it. I have vodka. Please, sit. I'll bring us some ice and the bottle."

"Thank you." Sam sat on the couch, and Duran brought in a tray with two rocks glasses and a bottle of middle-shelf vodka.

"Sorry, I know you're used to Belvedere." Duran moved to pick up the bottle and fill their glasses, but Sam beat him to it.

"This is fine. It has alcohol in it. Today I would even drink some of that brown stuff you love so much." His hands shook as he filled Duran's glass about halfway and his own to the brim. He brought his glass to his lips, and the shaking subsided after two large swallows. "I shouldn't be here."

"That depends who you ask. I have my own code."

"Interesting choice of words. I imagine you have a lot of code. Probably in C and C++." He looked at Duran and raised his eyebrows. "I don't know all of your sources, but you've discovered some things there aren't many ways of finding out, certainly not many legal ways."

Duran gulped. "Seems we both have our secrets, then."

"With all due respect, Detective, my secrets make yours look like playground whispers. Don't ever mention MKUltra to me again." Sam's voice was firm and commanding.

He felt himself shrinking. "I won't."

"I like you, but after today, we've never met. I don't recommend you do anything with any of what you're about to hear from me. I'm not going to tell you what might happen if you do, because it would sound like a threat, and I promise I am not threatening you."

"Understood. I can use my imagination."

Sam took another sip of his vodka and set it down on the tray. "Do you have a dark imagination?"

"I'm sure I do, compared to most people." Duran's hands trembled, and the ice in his drink rattled against the glass.

"Then your imagination would be right." Sam's voice deepened, and Duran stared at him wide-eyed.

"That's rather terrifying."

"It should be." Sam reached for his drink and reclined on the couch. "You spoke to the prisoner."

He nodded. "I did, but he's not a prisoner. He's a patient. He's in a psychiatric ward at Bellevue. He's also missing an eye, and the eye he has left might be the most gruesome thing I've ever seen." His stomach twisted from curiosity and fear. He was sick at recalling the image of Casey's infected eye.

"And how did he tell you this happened to him?"

Sam listened as Duran relayed Casey's wild account of what happened at Lonnie's Pub. He nodded as Duran spoke, seemingly unsurprised by anything he heard.

"If I hadn't seen the glass in his eyes right after it happened," Duran said, "and if the only facts I had were the ones the doctors do, I'd think he was nuts too. But I *don't* think he's nuts, Sam, I believe everything he told me is the truth."

"Whether or not he's sane is irrelevant." Sam leaned forward.

"He *is* telling the truth."

"Then the only conclusion I have would make me sound crazy enough to be in that ward with him. Velma Bloom can shatter glass with her mind." He looked to Sam for a reaction. He didn't get one.

"I don't know what, if anything, this has to do with Velma's disappearance. That's for you to speculate. I choose not to. I also don't know the extent of her abilities, but I do know where they came from.

"As I'm sure you've pieced together on your own, I was, from 1970 until 1985, employed by the United States Central Intelligence Agency. I spent those fifteen years doing things I've been regretting more than twice that long. I had no involvement with espionage as you may be thinking. I'm a neurologist. I should say I *was* a neurologist. I have done nothing in my field since I retired from the CIA."

"You retired young."

Sam nodded. "I was forty-two when I left."

"Why did you leave?"

"Jackson, don't you find it disturbing that the CIA would have reasons to employ a neurologist?"

"Now that you mention it."

"Use your dark imagination. Think about the things a neurologist might have been employed to do."

He forced himself to remain in the moment. "I'll wait to do that until I can drink enough to pass out."

"Smart man."

"After you left, you didn't want to get another job? You didn't want to do something different in neurology? Something less…"

"Sinister?"

"I was just going to say 'unsettling,' but sinister works."

"Unsettling is the perfect word here, but it's a rather an egregious understatement. To answer your question, no, I didn't. Neurology is the science of the central nervous system. After what I'd seen, I wanted nothing to do with the central nervous system ever again. Not even my own." He tilted his head toward the vodka bottle. "Now, to the point. Among the things I have seen, although far from the most unsettling, is something that happened during a test I conducted in 1981. The CIA was working with other groups, including the Department of Defense, on what you might know as a black project. This is something hidden, unacknowledged, even within the agencies involved. In this case, it was what we call an Acquisition

Special Access Project. I was dealing with the research, testing, and evaluation of a highly classified, unacknowledged project with an unknown application.

"Because of the nature of the project, I was required to have a top-secret security clearance. It was a compartmentalized clearance, meaning I only knew what I was required to know in order to do my job. What I'm telling you, is that there are parts of this story I do not know. I have a dark imagination too, Jackson, and in my line of work, that proved a curse. I was told just enough to feed it. I have demons in my head. The skeletons in my closet have demons in their skulls. Use your imagination at your own risk."

Duran's heart raced, and with each beat his chest filled with cold splinters. "I guess I appreciate the warning."

"You already know much about MKUltra. You're not supposed to. The parts of it that were declassified a few years ago were never intended to be. After information about it began to reach the public in the mid-1970s, the CIA got much better at keeping dead projects buried. This is why you have never heard of what became known after the fact as Project Shatter.

"Thousands of documents related to MKUltra that should have been destroyed were not. Then, of course, there were the subjects of the experiments. Not all of them were knowing and willing participants. Ironically, so many of those experiments were to help develop new interrogation methods for Soviet spies, ways to get people to talk. The subjects weren't the ones who were supposed to talk, especially not about those experiments. No one wanted to make that mistake again.

"The subject of the experiment I'm going to tell you about, however, was a CIA agent. He was a knowing and willing test subject who even had his own security clearance. He might have even known more than I did. What I knew was this man was to undergo some kind of experimental genetic alterations and part of his brain, his limbic system, was supposed to be affected. My job was to map his brain at different stages of the experiment and report any changes in his limbic activity. My reports were to be objective, and my clearance did not include knowing the ultimate goal of the experiment. I don't know what was *intended* to happen to this man's brain—but I saw what did happen."

Duran's stomach lurched. "And you didn't even know what

you were testing for?"

"Correct. The man being tested had his head and body covered with sensors, and he was attached to a machine that allowed me to view his brain on a monitor. He was shown projected images that were meant to stir up different emotions. The second time the test was performed, after the subject had undergone the experiment, what I saw on my screen was a level of limbic activity unlike anything I had ever seen before.

"I had been a neurologist for over a decade. I had mapped many people's brains. Hell, I did a lot worse than that to people's brains. I knew what I was doing. I knew what normal brain activity looked like on that screen and what a normal brain would look like in response to emotion. When this man was shown a picture that made him angry, a section of his brain went haywire. I couldn't take my eyes off my monitor. It was terrifying, but not as terrifying as what else happened. At the same time I saw what I saw on the screen, my coffee mug shattered in my hand. The next time the man became angry, the glass of the projector lens cracked into a thousand pieces. At that point, I called for the test to cease. It was meant to continue, but I had seen enough. My fear got the best of me."

"What were you afraid of?"

"One of two things had happened. Either the experiment had failed and done something to the man it wasn't supposed to do, or worse, it had done what it was supposed to do. It's a horrible thought, isn't it? That this had been their intent? Something was done to this man's genes that caused his brain to react so powerfully to anger that it produced *external* energy. *Destructive* external energy. Can you imagine a military application of that?"

"I don't want to."

"No, you don't. I might not have been cleared to know everything, but I knew who I was working for. My worst fears were of what their objective might have been, and that the experiment had been a success."

"Was it?"

"I'll never know for sure, but I don't think so. I was ordered to destroy the brain maps as well as all my notes, records, and any other documentation relating to the tests on this man. So my guess is that the truth is the less horrifying idea that the experiment had gone wrong. Still, that man's life was destroyed along with the records of what had been done to him."

"This happened in 1981. Before Velma was born?"

"Yes."

"So some record must have been kept? So they could do this to someone else?"

"No. Jackson, listen. My test subject—to put the sensors on his head, had to be shaved. I wasn't the one who shaved it, but whoever did missed a spot. He had red hair."

Duran was aghast. "Velma's biological father."

"Yes."

"What was this man's name? What happened to him?"

"His name doesn't matter, and I have no idea what happened to him. That man and that name no longer exist as one. If he's still alive, it's because he was smart enough to change his name twenty-seven years ago. If he did, it wasn't to Franklin Bloom. I did some homework of my own after I heard the story of Velma's Tabasco bottle. When I confirmed she was adopted, I knew my suspicion was correct. That's when I called you. That's when I broke."

Both men sat in silence, sipping vodka and staring at nothing.

"Fuck. Now what?" He growled under his breath. "This all blows my mind. I'm glad I know it, but I have no idea what to do with it."

"For my own sake, I hope you do nothing. For Velma's, that's up to you. Just keep in mind that while documents can be destroyed, people have long memories. That's why I think you should stop looking. It wasn't my intention to make this more difficult for you. In your position, I wouldn't know what the hell to do with this information either."

Duran was thunderstruck by all he'd learned. He tried to suppress his thoughts. Each one fired like a cannon inside his head. "At least now I have information to not know what to do with. That's more than I had before."

"And I feel unburdened, if only a little." Sam closed his eyes. He began to cry and covered his face with his hands.

Duran went to the kitchen and reheated a cup of cold coffee. He brought it to Sam along with a box of tissues. "You're a good man, Sam. Thank you."

"I made years and years of mistakes, but I'm not a bad person." He dried his eyes then winced as he took a sip of the coffee.

"I regret all of it. My only comfort is in knowing that if it hadn't been me doing the things I did, they still would have been done. By doing those horrible things, I spared someone else."

"There's no way I can ever understand the risk you took by telling me this, and I'm grateful." Duran wondered if he was capable of feeling as much regret as Sam experienced and hoped he'd never find out.

"I'm trusting you, Jackson. I'm an old man, and I would prefer not spend what years I have left in prison. I'll drink myself into an early grave no matter what, but I'd like to be free to choose where I do it."

"I promise everything you've told me is safe. I just hope we can say the same for Velma."

"So do I. Like you said, my skeletons have enough company."

Twenty-Eight

Jackson paced around his apartment, unsure of how afraid he should be. He just learned things he was forbidden to know. This excited him, but his excitement was tempered by his logic. There were reasons certain information was forbidden. Unanswered questions were torture, but in this case, he wondered if knowing the answers was worse. The answers frightened him. They also gave him more questions, ones that might have even more vexing answers. How badly did he want to connect these dots? Badly enough, he decided. He called Brett Riley.

"Brett, this is Jackson Duran."

"The detective?"

"Yeah. We talked a couple weeks ago. But listen, I'm not calling you from the police station. I'm working for myself today. And I would like your help."

"Did you find out anything about Velma?"

"I damn well did. May I come over and talk to you?"

"Am I in some sort of trouble?"

"What? No!" He realized how over-excited he'd become and how frightened Brett must have been to get his phone call. "Like I said, I'm working for myself today. I want to talk to you as Jackson, not as Detective Duran. You, my friend, are the one person who can help me connect some dots."

"Okay." Brett sounded suspicious, but conceded. "You can come over."

"Great. I'll be there in twenty minutes. You and I have some notes to compare." He called a cab and grabbed an unopened bottle of Johnny Walker Black. He wore jeans and a black T-shirt, looking very unlike a police officer. He left his badge and his sidearm at home.

He arrived at Brett's apartment exactly when he said he would. The door made a sinister creak as Brett opened it.

"Come in, Detective." Brett was fully dressed, and without his Chewbacca slippers.

"Thank you. Don't call me 'detective' today. No one knows I'm here."

"Okay. So, Jackson, I thought you guys were never really supposed to be off duty."

"Yeah, well, I have my own ways of doing things."

"You mean drinking whisky?" Brett looked at the bottle in his hand.

"That's one of them." He sat on Brett's couch. "And as to that, would you mind getting us a couple glasses, please?"

"Sure." Brett went into the kitchen and returned with two plastic cups. One was empty for Duran, and the other was full of red wine for himself.

"Not going to join me?"

"I am. It's just that I only drink red wine. Actually, I don't drink at all when Velma's not around. I've never tasted whisky before."

"What? Brett, how old are you?"

"Twenty-seven."

"You've got to be kidding. You're only three years younger than I am, and you've never tasted whisky?"

"Does kissing Velma count?"

He started to laugh until he saw how serious Brett was. "Well, if it's just me, I won't need the cup." Duran opened the bottle. "This is good stuff. But I guess it's an acquired taste. One worth acquiring, though." He brought the whisky to his lips.

"Maybe someday I'll try drinking it."

"If that someday is today, feel free to help yourself."

"Thank you. Can you tell me why you wanted to talk to me?"

Brett's voice was somber, and Duran didn't like it. He was charged, almost manic, and he wanted Brett's energy level to match his own.

"As I said, I would like your help. I have a proposition for you. I've learned some things I think you will find very interesting, and I'm willing to share them if you'll share some information with me. There's a lot we might be able to figure out, but we have to do it together. I need you not to hold anything back. If you do, I'll know. Call it a superpower, but I can always tell when someone is hiding something from me. I say we make a gentlemen's agreement. I will be honest and transparent with you, and you will be honest and transparent with me."

"Very well." Brett nodded and took a large gulp of wine from his cup. "A gentlemen's agreement. But only on the condition that you show me there's no wire under your shirt and you promise me you won't repeat *any* part of what we talk about, no matter what it is."

He lifted his shirt. "Someone once told me I'm a sneaky cop, but an honest man. You have my word that nothing we talk about today will leave this room. I promise I will not repeat anything you tell me."

"No matter what it is?"

"No matter what it is. I promise." He struggled to keep his voice calm.

"Okay. I believe you."

"Good. Now, will you promise me your complete honesty and transparency?"

"I guess I have to."

"You do. That's part of why they call it a gentlemen's agreement."

"Okay. I promise." They shook hands.

"Excellent." Duran let some of his excitement back into his voice. "Now, the way I see this, you and I each have a piece of a treasure map. There are pieces still missing, but if we put the pieces we have together, we might be able to fill in the gaps. Just maybe, the map will lead us to Velma."

"You really like metaphors."

Duran laughed. "Yes, I do, and I want to see your piece of the treasure map."

"What makes you think I have one?"

"You're not being transparent with me, Brett. Gentlemen's agreement, remember?"

"Oh, I forgot, you have some kind of superpower to know when people are hiding things."

"That, and last time I was here, I installed spyware on your computer while you were taking a piss." Duran took a gulp of whisky, waiting for his reaction. He just sat, wearing a look of shock as he realized how much Duran already knew. "I wasn't trying to violate you. I only wanted to see if you were communicating with Velma."

Brett stared at him with his mouth open. "You are a sneaky cop."

"Like I said, I have my own ways of doing things. But as I've just demonstrated, I'm honest." He flashed his friendliest smile.

"I would be furious," Brett said, "but I'm too impressed that you knew how to do that."

"Thank you, I think."

"So you know I haven't heard from Velma since she disappeared, but you probably saw things that made you think I'm some kind of lunatic conspiracy theorist."

"Actually, I think you are a brilliant and sane conspiracy theorist. And I think you'd be a great secret agent."

"You saw that too?" Brett blushed.

"What I need to know is why you started researching that stuff. Why MKUltra? Why mind control? What made you think there was a connection?"

"I'll show you." Brett stood, walked over to his desk, and took something out of his drawer, keeping his hand closed around it as he returned to his seat. "I lied to you when you were here before. You asked me if I knew of a reason Velma might be in danger. I said no. That wasn't true. I *don't* know of anyone who would want to hurt her, no one specific anyway, but there is a reason she could be in danger." He opened his hand and presented what he was holding to Duran. "Do you know what this is?"

"Oh my fucking god." In the palm of Brett's hand lay the broken-off neck of a Tabasco sauce bottle. It had a bright red lid on it. "Yes, I do."

"So you know her secret?"

He nodded. "Brett, where did you get that?"

"It was in an envelope on my windshield. I found it the day I realized she was gone."

"Do you think *she* put it there?"

"I don't know. Either she put it there to let me know she's okay, or someone else put it there to tell me she's not. When she disappeared, I stopped sleeping. I did nothing but think about her. I guess I am a conspiracy theorist, because a connection occurred to me right away. It sounds extreme, but think about it. If the CIA knew there was a woman who could shatter things with her mind, don't you think they'd want to get their hands on her? Study her? Make a weapon out of her? That was my first thought."

"But you don't think that anymore?"

Brett shook his head. "Do you know Velma was adopted?"

"I do."

"After I found out a few things, I realized the actual connection was to one of her biological parents."

"You really would be a great secret agent, Brett. Or a detective. We could use more conspiracy theorists. You're right, you know, about the connection."

"I thought so, but I was hoping I wasn't."

"So was I. I shouldn't be telling you any of what I'm about to tell you, but you've figured out a lot on your own, and we need to put things together. I was able to locate a credible source who told me that some kind of genetic experiment was done on a CIA agent a couple years before Velma was born. It was covered up and there's nothing left to prove it ever happened. But whatever was done to that agent altered his brain somehow, giving him something in common with her. When he got angry, something around him would shatter. This agent also had red hair. I don't know his name or if he's still alive, but it has to be her father."

Brett cocked his head. "Don't you mean her mother?"

"No, her father." They looked at each other with distinct confusion.

"I thought for sure it was her mother." Brett's face became even paler than it already was.

"My source told me the agent was male."

"Goddammit." Brett became visibly upset. He took a swig of the whisky, gagging and coughing after he swallowed it.

"I should have warned you not to do that if you've never had whisky." He took the bottle from Brett. "Why did you think her mother was a CIA agent?"

Brett winced and wiped his lips. "You promised me none of this is leaving this room."

"I did. I will hold to that."

"Okay." He took a deep breath, and his voice became a shaky whisper. "Velma's mother was killed by a Russian doctor."

"What?" Horror washing over Duran.

"Velma told me her mother's name. Annalise Miley. Everything else is public record. She died giving birth at Coney Island Hospital. She was having trouble delivering and had a bad reaction to her epidural. Her death was recorded as accidental."

"But you're like me. You could tell it wasn't."

Brett nodded. "I had to call the hospital nine times. I knew no one would be allowed to tell me who gave the epidural, if anyone there even knew, but finally I was able to get a hospital staff directory from 1983. One of the names might sound familiar to you: Alexei Novikov. He was an anesthesiologist. You showed me a picture of his house last time you were here."

Duran's stomach roiled. If Brett's theory was right, Velma might be more than just missing. "Brett, I'm going to keep my promise to you. I won't repeat a word of this, but Velma is already a person of interest in that homicide case. Do you realize that what you just told me could make her a suspect?"

"That's why I made you promise."

"Do you think she is capable of murder?"

He took another swig, squinting and pursing his lips as he swallowed it. His answer shocked Duran. "I don't know."

"This is crazy. Novikov and the man who broke into his house, Boris Ivanov, shot each other. But here's the thing, there was a second shooter. Ivanov shot Novikov in the stomach, which didn't kill him. He was able to draw his gun and shoot Ivanov in the back of the head as he was running away. Ivanov was killed instantly, but after that there's a mystery. Novikov was shot a second time, in the head, with Ivanov's gun. Someone else had to have been in the house, and picked up Ivanov's gun after he was already dead. Whoever that was, is the one who killed Novikov."

"Do *you* think it was Velma?"

"No. She'd have to be an idiot to bring a car that noticeable to a crime scene, and why would she bring her own car at all, unless she was planning on leaving in it?"

"It doesn't make sense."

"No, it doesn't, but that doesn't mean it didn't happen. Still, there wasn't any evidence she was even inside the house at all, and no one knows what time her car showed up there. It could have been after they were already dead. The only reason she not a suspect is lack of evidence. They found no way of linking her car, or her, to the victims. You and I have, but we're stuck with questions. I mean, is she capable of killing? Was she Novikov's second shooter? Either way, why was her car left in front of the house of a man who might have killed her mother on the night of his murder?"

"I wish I could ask her."

"That's another question we're stuck with. She now has two

links to a homicide. The car and a motive. What the fuck do we do if we find her?"

"I think we should stop looking."

"I'm probably going to end up agreeing with you, but I'm not convinced yet. Do you have a key to her apartment?"

"Yes."

"Good. Call a cab, we're going."

"Why? Didn't you already search it?"

"We made sure it wasn't a crime scene, and we looked for any signs she'd run away. A note, missing clothes, that kind of thing. But that was before I knew what we know now." Duran felt himself beaming and his excitement rising. "I want to look for something different. Something that might be connected to dead Russians or CIA experimentation."

"Like what?"

"I have no fucking clue. But I'll know it when I see it."

Twenty-Nine

Wednesday, April 16 2008

Velma approached Leo Volkov's front door just before nine a.m. As always, he was there to open it the moment she approached. She was not happy. She had only slept, off and on, for a total of four hours since leaving his house the night before.

"You look tired," he said when she entered. "I don't blame you. Did you sleep?"

"A little. Not well enough for it to count," she grumbled.

"I scared you, and for that I am sorry, but you will understand why." He led her to the basement.

"I think I have an inkling."

"You are a smart girl. I'm sure you do. Still, there is much you do not know. When we first met, I hoped you would never be in this position."

"Well, fuck. Isn't that just what every woman wants to hear first thing in the morning?" She sat in her usual chair and crossed her arms.

"You are upset. You should be. And you are tired. May I make you some coffee, Velma?"

"No, thank you. I've actually been awake for a few hours. It feels more like happy hour than coffee hour."

"I understand. I will get you a drink then."

"Thank you."

He fetched the bottle of whisky and a rocks glass. He placed them in front of her and returned to his chair. "Make sure you are comfortable. I promise you that you are not ready for what you are about to hear."

She poured herself an inch and a half of whisky. "I always thought it was just me. It's not just me, is it? Or at least it wasn't."

"No." He poured a drink of his own. "As I have told you, like yourself, your father enjoyed more than his share of liquor and cigarettes. Now you know why. There are many things that can calm the limbic system, that distract a person from anger or cloud the mind, and these are the two most available. Like you, he did not always have control over this power. Certainly not in the beginning."

She focused on his words. Her feelings of frustration disappeared and turned to excitement. She was about to hear more than she ever thought he would share with her.

"Your father's real name was Agent Gabriel Majors. In the early 1980s, before you were born, before he even met Annalise, your government's Central Intelligence Agency oversaw an experiment being conducted by the Defense Advanced Research Projects Agency, which you may know as DARPA. The experiment was the last phase of a project that had been in the works, so far as we could confirm, for approximately three to five years prior to your father's involvement. He was a key player in this experiment, but he was not on the research team. He was not a scientist—he was their subject.

"The ultimate purpose of the project was to improve and protect the United States Military, from the inside out. The intention of DARPA's research team was to create a synthetic gene that would alter a soldier's DNA in such a way certain activity in his limbic system was linked to his overall mental acuity and his physical strength. In simpler terms, when the soldier felt threatened enough, the activity in one part of his brain would enhance the function of his overall brain, including his brain's control over his body."

She was still. She'd forgotten about her whisky, intoxicated by what she was hearing. "That's actually kind of a brilliant idea."

"It would have been a brilliant idea if it didn't seem so impossible. Imagine the fight or flight reactions of a soldier in battle. Imagine then, that he is able to remain lucid. His grasp of logic, his ability to plan, his ability to assess and respond to danger, are no longer overshadowed by impulse. Beyond this, these abilities are enhanced, as well as his physical strength and his control over his actions. Imagine the wartime advantages of having an entire military force in possession of such abilities when their opposition is not. Imagine that their opposition knows nothing of their abilities and continues to expose them to the very dangers that are the triggers for their brains to become their greatest weapons."

Velma shuddered with a rush of excitement. She moved forward in her chair, thirsty to hear more.

"Had this project been a success, it might have meant that your country's involvement would bring a swift end to any war. Needless to say, it was not a success. Things went terribly wrong, and the results could have meant widespread devastation for military personnel and civilians alike. When the CIA learned of your father's test results, of what had happened to him, they ordered all versions of the experimental gene be destroyed. All written records of the project and all test results were also destroyed. Mention of the project in conjunction with any of the scientists involved was wiped away. The greatest care was taken in making sure it was as though this project had never existed. Your father, however, was living evidence that it had."

Velma picked up her forgotten whisky glass. Her excitement remained, but was now infused with dread.

"When, in 1981, it was decided this project required a human subject, your father was selected by his agency for many reasons. At age thirty-two, he was younger than many of his fellow agents, so closer in age to the average enlisted man in the armed forces. He was even-tempered and known for this by his superiors. He had no physical or mental infirmities. He had no genetic anomalies, and, at the time, he had no personal attachments.

"His agency explained only the bare basics of the project to him, much less even than I have explained to you. He thought the project's goal to be noble, and was fascinated by the science behind it. After being briefed, he agreed to participate. He was required to agree to an uncommonly high level of confidentiality. Things of this nature were referred to as black projects. Details of such projects are not only hidden, the very existence of the project is hidden. The scientists at DARPA who injected him told your father nothing of their research. The doctors at the CIA who conducted his testing kept him informed of what they would be doing to him, but told him very little else.

"They tested him for baseline physical strength and baseline limbic reactions to various emotions. They did this using an electroencephalograph, a brain-mapping machine. With sensors on various parts of his body, especially his head, he was connected to this machine and shown slides of various images meant to provoke different emotions. He was shown things that would evoke joy, sympathy, fear, sexual arousal, comfort, and of course, anger. Essentially, they created a stage zero picture of his brain." Volkov paused to take a breath.

She remained motionless, numb with fascination.

"Their hope was to compare this baseline brain map to future brain maps made after he had been injected with different variations of the gene. Had early testing not shown what it had, the plan was to advance him to strength tests, and eventually to simulations of situations evoking a fight or flight reaction. They never got beyond the second electroencephalogram. The results, the first brain map made after his first injection, never saw the light of day. It was the very first thing to be destroyed.

"During that second test, just after your father was shown an image that made him angry, he heard the doctor curse from behind his machine. The doctor said he had spilled his coffee. After that, another image evoked more intense anger. The lens of the projector broke, and the doctor demanded they stop the test. According to your father, the doctor was panicked, but told him everything was fine and to go home and get some rest. He would be contacted when they needed to see him again. Your father, of course, knew that the projector lens had broken. He heard it shatter, and he saw the picture on the screen split into pieces. As he was escorted out of the laboratory, he also saw the shards of the doctor's coffee mug on the floor.

"He did not connect these things, at first. He went home that night and ruminated on what had happened. He was an intelligent, observant man. It did not take him long to figure things out—the timing of the spilled coffee and the broken lens. He was hesitant to believe it. He wanted to test the theory for himself, make sure the synthetic gene was not just making him crazy. He got out a wine glass and sat in front of it, trying to summon the anger he'd felt in the laboratory."

Velma shifted in her seat. "What happened?"

"Nothing. He told himself he might have been wrong, that the notion was farfetched. The next morning, he sat in front of the wine glass and tried again. He recalled the image he had seen the day before that most provoked him. Still, nothing. Then he thought about what the experiment had done to him, and that his life could never be normal. He thought about other things the CIA had done, other lives destroyed years before. A crack appeared in the wine glass."

"Did he ever learn to control it? Could he do it at will?"

"It took him many years, but yes. He spent hours almost every day working to harness his power. Eventually, I believe he began to see it as more of a gift and less of a curse, but it took a very, very long time."

"What happened after he broke the wine glass?"

"He got out a new one and filled it. Soon after that, he figured out one of the same things you did, that drinking would help keep him from breaking anything involuntarily. The CIA did not contact Agent Majors for several days. When someone did contact him, he was not summoned back to the laboratory, but instead to a CIA office for debriefing. Something you must understand about government secrecy is that no one knows everything. There are people who know a little bit about many things, but not the fine details of any one of them. There are people who know all there is to know about one piece of a puzzle, but are never told where their piece fits. It is designed this way. The person who knows where the piece fits will never know everything the piece contains. The doctor who performed the tests on your father, who ran the electroencephalograph, had no hand in developing the synthetic gene his subject was injected with. It is possible that this doctor was not even cleared to know the end goal of the project. People are told only what they *need* to know.

"This is how clearances work. There are compartments within compartments within compartments. But no one, *no one*, gets to know everything. It would be impossible, and dangerous. The scientists who did develop the gene were never told what their creation had done. They didn't need to know, but beyond that, imagine what could have become if they had been told. Just think of what a person with that knowledge could do to the world. Imagine if someone knew they had created something that would allow a human being to break the laws of physics, as we know them. Imagine they knew how to recreate it, that they could research it further, and where that path could lead. No, those scientists could never know the effects of their creation on a man. Instead, they were told only that it had failed."

"What about my dad?" Velma asked. "Did he ever get to know all this?"

Volkov sipped his whisky and leaned back in his chair. "Your father was among those who knew of the broader picture. He knew nothing of the details of the work of the geneticists and the chemists. He also never saw his brain map. He did know, albeit in an even more general sense than you now do, what was *supposed* to happen to him, and of course, he knew what actually happened to him.

"When he went in for his debriefing, he was told the project was being cancelled and his participation would no longer be required. It was then they told him he would be put on paid leave until he was told otherwise. He was relieved, for a moment, then suspicious. There was much he didn't know and still wouldn't be told. He was also uncertain who, if anyone, among his colleagues knew about the results of his testing. The only other people in the laboratory had been the doctor and the projectionist. Would their account of what happened be believed? Your father found out later, though not then, there was a two-way mirror in the laboratory, and behind it, were three CIA agents watching and recording the test. There were witnesses and recorded evidence to support the doctor's far-fetched report. Those agents were immediately debriefed and given other assignments. So how did your father find out they were there? How did he find out that factions of the CIA knew without any doubt about his new power? One of those three agents was working for us." Volkov sipped his whisky and paused so she had a moment to process what she was hearing.

"Was it you?" she asked.

"No," he said as he brought his glass to his lips and tilted his head back to swallow his remaining whisky. He put down his glass. "It was not me, but it was a man who reported to me. I mentioned him to you before. He was an American. He was not GRU, he was CIA. He needed money, and we needed secrets, so an arrangement was made.

"It is here there is a change to the story you know. The man was never caught. As far as I know, he retired years later and collected his pension. This man himself is not important. He was simply a peddler of information. What is important is that his information allowed me to save your father's life.

"After your father was put on leave, he was left alone for over a year. His agency had gotten him out of the picture and moved on. However, something weighed heavily on the minds of the CIA members who had overseen the project: as long as Gabriel Majors remained alive, there would be proof of one the most terrible, frightening, and inexplicable mistakes ever made by government scientists.

"For the most part, the rest of the story you already know. It is a relief to me you now know the truth about why your father was in danger, that you know he was not only an honorable man, but an innocent man. However, we would be fools to think there isn't someone, or several someones, in the CIA who remember the name Gabriel Majors. I thought, though, when your father passed away, that the last evidence of this mess died with him."

"But it didn't. Whatever they did to him, whatever artificial genetic mutation he had, he passed to me. So as long as I'm alive, there's still evidence."

"You are a threat to the United States government, Velma. Which means they are a threat to you."

Her thoughts ran wild but she didn't take her eyes off him. His face was as serious as she had ever seen it. "I'm sure what I'm about to say is going to make you angry, but assuming nothing's going to break, I'm going to go ahead and say it. Knowing my existence is a threat to the US government makes me feel really fucking cool."

"Velma." He brought his left hand to his face and rubbed his eyes with his thumb and index finger. She wasn't sure if he was trying to suppress anger or laughter. "If I did not know you had predominantly good sense, this would make me angry." He released his smile and then forced his facial muscles to return themselves to their previous position.

"I'm guessing… I'm in some kind of danger?"

"Yes. You've been seen, Velma. Whether or not the witnesses knew what they were seeing, you used your power in public, and in a way that can be traced to you. Right now, we still have a small amount of time to get some things in order before anyone who would want to hurt you has time to make plans of their own, but you must run."

"Run?" She hadn't expected to hear any of what he told her today, but least of all this. *Run?*

"Run. You understand, I gather, that what puts you in danger is that you are your father's daughter. Now, there is nothing on paper, nothing on your birth certificate, nothing on your adoption papers, nothing documented anywhere, that links you to Agent Gabriel Majors. Two of the three other GRU agents who passed me information on you did not even know why. Only five people in the entire world know ever knew the truth about your paternity. Two of them are not among the living—your biological mother and father. One of them is in Russia, and very good at keeping secrets. The other two are sitting in this room.

"But even though there is no documentation, and your father is no longer alive, there is still your…ability, and it is unique to you. Information travels. Now that you've been witnessed, *this* information will travel. Over time, it will travel to the people who mean you harm.

You believe your witnesses to be ignorant, so this may seem unlikely, but the probability of an unlikely thing happening increases on a longer timeline. You are young, so the timeline of the rest of your life is a long one. If you stay here, you will either shorten it, or spend the rest of it wondering if every person you meet is the spy sent to kill you. You now have the same choice your father had."

"Stay and run forever, or run to a place I can stay."

"Yes, and a decision must be made now about what place that will be."

She forced herself not to think about everything she'd be leaving behind. Those were thoughts for another time, and she knew he was right.

"Mexico," she said after a brief silence. "Somewhere in Mexico. It's pretty there, and I like the food."

"Better yet, you speak the language."

"I do work in a restaurant." She hoped Volkov would laugh. He didn't.

"Very well then. I will make travel arrangements for you, but when you arrive at your destination, you will be on your own to find lodging and employment if you wish to work. You have more than enough money for now, but your money will not last forever. I will arrange to get you identification and a passport under a new name. I only need for you to do three things."

"What are they?"

"First, meet me at Mount Vernon East station tomorrow morning at this time with your money. I will convert it into foreign currencies and other forms so you may travel without suspicion."

"What's the second thing?"

"Second, be ready to go. I do not mean pack your things. You will be packing nothing. I mean, *be ready*. You are leaving this country in less than a week, and you are never coming back."

"What's the third thing?"

"It will not be Velma Bloom who is traveling abroad. Velma Bloom is going to disappear without a trace and without a trail. The woman I will safely transport to her new home abroad, for whom I will procure a passport and identification, she must have a name. Since she can never get her old name back, I hope for her to be happy with her new one. I want you to choose what that name will be."

A crushing sensation seized Velma's chest as she thought of

Brett standing at the door of her empty apartment. She stopped her train of thought before it went any further. Her choice was clear. "I'll be ready, and I know the name."

Thirty

Monday, April 21, 2008

Cloaked by hordes of morning rush-hour commuters, Velma made her way to Volkov's. It was time to learn the logistics of the beginning of her life on the run. He gave her a simpler route to Mount Vernon East Station for this visit, and this time, he said, he would be there to pick her up.

"There is my lovely niece," he said as she as she got off her train. "Come, walk with me to the car."

When they arrived at his grand suburban home, he pulled the car into the garage and they entered the house from the side door. She hadn't seen this entrance before. It was hidden and made for a shorter walk to his basement sanctuary.

"Thank you for coming. I know this is early for you."

"Did I have a choice?" She smirked.

"You always have a choice, but for practical purposes, today—no, you did not."

"Now that I'm here, do I have the choice to have some coffee?"

"I already have it made. I will go upstairs and fetch it. Milk or sugar today?"

"No thank you." She forced the obvious frustration out of her voice. "Black is fine. As usual, I will be drinking it for effect."

"I think it would be wise if you did not stay too long today," he said after he returned with the coffee and sat. "I have information for you regarding your passage abroad as well as your new identity. Everything has been planned so no trail will be left. I am sorry to say this will be our last meeting prior to my escorting you to an airport to ensure your safety until you board. I will miss you, Velma."

"I'll miss you, too, Leo. It's nice having an uncle."

He handed her a thick manila envelope. "Driver's license, passport, plane tickets, itinerary, travel instructions. Velma Bloom no longer exists. You will also find your traveler's checks, pre-paid Visa cards, pesos, francs, pounds, and American dollars. You will also find some bank account information. What remains of your money has been deposited into an overseas account in your new name. You will be able to withdraw cash, should you need to, in the form of whatever the local currency happens to be. Now, take out the papers, please."

"There's so much." She began to look over her flight schedule.

"It is not as complicated as it seems. Tomorrow night, a woman no one has ever seen before will board a plane at JFK International Airport. Seven and a half hours later, she will arrive at Charles De Gaulle Airport in Paris, France. She will have a two-hour layover and will then board another plane. This one will take her to Heathrow International Airport in London, not far from where, I imagine, she grew up." He winked at her, and she nodded to indicate she understood. "She will spend one night in London. The hotel information can be found with the plane tickets. The following day, she will return to Heathrow, this time to depart from London. She will have a short layover in Munich before one last plane takes her to her final destination."

"Cancun?" Velma saw the name of the airport on her itinerary.

"Perhaps not her very final destination, but that will be the last airport at which she will arrive. Look at the next page."

She flipped to the next page in her stack of papers. This one was handwritten. There were no tickets purchased and no times designated for this part of the journey. "I need to take a boat?"

"It is possible to fly, but this is more anonymous. After the number of planes the woman of whom we are speaking will have taken, this part of the trip will be quite simple. After her arrival in Cancun, she will go outside the airport and get into a taxi. She speaks Spanish, so she will not be tricked or overcharged by unethical drivers who prey on tourists. Her taxi will take her to Turtle Beach, Playa Tortugas. From there, she will purchase a ticket for a ferry. That ferry will spirit her across seven miles of the Caribbean and deliver her to her new island home."

"Isla Mujeres?"

"Isla Mujeres. It's about five miles long and a half a mile wide. Its southern tip features a cliff formation that is marked as being the eastern most point in Mexico. It has residential neighborhoods, though not particularly upscale ones, where she can live comfortably. It also has downtown areas full of dining establishments where, she will discover, bilingual staff is always in demand." He winked again.

"Oh, Leo! It's…perfect."

"She fancies Latin men, I hope?" He cocked a brow at her.

"Not particularly, but she'll be fine preying on tourists."

"I have no doubt, but she must be mindful of what she says and how she speaks around those tourists. If she is not, on her own head it will be. Does she understand this agenda?"

"She does. I do." She returned her papers to the manila envelope.

"Excellent. Now, you have thirty-six hours left to be Velma Bloom. I advise you to spend them cautiously. When you return here tomorrow night, you will do so for the first and only time in your own vehicle. As I have said, I will escort you to the airport. You will fly east first, and when you land, it will be the day after tomorrow."

"I'm just going to leave Smiley here?"

"You are."

"Won't that leave a trail?"

"By the time you board your first plane, there will be a yellow Dodge Challenger at the bottom of the Hudson River."

She dropped the envelope onto her lap. "Whoa. So we're faking my death?"

"We are hiding your car."

"We have to hide it at the bottom of the Hudson River? I didn't realize secret agents had such a flair for the dramatic."

"We have to hide it where it is not likely to be found. In the event that it is found, we do need to hide it in a place that indicates you are dead."

"So people don't look for me."

"So they won't look for you as long, but people *will* look for you, Velma. The police, your loved ones. We need to minimize their search efforts. To do this, we must make them think you ran away of your own free will. For this to be believed, your car must disappear with you. Should the car be found, you are safer having them search for you dead than alive."

She began to cry. She hated this part of the plan. She imagined the heartache her parents would be going through, that Brett would be going through, but she knew that without hiding the car, they would search for her with fervor, assuming she was alive and in danger, or kidnapped and dead. She had to go through with this. The alternative was either being killed, or, as Leo said, spending the rest of her life wondering if everyone she ever met had been sent to kill her.

"You know, Leo, the day after tomorrow is my birthday."

"So it is. Happy birthday, Velma. If you don't want it to be your last, make sure you learn your new one."

Thirty-One

Monday, April 21, 2008

When Velma returned home from Volkov's, she stashed the folder with her money and travel itinerary in a tote bag. She looked around her apartment, wondering if she had forgotten anything. As she glanced over her belongings, she realized she had. For a moment, she had forgotten that she needed to forget everything, but she realized she'd forgotten one thing she shouldn't have. It was almost eleven a.m., and it was Monday. She was supposed to be downstairs opening the pub.

"Fuck this," she said to Carrot. "I have to flee the country because the goddamn government couldn't clean up its own mess before I was conceived, *and* I have to work a double shift?"

He meowed.

"I know. It's the last double shift I'll ever have to work. At least in the United States." She changed into her work clothes. She had to play the part of the waitress for one more day.

It was a long day. She forced herself through it, more conscious than ever of not doing anything differently than she would any other shift. On Monday nights, in her boss' absence, it was her job to be the last person to leave and lock the front door of the pub.

Just after midnight, she walked outside through the front door of Lonnie's Pub for the last time. She wished Brett were there to pick her up. They had spent most of the weekend together and done nothing out of the ordinary. All that had been different from a typical weekend was that when they parted on Sunday night, she kissed him knowing it meant goodbye. She was tempted to call him, but she knew she couldn't. For the next twenty-one hours, she had to continue to do nothing out of the ordinary. On an ordinary Monday night, she wouldn't call him for company after working a thirteen-hour shift.

After locking the building's outer door behind her, she started to turn left to walk around the corner to the back of the building. It made her sad to think she would be ascending the rickety metal steps to her back door for the last time and spending her last night with Carrot. She tempered her sadness by fantasizing about dangerous ways she could come back and see her loved ones again and knowing her father had done the same.

The street was quiet. A lone car approached as she tucked her keys into her jacket pocket. She turned her head. In front of the oncoming headlights, she saw the shadow of a man being cast onto the sidewalk. The shadow moved in her direction. She paused before turning, and the shadow's pace quickened.

The car rolled by and the shadow disappeared. Her eyes adjusted to the darkness that the headlights of the passing vehicle had left behind. The shadow was gone, but its owner remained, and he was running.

Panic stung her. She turned right instead of left and bolted. From behind her, she could hear the man's feet landing, closing the gap between them. She ran faster, looking back at her pursuer. He was encumbered with a heavy jacket and the bulges of whatever he was hiding beneath it, but his legs were long and his strides covered twice the length of sidewalk that hers did. She wouldn't be able to maintain her pace, and even if she could, she didn't have enough of a head start to outrun him for long.

Every muscle cried out for her to slow down. If this was a race, she was going to lose. She couldn't run any faster. She had to change this from a race into a game she could win. The man in the heavy jacket had speed and stamina on his side, but she had the advantage of knowing her own neighborhood. She thought of a place that would surround her with something she could turn into a weapon. Windows.

She forced herself to keep running. After four blocks, she made a swift turn down an alley. The man was close behind, but the alley was lined with buildings whose crumbling, second floor apartments had long been unoccupied. She was halfway down the alley when the man in the heavy jacket turned after her.

He sped up even more, but she timed her pace so he would be where she needed him to be when she reached the other side. The faster he ran, the more she could use it against him. Seconds before the man reached the halfway point, two of the second-floor windows shattered, one on each side of the alley. Broken glass flew outward into the street from all directions. The man in the heavy jacket was going too fast to stop before one of his feet landed in a pile of shards. He slipped and started to fall face first. He put his other foot down and tried to catch his balance, only to fall backward as though he had run over a cluster of marbles.

She watched him land and chose a direction to run before he could lift his head enough to see where she'd gone. She couldn't stop yet, but her heart was pounding from panic and exertion. She couldn't keep running forever. Eventually, the man would get up, and he would reach the end of the alley. He would run either right or left. Even if she could maintain her speed, she would only cut his chances of catching her in half. She had to do better than that. She had to hide.

Velma ran left in the direction of a tiny corner bar. She had never been inside it, but she remembered seeing it from the window of a cab at night. It would be open. When she reached the door, she looked behind her as she rushed inside. She didn't see the man in the heavy jacket. Either he hadn't made it out of the alley, or he had run in the other direction. With the bar door shut behind her, a great rush of relief washed over her until she remembered how many reasons there were for someone to chase her.

She tried her best to catch her breath. She needed to blend in until she could figure out what to do. She looked at what she was wearing. No one would believe she was out for a jog after midnight wearing a leather jacket, jeans, and an apron. Thank god, the bar was more crowded than she thought it would be. She was able to walk to the back of the bar and reach the bathroom without attracting attention. She ducked inside a stall and waited for her stomach to settle and her breathing to steady. She collected herself as quickly as she could before finding an empty seat at the bar.

Two men stood behind the bar. It was easy to discern which was the bartender and which was the bouncer. One of them appeared to be working while the other stood quietly looking around, and the one working was a head shorter than the quiet one.

"What can I get you?" The short man leaned over the bar and smiled at her. The tall man was staring in the direction of a group of young women.

"Sailor Jerry on the rocks, please."

"Six-fifty." He poured her drink and handed it to her. She was pleased with the portion size and handed him a ten-dollar bill.

"Keep it," she said. Under different circumstances she would have given a generous bartender more, but tonight she wanted to attract as little notice as possible. "And may I have a glass of water please?"

She was parched from her unexpected dash. As the bartender filled her request and busied himself with his other customers, Velma looked at the group of women who had the attention of the bouncer. They looked like local college students, and they were probably underage. This was a good sign. It meant she was somewhere that didn't get a lot of attention and probably didn't have cameras. She downed her water, sipped her rum, and let herself relax just enough to think through her next move.

The man in the heavy jacket wasn't likely to come after her again tonight. He would be bleeding from his fall in the pile of glass. If the man meant her harm, he wouldn't want to be followed by a trail of his own DNA.

She wondered if the man in the heavy jacket was just hoping to steal her tips. Thieves often targeted people, especially women, coming out of closed restaurants. A server or bartender just finishing a shift was guaranteed to be carrying a lot of cash. Could the man simply have been a very enthusiastic mugger? She didn't think so. It had been one week since the attempted robbery at Lonnie's Pub. Had the gunman sent someone after her for revenge? Maybe.

Though she knew what was going on, she was searching for any possible explanation other than the one she most feared. She had used her power in public. As Volkov told her, her power made her a threat to the government, which made the government a threat to her.

Somehow, the story of the bursting Tabasco bottle in the robber's face traveled. Her name had been kept out of the papers, as she requested, but the police would still know about it. They would have documented the incident. Her story could have been whispered from one law enforcement office to another until someone connected her to her father.

She forced herself not to dwell on her uncertainties. She was mere hours away from fleeing the country and starting a safer life as someone else. The safest thing she could do was to go forward with her plans. To do that, she needed her passport, her plane tickets, and her money. All of those things were in her apartment. If she wanted to get to Mexico, to permanent safety, she had no choice but to go home and hope no one was waiting there for her. She wished she could call someone for help, but who would she call? She couldn't call the police. Leo Volkov was the one person who could help her, but she had no way of reaching him.

She wanted to call Brett. He could pick her up and take her to his apartment to keep her safe. But what would she tell him? The truth? That would only put him in danger too. An image popped into her head of him being tortured for information on her whereabouts, all because he had been seen spiriting her away from a dive bar in his El Dorado. He might already be in danger just by knowing her. If he got any more mixed up in this, he would have nowhere to flee. She couldn't take him to Mexico with her. He had no fake passport, no documented pseudonym. Not only could Brett be tracked, his tracks would lead straight to her.

She listened to the drunken laughter from the bevy of college girls. She closed her eyes and used the sound of their voices to keep herself centered and remember where she was. The bouncer was still looking in the girls' direction, but Velma saw him lift his head and look over them. She watched as he took a step sideways toward the bartender. The bartender had his back to the crowd as he wiped the dust off the seldom-used top-shelf bottles. The bouncer nudged him, wearing a look of concerned sternness.

"Remember those cops who were here for happy hour? One of them is still here." The bouncer nodded in the direction of the back wall of the bar. The bartender looked over his shoulder.

"Oh, that one. I'm not worried about him."

Velma turned her head. A man wearing a white shirt and a loosened tie sat alone at a small table. He reclined against the wall and held a book with his left hand. With his right, he alternated between turning pages and picking up his drink. She froze and tried not to gasp.

"Fuck," she said under her breath. Of all the bars in Yonkers, she had chosen to hide in the one inhabited by the only Yonkers police officer who would be sure to recognize her, Jackson Duran.

She looked down and sipped her drink, hoping he wouldn't look up from his book and recognize her hair. She was grateful her signature curls had gone limp from running. The bartender was getting ready to say something to the bouncer. She called him over for another drink. Whatever he was about to say, she wanted to hear. She also wanted another drink.

"He's one of the good ones," the bartender continued in a low voice. "How long has he been here now, anyway?"

"Seven hours. Quiet motherfucker. His buddies left after happy hour and he's been parked there ever since."

Velma tuned out the sounds of the crowd around her and strained to hear the conversation behind the bar.

"Let him be. Do you recognize him? He's not wearing his uniform, but that's the guy who was here last month."

"When someone called the cops who saw you selling weed?"

"Yeah. That's the guy they sent. I tried to bribe him. I handed him five hundred bucks. He wouldn't take it, but he let me go. He said he could tell I'm not a real criminal and it would be against his personal code to arrest me just for being stupid."

"Selling weed in your bar is fucking stupid."

"Yeah, except I paid off a couple of the other guys to look away."

"This guy didn't take your money, he just let you go? I find that hard to believe."

"This guy's not like any cop I've ever met. He said he knew I wasn't hurting anybody and even told me what the punishments were for selling different quantities. Then he fuckin' winks and says to me, 'If you're going to break the law, at least have a little class about it.' And then, 'They're not mutually exclusive' or some shit like that."

Velma fought to contain a smile. It sounded like something she would say if she were a cop. She glanced back at Duran. He was reading *The Adventures of Sherlock Holmes* and drinking what appeared to be whisky and club soda. She released her smile when she thought about what a perfect drink choice this was. Then something else occurred to her. Duran had come into the bar with a group of other cops. He was wearing a shirt and tie, and he was reading a book starring one of literature's most famous detectives. *He must have gotten promoted. Good for him.*

What a great detective she would make. Here she was, hiding after being chased by a man she suspected was a government agent, and still managing to apply logic to her surroundings. The world would have to survive without Detective Bloom; she didn't plan on sticking around. Even if circumstances were different, she didn't know if she could tolerate the time she'd need to spend as a uniformed police officer. She had too much of an aversion to authority. *But I would be an amazing vigilante.*

She decided to leave. She couldn't let Duran see her, especially if he was now a detective. He would have no reason to think she was in this bar tonight was to hide. He would probably think she was there for the same reason he was, to have a drink alone. But that was the problem. She was alone. If all went according to plan, she would continue to be alone until Volkov took her to the airport. This would mean that, of the people who could identify her, Jackson Duran would be the last to see her alive before she disappeared. She couldn't do that to the man who thought of James Joyce before Scooby Doo.

She scanned the group of college girls. She could use them as cover. There were five. When they left, they would have to call two cabs. She could slip into the back seat of one of them, camouflaging herself. Around one-thirty a.m., one of them pulled out her phone and did as Velma predicated. When their cabs arrived, she followed the girls outside. She was planning to ask if it was okay for her to ride with them, but realized they were too drunk to even notice she wasn't a fellow student. One of the girls gave the driver a Bronxville address.

She opened her mouth to give her own, but caught herself. She couldn't go directly home. As intoxicated as her fellow passengers were, they would still be witnesses that a cab had been to her address tonight. The driver would not only be a witness, but would have record of the fare. She didn't forget her peril, but took a moment to reflect on how much she was thinking like a secret agent.

She was tempted to ride with the girls back to their campus. She could follow them into a dorm and find a common area where she could spend the rest of the night. She might even be able to sleep. When the sun came up, she could take a series of buses home. A few safe hours of sleep then traveling home by daylight seemed like a wonderful option, but it wasn't. While it wasn't safe for her to go home, it was even less safe to leave her new passport, her flight itinerary, and her offshore bank account information unattended in her apartment.

Velma asked the driver to bring her to an address two blocks beyond her back door. As they rode by the front of Lonnie's and then passed the rear parking lot, she used the illumination from the headlights to look for broken glass, trails of blood, or lurking shadows. She didn't see any of them. This didn't mean no one was waiting inside for her, or that no one would be coming after her between now and her departure, but the only other options she had all meant staying apart from the contents of her tote bag, her means of escape.

Velma got out of the cab and waited until it was out of sight before walking the two blocks home. She climbed the metal steps to her back door, having long forgotten it was her final ascent. She went inside and took a moment to look and listen before locking the door behind her. No one was waiting for her except Carrot, who was curled up in the empty bottom shelf of her bookcase, his fluffy tail spilling out onto the floor.

She collapsed onto her bed. She hadn't thought she'd be able to sleep tonight, but running, rum, and relief changed her mind. She wondered if, in the next nineteen hours, anyone would come after her. After what had happened in the last two hours, that didn't feel so terrifying. When she broke the windows in the alley, something happened that had only happened once before, with a bottle of Tabasco sauce. The glass flew outward. When she had thrown the bottle, she thought the glass had flown into the robber's eyes because the bottle was moving. Thinking back, it was more than that. The pieces of glass that had once comprised that bottle had some direction and propulsion of their own.

When she smashed the windows in the alley, some part of her felt she wasn't just breaking the glass, she was pulling it out into the street in the direction of the threat. Danger seemed to enhance her control and her capacity for destruction. With that in mind, the idea of someone breaking into her apartment wasn't such a scary thought. She had windows, so she had weapons. This meant that, in some small way, the experiment on her father had been successful. It was a scary thought. Velma recalled the times she had used her ability to protect herself or someone else. She once saved a woman from being drugged and raped. She could protect herself for another nineteen hours.

She couldn't figure out why, but thinking about Jackson Duran gave her a sense of comfort. She wished she had a way to telling him, and only him, she was okay. She trusted him more than she thought she should, but he was the only Yonkers police officer she had ever met, so her trust didn't extend to anyone else who might be hunting for her, even if they were working with him. In a couple of days, he and his colleagues were going to have a mystery on their hands, and she had no intention of making their jobs any easier. If she could help it, she wasn't going to let anyone follow her, even with good intentions. If she ever returned to New York, it would be because she'd chosen to, not because she'd gotten caught.

She wanted to come back someday. Maybe she could give her vigilante idea a try. If she did, she would want a friend who worked inside the system. Jackson Duran was someone she wanted in her corner.

Velma heard the scuffling of Carrot's feet as he emerged from the bottom shelf of her bookcase. He jumped into bed and curled up next to her, purring. As she drifted off to sleep, her eyes stayed on the empty bookshelf where the cat had been.

Thirty-Two

Jackson and Brett exited a cab in the parking lot of Lonnie's Pub.

"It looks so empty back here without her car." Brett pointed to the spot that had been the home of Velma's Challenger.

"Give me your key. Let's see what we find up there before you get sentimental." Duran took the key from Brett and they ascended the rickety metal steps that led to the back door. The hinges made a horrible creaking sound when they opened it.

The apartment had been vacant for two weeks. The air was stale. He entered and looked around without touching anything.

Brett lurked in the doorway. "I've never seen this place without her in it." His face looked lost, and he stood as though an invisible barrier kept him from walking inside.

Duran grabbed his arm. "Hey, Brett. Come on, buddy. You knew her better than anybody. I need you." He tugged Brett's arm, and he stepped inside the apartment.

"I feel like we shouldn't be here." Brett looked at the bed. The sheets were pulled off from when the Yonkers Police searched for evidence two weeks before.

"We probably shouldn't be, but that's why we are." Duran scanned the room.

"Could we get in trouble for being in here?"

"No. We determined it's not a crime scene. Lonnie hasn't changed the locks, and you have a key."

"Then why do you say we shouldn't be here?"

"Because we know some bizarre shit we're not supposed to, and we might find something that would get us in trouble. In fact, that's what I'm hoping we find."

"What should I look for?"

"You know this place well. That's why I need you. Look for anything you've never seen before, or anything that might be in the wrong place... and anything that makes you think of secret agents, human experiments, or dead Russians."

Duran went to the kitchen, and Brett went to the closet. Duran felt a pang of guilt for bringing him here and stirring up his memories.

It didn't take long for the two of them to give up. It was a small apartment, and she didn't own much. What she did own, Brett said, was all where it had always been, except for what the police had moved during the original search. Nothing was missing, nothing was there that hadn't been there before she disappeared, and nothing of hers suggested she had any connection to any of the things that made her disappearance suspicious.

"I'm sorry, Brett. It's got to be heartbreaking for you to be here. We just have so much information now that I really thought we'd find something to, you know, help tie it together. Like a Cold War relic or a cryptic message or something. Maybe I just hoped we would."

"Maybe if I sit here and wait, she'll come home." Brett sank into one of the thick couch cushions. "Do you think she's dead?"

"I don't know. She might be dead, or she might be hiding." He sat beside him and did his best not to sink. "We know she had a reason to hide. I just wish we knew what she was hiding from. Or who."

"If she is hiding, she wouldn't want to be found. If she's dead...I don't ever want to know for sure."

"So we're stuck. She doesn't want to be found alive, and we don't want her found dead. There's only one thing for us to do."

"Stop looking."

Duran nodded. "Stop looking." He took a deep breath and leaned back on the couch. This wasn't how he'd imagined concluding his first big case. He didn't know what to do next. He felt lost, disappointed, and exhausted. He despised the idea of giving up, and struggled to accept the fact that it might be the right thing to do. He turned to Brett. "I need a fucking mental break. I don't think she would want us to sulk like this. I think she would want us to drink her liquor. What does she have?"

They crouched by the liquor cabinet and one by one, removed the bottles to peruse her collection. He was impressed. She had four different whiskies, any of which would have pleased him, as well as a diverse selection of rums. Duran's eye caught a flash of green. "Is that...absinthe? She drank absinthe?"

Brett shrugged. "I only saw her drink it once, while she was reading."

"That's the best time to drink absinthe." He wandered over to her bookcase and scanned the spines of her books. They were in no particular order, and many of them appeared to have once been property of the Vassar College Library. "Does she have some sugar in the kitchen?"

"I think so."

"Why don't you mix us a couple glasses of that, and I'll grab a couple things to go with it." Duran mused over what he might read with absinthe, and wondered what she would choose.

Brett took the bottle into the kitchen and got out two dusty rocks glasses. "Doesn't this stuff make you hallucinate?"

"Only if you live on it for years and you're already a little nuts, which most great writers are." He chuckled but didn't look away from the bookshelf. "Just mix it with sugar and water. I promise you'll live."

Duran continued to scan the spines of the books and look for things written by authors known for their absinthe habits. The disorganization of her books frustrated him. They weren't alphabetized or sorted by genre. Starting with the top shelf, he looked the books one at a time from left to right, pulling some selections along the way, including her ragged paperback copy of *Ulysses*. It was next to three other books by James Joyce. She at least kept books by the same author together.

When Duran reached the bottom shelf, he saw it had only eight books on it. He glanced over them from left to right. Irving, Goethe, Orwell, Thoreau, Thoreau, Heller, Irving, Steinbeck. He grimaced. It annoyed him that she had broken from her one means of organization, keeping Henry David Thoreau's works together, but not John Irving's.

He took his chosen titles and placed them on the coffee table. Brett returned with two cloudy green drinks and handed one to Duran.

"Edgar Allen Poe?" He sat on the couch and stared at the books on the table.

Duran joined him. "Famous absinthe drinker. The green fairy inspired a lot of genius." He lifted his glass in tribute before taking a large sip from it.

Brett reached over to the table and picked up one of the books. "I think this is the book she was reading when I saw her drinking it." He showed her copy of *The Tell-Tale Heart*.

"Really? That's one of the first things I would pick to go with absinthe." Duran took another sip of his drink and sat up straight. His mental break had ended. "You know how a lot of people pair their wine with their food? Not many people pair their cocktails with their books." His head cleared. Suddenly, he was sober and alert. Brett had just given him a glimpse inside her head and what he saw looked much like his own. "I just got a crazy idea. I think my mother might have been right about something."

He reached for *Ulysses* and flipped through the pages. A plastic bag, folded flat and containing a piece of paper covered in writing, fell to his feet. He and Brett stared down at it.

"What do you think that is?" Brett winced as he swallowed each sip of absinthe.

"You've never seen it before?"

He shook his head.

Duran picked up the bag. "Drink up. If we don't like what find in here, we can tell ourselves we hallucinated it." They swallowed what remained in their glasses. He opened the bag and took out a letter written almost twenty-six years ago. He unfolded the paper and held onto one side while Brett held onto the other. They read the letter in silence and gaped.

Brett looked up. "Jackson, do you think this was written to…"

"Alexei Novikov."

"Then he was a friend of Velma's father."

"And Velma's father was in danger six months before she was born. Novikov helped him escape from… something. I wonder if he's still alive."

"He's not. Velma told he was dead. I don't know how she knew, though. It must have been Novikov who gave Velma the letter. Do you think he was helping her?"

"Yeah, I think he was, but something went wrong. Novikov might have been helping Velma the way he helped her father, and there were people who weren't supposed to know about it. Ivanov and whoever the other shooter was."

"Novikov killed her mother, but I don't think Velma shot him."

"I don't think she shot him, either. We don't even know if Velma knew Novikov killed her mother."

"Could the letter have been written to someone else?"

"I don't think so. Whoever R.D. is, he loved this woman. I bet she knew his secret. I think he told her more than he should have, and I think Novikov knew that. He killed Annalise to keep Velma's father safe."

"Then why would he help Velma all these years later?"

"Maybe to atone for what he did. Or maybe he had another agenda. We don't know what happened to Velma's father since this was written, and something tells me a Russian man wasn't helping an American agent during the Cold War out of the goodness of his heart."

"Then maybe Velma did want to hurt him."

"Maybe. Aside from her, the only person who could answer these questions was found dead in his basement three weeks ago. But this letter does confirm that her power puts her in danger, and it makes me wonder who the real danger to her is."

"It might be Russian sleeper agents, or it might be the U.S. government."

"It might be both. I just hope she's somewhere far away from both of them." None of what they had learned could tell them for sure if she was dead or alive, or if she had played any part in Novikov's murder. But between the contents of her bookshelf and the contents of her father's letter, Duran finally knew who had sent him his copy of *Ulysses* and why. Then it hit him; she *had* to be alive. He leapt off the couch and over to the bookshelf.

"Jackson, what is it?"

"Hang on." He scanned the spines of the books on the bottom shelf again. Irving, Goethe, Orwell, Thoreau, Thoreau, Heller, Irving, Steinbeck. *Irving, Goethe, Orwell, Thoreau, Thoreau, Heller, Irving, Steinbeck.* "Holy shit. Brett, call a cab for us and then get over here."

"What's wrong? Why are we leaving?"

"Nothing's wrong, but I have to show you something in my apartment. Call."

"Okay." Brett dialed, frightened of the excitement in Duran's voice. "They'll be out back in ten minutes."

"Good. Now come look at this." When Brett joined him at the bookcase, Duran pointed at the bottom shelf, moving his index finger over the spines of the books from left to right. Brett looked perplexed.

"What are we looking at?"

"It's a note."

"Inside one of those books?"

"Right in front of us."

"I don't understand."

"There are only eight books on this shelf, and these are the only ones she has in any kind of order." He pointed to the spines one at a time. "Irving, Goethe, Orwell, Thoreau, Thoreau, Heller, Irving, Steinbeck. I, G, O, T, T, H, I, S. *I got this!* It's a note. She's alive."

"Goddammit, Velma." Brett laughed and cried at the same time. "How the hell did you figure that out?"

Duran smiled. "I guess she and I think alike. Let's go wait for our cab. Bring the letter. And the absinthe."

Thirty-Three

When they arrived at his apartment, Duran offered Brett a seat on the couch and snatched the absinthe bottle from him.

"I got another message from her!" Duran called from the kitchen as he mixed two drinks. He stirred furiously, drowning the sound of his own voice in the clanking of the spoon against the glass. He carried the glasses out of the kitchen and watched the undissolved sugar still swirling in the drinks, making them look like polluted snow globes.

He handed Brett a glass of the cloudy, green combination of absinthe, water, and sugar, trying not to think about how much it looked like algae-filled pond water. He sat on a chair across from Brett and placed the book on the table between them.

"What's this?"

"It was sent to me from a bookshop in London. At first I had no idea who sent it or why. I called the shop and no one could tell me anything about it. Now I know it's from Velma, and it's part-gift, part-bribe."

"All she sent was a book?"

"My favorite book, *Ulysses* by James Joyce."

"This is the book she hid the letter in."

"It is. But I don't think that's why she sent it."

"Are you sure it's from her?"

"I'm positive. This isn't just any copy." He opened the front cover. "First illustrated edition from 1935. It's signed by James Joyce himself and by Henri Matisse. If she only wanted to lead us to the letter, she could have sent an eight-dollar paperback."

"You met her one time. Why would she send you this?"

"Like I said, it's part gift and part bribe. After the robbery, she asked me to keep quiet about the incident with the Tabasco bottle. I kept her secret for her, what I knew of it. I kept it out of the papers."

"How did she know…?"

"I said something about it when I was taking her statement. She has the same last name as the main character."

"Could she be leaving a trail?"

"No. You know her better than I do, but I think if she wanted to leave a trail, she would make it one we could follow. She's not leaving a trail, but she's sending a message."

Brett nodded. "So what does the book mean?"

"I don't know if you're a literary man. I don't know if you appreciate the value of what you see before you, but not only is *Ulysses* my favorite book, *that* particular copy of it is worth tens of thousands of dollars. It means Velma Bloom is alive and having me keep her secret is worth that much to her. She knew the Yonkers Police would be searching for her. She's thanking me for my silence and buying more of it. She doesn't know me well; all she knows about me is my favorite book and whatever that might tell her about me. This is the one way she knew to tell me how valuable my keeping her secret is. If the secret is safe, so is Velma. I'm not saying I'm not worried about her, but between this and the message on the bookshelf, I know for sure she does not want to be found." He took a sip, feeling some peace with the decision to stop looking for Velma Bloom. "You know, she's like Heisenberg's Uncertainty Principle made flesh. As long as we don't know where she is, we know she's safe."

"And if we did know where she was, we'd have no idea if she was safe. If we knew where she was, the wrong people probably would, too."

"Exactly, and we have no idea where she is. Something tells me she has everything under control."

"So what will you do now?"

"Drink. Then on Monday, I'll go back to work and hope another case comes along to distract me. What about you? Were you serious about a job at the CIA?"

Brett peered into his drink. "I don't know. All I know is someone out there wants to hurt the girl I love, and I can't let that happen."

"Do you trust her?"

"Yes."

"I do, too."

"Do you think she'll ever come back on her own?"

"She's the last remaining evidence of a Cold War black project. Coming back would be pretty fucking dangerous, but that doesn't mean she won't do it. What do you think?"

"I think she'll come home."

"I hope you're right. I want to thank her for the book, and we owe her a bottle of absinthe."

"She trusts you, Jackson. Will you keep her secret?"

"I will. And I need you to keep mine so I can keep my job. If or when she does come back, hopefully she and I can help each other. She has a superpower, and I have a badge." Duran raised his glass and smiled. "Empires have been destroyed by less."

Thirty-Four

Tuesday, April 22, 2008

A bright yellow Dodge Challenger sat on the side of a road in a well-kept, upper-middle-class neighborhood in White Plains. It was dark, so the car was not as conspicuous as it might have been. The woman in its driver's seat wore large black sunglasses, black gloves, and a scarf over her head. She watched the comings and goings of the people in the neighborhood, circling the block sometimes to look less suspicious. Finally, she saw the downstairs lights go out in a certain house.

When they had been out for about five minutes, Velma lifted her dark glasses onto her head so she could see and pulled her car closer to the front of the house in which she'd grown up. She got out of the car and removed a large cardboard box from the back seat. She carried the box to the front door and placed it on the doorstep. In the box were a case of twenty-four cans of wet cat food, a five-pound bag of dry cat food, a litter box, a small collection of cat toys, two small bowls, an up-to-date rabies vaccination certificate, and ten one-hundred-dollar gift cards to PetSmart.

She went back to the car and picked up a cat carrier off the front seat. She set it on the doorstep beside the box, then opened it and lowered her huge, dark sunglasses so she could cry behind them. A big orange cat with long hair and white paws stepped out and rubbed his body against her. She picked him up, and he rubbed his nose lovingly on her face. She kissed him on his fluffy orange head and then put him back in the carrier. After taking out the small bowls, she filled one with some dry food and emptied a bottle of water into the other. She hoped it wouldn't be too long before the Blooms found their new feline family member.

"You're going to like it here, Carrot. I promise you'll be happy. Franklin and Elizabeth are really good at being parents. I love them very, very much. You'll love them too." She dashed back to her car and drove away from White Plains for the last time.

Her second to last stop was a residential Yonkers neighborhood lined with aged and alternately dilapidated duplexes. Near one of the less dilapidated ones, she found a 1995 Cadillac

Eldorado. That car's sparkling white exterior was easy to spot on the dark street. She placed an envelope under one of the windshield wipers. In it was the broken neck of a Tabasco sauce bottle, its lid still screwed tightly onto the threads. If anyone found it aside from its intended recipient, they would have no idea what it meant. She hoped.

Her final stop was a place she had been before, but her car had not. She parked Smiley in front of 101 Forester Avenue. She was traveling light. All that remained for her to carry was a lightweight tote bag. She strapped it across her shoulder. It contained a passport, a British driver's license, an assortment of dollars, pesos, and francs totaling nine thousand nine hundred and ninety-nine dollars, and an additional ten thousand dollars distributed between twenty prepaid Visa cards. Three more with lower balances were tucked away in one of the bag's inside pockets. She would need to scan these at three separate airports to get her boarding passes. In another of the inside pockets was an envelope containing information on an offshore bank account under the name Daphne Kelly, a woman who would come into existence in just under three hours.

Velma got out of the car and placed the keys under the front passenger seat. She strapped on her tote bag and shut the Challenger's door with a gloved hand. She walked up the driveway and through the open garage door, then passed the navy blue Nissan and approached the house's side entrance. She knocked on the door.

"Oh, fuck!" She tried the knob and found the door unlocked. As soon as she opened it she heard a scream.

"Stop!" The voice was strained, and she heard faint coughing. "Take off your shoes."

"My shoes? Leo, where are you?"

"Take off your shoes. Come to the basement door. Do not come downstairs!"

Velma did as she was told and left her shoes in the garage. She dashed to basement. What she saw stopped her in the doorway.

"Velma. Do not come downstairs." Leo's voice came from a supine figure on the floor about six feet from the base of the steps. "Stay there. You mustn't leave tracks. There can be no sign you were here." His voice was strained, and he held his left hand over his stomach. The reservoir of blood on his torso drained down his sides and became part of an expanding puddle on the floor.

"Fuck, Leo! No!" She wanted rush to his side but was stopped by his warnings and her own shock.

Her gaze traveled away from Volkov's wound and over the space between them. A man's lifeless body was face down on the steps. His feet hung over the bottom step onto the floor. She couldn't see the man's face, but the hole in the back of his head told her he didn't have much of a face left. That didn't matter; she recognized him by his heavy jacket.

"Velma, stay. Do not move."

"Leo! Let me come help you!"

"No! You must stay alive. Get to the airport. Any way you can, get to the airport and get on the plane! I'm so sorry. I'm so sorry."

"Why? Sorry for what? Who is this guy?"

The dead man's arms were stretched out in front of him as though he were still reaching for his gun. The gun had fallen on the second stair from the top and rested near the center of the splatter created when a bullet exited near the top of the man's head. She could see small pink pieces of his brain close to where she was standing.

"It wasn't the CIA."

"Leo, what do you mean? What should I do? Please, tell me what I should do." She wanted to call 9-1-1, but she knew why she couldn't.

She wanted to hold his head in her lap and comfort him, but couldn't. She looked down at the steps again. The splatter of blood around the gun didn't move. There were red stripes from the gun and the splatter leading to the man's fingers. He must have been alive until he was almost out the door. He had been so close to escape, only to become an instant corpse. His body draped over the bottom of the steps, posed as though he still clung to the hope of climbing to safety.

"Velma, I want you to listen to me. You are going to the airport. You are going to run out of here and put on your shoes. You will not touch anything." Leo tried to lift his head, and a drop of blood seeped over his bottom lip. "You must move only between here and the side door. There can be no trace of you. I need you safe. You are the last one who can protect him."

"Protect who? Leo, please…"

"I am so sorry. Do not forgive me, just protect him."

"I don't understand. You have to tell me what you mean!"

"She knew too much. She knew…" Leo coughed and blood trickled down his chin. "She knew everything. I had to do it."

"Leo, please. Who are you talking about? Had to do what?"

"It wasn't the CIA. I am so sorry. Velma, you have to help me."

"Tell me what to do."

"Look down. Look at the gun. Do not touch it. Memorize where it is, the angle, the position. Print this picture in your head."

She did. The gun had a red outline, and she memorized its distance from the largest of the slimy pink scraps of the dead man's brain. "Okay."

"Pick up the gun."

"Pick up the gun!"

"Pick it up! Do not forgot the picture in your head. You are going to put it back. I told you to wear gloves. Are you wearing gloves?"

"Yes."

"Pick it up now!" His speech quickened as though he no longer cared about worsening his pain.

She lifted the gun. It was heavier than she thought it would be and had a long, black extension on the front of it. "Tell me what to do."

"Do you know how to use it?"

"Kind of? You point it at something you want dead?"

"The sights. Find the sights."

"Okay."

"Line up the sights. That is where the bullet will go."

"Do you want me to take this with me? I don't think…"

"No! Don't be stupid. You are going to put it back where you found it, in the place you memorized, after you shoot me."

"What? No, Leo, I can't, please don't ask me…"

"You are going to line up the sights and shoot me in the head. Otherwise it will take hours for me to die. This will be easy. I will not move. You can do it. I hit that man while he was moving." He summoned enough strength to lift his right hand off the floor and point to the dead man.

"You've been killing people for longer than I've been alive! That's not what I meant! I mean, you're my uncle. I can't shoot my uncle."

"You can, and you will."

"You saved my life. I never got to thank you. Not really." She started to cry. "You were going to take me to the airport. I was going to say thank you. For everything."

"Velma, you mustn't cry. I need your eyes clear. You can't miss."

"Don't make me."

"Save me from dying in pain with no dignity."

"How is there dignity in me shooting you in the head?"

"Because you are the only person who deserves to kill me."

She reared back. "What? Why?"

"I wronged you. I am sorry." He rolled his head to one side and spit out a mouthful of blood.

"Leo, how did you wrong me? I don't understand."

"You must stay alive. You must get to the airport. Get to London. Get to Mexico."

"I will, I promise. Just tell me what you mean, how did you wrong me? I owe you my life."

"Then you must do this for me. All I have done... I have done to atone."

"Atone for what?"

"I killed your mother. I killed Annalise." He tilted his head to rid himself of another mouthful of blood.

Alarm seized her chest as her insides twisted. It wasn't the grisly sight before her that churned her stomach, but the shock of his confession. Her mind was a cloud, and any thoughts and emotions she might have had disappeared into the fog. "But she died giving birth to me."

"I was there... in the hospital. I-I botched her epidural. She knew everything. I had to protect your father. Please..." He coughed, and this time blood came straight up out of his mouth like a geyser. "If it is you...that is the only way I can die with some peace. I don't need you to forgive me. Just stay alive."

"Oh, Leo." She used her sleeve to wipe away the tears fogging her vision. She lifted the gun and pointed it at Volkov.

"Velma." He strained his neck to look up at her as much as he could, and a river of blood rushed down his chin. "I did say thank you."

She lined up the sights and fired. His head collapsed. She stood at the top of the steps, unable to turn away from the scene in the basement. Blood oozed like syrup out of his wounds, flowing into stagnant puddles on the floor. She conjured up the image she had printed in her mind of where the gun laid and returned it to its resting place. She looked down. Everything in the basement was peaceful and still.

She was numb. There was information she needed to process, and there were feelings she needed to feel. But not now. One thought escaped the fog in her mind. She had to get out of the house.

She turned on her heels. She would have time to grieve later, but only if she made it to the airport. She ran.

Thirty-Five

Thursday, April 24, 2008

The woman who had abandoned the name Velma Bloom walked into a bookshop on Fulham Road in London. She had just eaten lunch at a nearby cafe, and no one seemed to suspect she was faking her English accent. She realized after departing that she had likely given herself away by committing the cultural faux pas of tipping over twenty percent. She hoped the waiter wasn't offended, but it didn't matter. She wouldn't be in town much longer.

"Pardon me," she approached a large counter in the front of the shop. "My name is Roxie Drake. I have an appointment."

"Yes, of course." The woman behind the counter pushed a button on her telephone console. "You'll be meeting with Mr. Pemberton, the owner of the shop. He wanted to meet with you in person, you know, after he heard what you were looking for."

"Miss Drake?" A man appeared from behind a massive bookshelf and greeted her.

She took a moment to react. It was the first time anyone had addressed her by that name. She realized now it could be a dangerous alias, but she had no choice but to embrace it. "Mr. Pemberton?"

"How do you do." They shook hands.

"How do you do," she replied, remembering that, in this country, the greeting was tantamount to hello and should not be inflected as a question.

"Please, let me take you to my office."

The woman who would be Roxie Drake until she left his shop followed Mr. Pemberton into a large, clean room with walls covered in books. "Please, sit. I know it's a bit early, but may I offer you some tea before we begin?"

"Thank you, no. I've just had lunch."

"Well, I am quite anxious to show you a few items in particular that I've selected for your consideration. I have nearly a dozen copies that may interest you. So I know where to begin, is there a particular edition you had in mind?"

"There is not. I am looking for something signed, if possible, and very old."

He laughed. "Very old is our specialty, Miss Drake. This is an antiquarian book shop."

"Something antiquarian in precisely what I'm after."

"That doesn't much narrow down your selection, I'm afraid." He laughed again. "When you phoned to make your appointment and I heard what you were looking for, I assumed you were a collector. You are not a collector, I take it?"

"No. This is to be a gift."

"A gift for a collector?"

"A policeman."

"Very well." He walked over to a small table on which he had arranged six books. "If you're looking for presentation, I've always thought the cover of this one was quite striking." He handed her a hardbound book with a gorgeous deep red spine on which *Ulysses* and J. Joyce were clearly printed in gold. "This is a tenth edition Paris printing from 1928."

"It's lovely. What would this one cost?"

"That book is five-hundred and twenty-five pounds." He spoke as though this was not a high number, but she took a moment to do a calculation in her head. The book would cost her over a thousand dollars.

She scanned the other books on the table. Some showed their age more than others. She knew the contents of each one was the same, so it felt appropriate to judge them by their covers. Mr. Pemberton allowed her to pick them up and examine them and delighted in telling her about each one as she did. He knew where and when each was printed, as well some additional history to which she paid little attention. The books came from all over Europe and dated back to as early as 1922. None of them impressed her enough.

"I really do think a signed copy would be the best gift, don't you?"

"Miss Drake, I mean you no offense, but as you are not a book collector, I must ask if you are aware of what a signed copy of this book will cost you."

"Quite a lot, I imagine."

Mr. Pemberton gingerly picked up a rather plain, off white copy she had ignored until now. "This is part of a two-volume set printed in 1933. You will find the signature of James Joyce on the title page." She opened the book as though it might crumble in her hands.

"It's quite a rare edition. At sixty-five hundred pounds, I believe it's the least expensive signed copy I have."

She handed the book back to him. "What if I told you I'm willing to spend quite a bit more?"

Mr. Pemberton maintained his composure, but his face gave away his excitement and intrigue. "I think you and I should have some tea and a chat." He got out a pen and paper and jotted something down, then reached for his phone and called the clerk. "Bring Miss Drake and me some tea, please. I have some books I would like brought in."

"You are very kind, Mr. Pemberton," said the woman who, for the moment, was Roxie Drake.

"I must apologize for my comments earlier, Miss Drake. You may not be a book collector, but your taste is quite exquisite."

"Thank you, but the person with exquisite taste is the one who will be receiving it. I want something grand looking and something rare. I'm willing to pay rather a lot for grandeur and rarity."

The clerk returned with a tray containing a teapot, two cups, a bowl of sugar, and a small pitcher of milk. Mr. Pemberton handed her the piece of paper he'd written on. She looked at it with shock, and then looked at the woman known as Roxie Drake. Her expression oozed disapproval.

"Are you sure?" She titled her head to Mr. Pemberton as though hoping what he wrote was a joke.

"I am. Fetch those for me, please." He nodded at the clerk and she departed. He poured each of them a cup of tea.

"Thank you so much."

"Miss Drake, forgive my impertinence, but I'm quite curious about something. I can't quite place your accent. Pardon me if I'm wrong, but you are not from London?"

"No, I'm from a bit west of here."

He sipped his tea and nodded. "Well, I think you will be most excited when you see what is being brought in."

He was right. Two clerks came in, each carrying what looked like a glass museum case. "Put those on my desk, please."

The clerks set them down and departed. Mr. Pemberton opened the cases. Each contained two copies of *Ulysses*. In one was a dark brown book with gilded accents and a larger blue book that appeared to be older.

In the other case was one with a beautiful royal blue cover and striking gold patterns on the spine and a lighter brown book with a ringed gold orb on the cover.

"Now, I am not going to tell you how much each of these books cost. Each is signed by James Joyce; each would make quite a magnanimous gift. Which, if you were to open a box and find it within, do you think would please you the most?"

"This one." She pointed to the light brown book with the golden orb. It was the only one with a design on the front cover, and it somehow struck her as being much more of a work of art than the others. "I fear that one is likely to be the most expensive."

"On the contrary. By far, the most expensive choice is this one." He indicated the larger blue book. "For the cost of this book, you could buy a rather nice house in some places. For the cost of the one beside it, you could attend Oxford twice over. The one you selected, you will be surprised to learn, is but a tenth of the price of the most expensive one. And yet, I believe it may be the most special." He took it out of the case. "Look inside."

She gasped. "Why, it's illustrated! These drawings... I can't take my eyes off them."

"Those are the work of Henri Matisse. Who, if you will look in the front, you will see has also signed the book."

"This is perfect. I'll take this one, please. I need it shipped to the United States."

"Certainly. Would you like to know the cost of the book, though? This one would equate to a rather nice car."

"While I appreciate the point of reference, Mr. Pemberton, will you kindly tell me the cost of this book in pounds so I can pay for it?"

"Sixteen thousand, two hundred and fifty pounds."

She quickly did a calculation in her head. Sixteen thousand two hundred and fifty pounds was a little over thirty thousand dollars. For Jackson Duran, she had that much to spare. She opened her purse and pulled out several bundles of money. To her, it was very unfamiliar money.

To Mr. Pemberton, the sight of it was enough to make him dart for his door and lock it. "Would you mind counting what you need, please? I'd like to peruse the drawings in this book a bit."

He sat at his desk and counted the money. He showed her that he had sixteen thousand two hundred and fifty pounds and returned the rest of the money to her along with a piece of paper and a pen. He looked at her with a curiosity that bordered on suspicion.

"If you would please write down for me the recipient's name and where you would like to have it shipped."

She wrote the name and the address of the Yonkers Police Station.

"Would you like to include a message?"

"No, the book alone is message enough. Now, I have a very important favor to ask. It is essential this gift remain anonymous. If this man were to phone, and I warn you he will, inquiring about who purchased it for him, it is imperative he not be told I was here."

"I will advise my staff to inform him that it was an online order and they cannot give out the name of the buyer, or to say they know nothing about it."

"Thank you, Mr. Pemberton. I should be most grateful for that."

"Miss Drake, you are an intriguing woman."

"Really?" She laughed. "You mean young women don't come into this shop and buy thirty-thousand-dollar books for policemen every day?"

She expected Mr. Pemberton to laugh with her, but he was silent. After a moment, she realized what she said and clasped her hand over her mouth.

"You did say you were from west of here. Quite far west, I see."

"Well, shit," said the voice of Velma Bloom.

"You needn't worry. As a wise businessman and an English gentleman, I value discretion, and I certainly wouldn't want to lose your business." His smile calmed her.

"Thank you. It is a relief to drop the accent."

"Roxie Drake is not your real name, is it?"

"It is today."

He stared at the piece of paper with the address. "Officer Jackson Duran must be quite extraordinary. He has exquisite taste."

"He certainly does. Most Americans don't."

Mr. Pemberton laughed. "I am a bit perplexed. I may be wrong, but I don't get the impression you know him terribly well, do you?"

"No."

"Yet here you are in my shop, spending the amount of money on a book for him that some people make in a year."

"He saved my life once. I'm not sure if he even realized it."

"That sounds like a fascinating story. I don't imagine you'll tell it to me, though."

"Truthfully, Mr. Pemberton, I would love to tell you that story, but I'm afraid you'd be disappointed, because I don't know how it ends."

Thirty-Six

January 2009
Isla Mujeres, Quintana Roo, Mexico

Robert Drake sipped a mojito, wishing it had less sugar in it. He imagined himself as Aragorn in *Lord of the Rings*, disguised as Strider, crouching in the corner of a bar, making sure the person he was watching would never look back at him. He smiled as he thought of this, but his smile faded. His smiles always faded quickly.

He wanted a different drink. He wanted straight vodka, or even tequila. Tequila would help him hide. Vodka might draw attention from the bartender. He had to wait for a server to walk close enough to him for him to order since he couldn't go up to the bar.

He waited with his acquired level of extraordinary patience, and watched with his well-developed skill for subtlety. The people in the bar were all foreign to him. Not because he was an American in Mexico, but because of the oppressive isolation he had endured over the past two decades. Many of his most prominent visual memories, at least those from his adult life, were of Russia, an apartment he hadn't redecorated since moving into it in the 1980s, and of the insides of underground laboratories. The places he knew were stuck in time, as stuck in time as he felt. He took in his surroundings, avoiding direct glances at the busty redhead behind the bar.

The tourists had all departed on their ferries back to Cancun for the day. The streets of Isla Mujeres once again belonged to its residents. Dogs and cats roamed the streets, seating themselves beside the outdoor tables of restaurants. Waiters cleared plates and gave the animals scraps of chicken, steak, and fish. People laughed with one another and delighted in the warm, late evening air. Women were given two drinks for the price of one. Bars were speckled with coarse salt, bitten lime wedges, and empty shot glasses.

The handsome stranger and the carefree, busty redhead caught each other's eyes. He admired the crease between her pale, sunburnt breasts as she leaned over the bar to remove some dirty glasses and wipe away the rings they left behind. She wasn't from here; that was certain. He too had fair skin and blue eyes, though his face was not as pink as hers. He had brown hair and a complexion less sensitive to the sun. Perhaps he just hadn't been in Mexico as long.

"Hoe-lah," the stranger said, taking a seat at the bar.

"*Hola*," she replied with a smile.

She spoke with no accent, as one who had learned Spanish as a second language so perfectly her inflection gave away nothing of her origin. He, however, spoke his one word greeting with the obvious accent of one native to the southern United States, who had a poor grasp of Spanish.

"It's okay," the barkeep continued in their native tongue. She leaned over and whispered to him with a wink. "You can speak English with me." She spoke with an unmistakable British accent.

He looked at her with surprise. "Well, don't I feel like a fool. You sound just like a proper lady in any language." He spoke like a true southern gentleman.

The bartender seemed to blush beneath her sunburnt face. "You're too kind. Can I get you something?"

"I would love a Sol, thank you kindly." He even pronounced the name of the beer like a *gringo*.

"*Sol*," she repeated back, pronouncing it almost too properly. She opened the beer bottle and placed it in front of him. "There we are. Have you missed your boat?"

"My boat? Oh, no ma'am. I'll be staying on this island for a spell. Cancun's too loud for me. Makes me nervous as a long-tailed cat on a porch full of rockers."

She cocked her head and looked at him for a moment with a quizzical expression. Then she laughed. "A long-tailed cat on a porch full of rockers?"

It sounded so funny in an English accent. He smiled back and looked down at the hand he had around the beer bottle, embarrassed.

"That's brilliant."

He chuckled, relieved, though perhaps still a bit intimidated by her. "Brilliant? I'm glad you think so." He took his right hand off the beer bottle and wiped the condensation onto his pant leg before reaching across the bar to make his formal introduction. "My name is Eric. Eric Thorn."

When she shook his hand she was gentle, but polite. "Daphne Kelly."

"I sure am glad to meet you, Daphne Kelly."

"It's a pleasure to meet you as well, Eric Thorn."

"When do you finish work, Daphne?"

"Well, I'm not sure. It gets busy in here around midnight. I'm sure you must have a clever expression for that," she said, flirtatious.

"You're as right as a ninety-degree angle, ma'am."

She rolled her eyes at him. "Mister Thorn, I'm sure you can do better than that!"

"Well, I'm sorry, Miss Kelly, let me try again. Sounds like around midnight it gets so crowded in here you're 'bout as busy as a stub-tailed cow in fly time."

Daphne paused and cocked her head again. A couple sat at the other end of the bar. She held up one finger, telling him she needed a moment. She went over to her new customers. She took their drink order in Spanish, and they exchanged a laugh. She turned around and muddled mint and sugar in two glasses.

After she served the couple their mojitos, she returned to him. "Cows use their tails to swat flies that land on their backs."

"Yes ma'am, they do." He brought his beer to his lips and drank deeply, all the while keeping his eyes locked with hers.

"Can you tell I'm blushing, Eric?"

"Yes, I can, Miss Daphne. Can you tell I like you?"

She turned around and opened the small refrigerator behind her. She took out a Sol, cracked it open, and put it down in front of Eric. "That one's from me. I can tell now that you've told me. Can you tell I like you?"

"Darlin', I can tell a lot of things." He downed what remained of his first beer. "I can tell you and I are both foreigners."

"Well, that one's easy. What else?"

"I can tell you don't mind me watchin' more than just those red curls bounce when you walk around."

"Why, Mr. Thorn, you were such a gentlemen until you said that!"

"I can tell you don't want me to be too much of a gentleman. I can also tell you're awful good at speaking Spanish. I bet you studied it real hard before you came here."

"Well, I certainly paid attention at university."

"But you ain't speaking Castilian Spanish, you're speaking Latin American Spanish. So I can tell that British accent of yours is 'bout as fake as the tits on a Las Vegas showgirl."

Daphne straightened and took a step back.

Eric grabbed her wrist. "It's okay, you ain't got to worry about me. I just want to get to know you. I don't care what you done or who you hidin' from, and you don't never have to tell me."

She pulled her wrist away, but didn't take her gaze from him.

He spoke again, and his Southern accent disappeared. "I just think the two of us might have a lot in common."

He lifted his beer bottle to take a sip, and a crack appeared in its side. He dropped the bottle as it split in his hand. Daphne handed him a clean towel. She put a shot glass on the bar between them and filled it to the brim with gold tequila. She raised it to her lips. Eric Thorn looked up from his puddle of beer and watched as she threw her head back and swallowed. She licked her lips and leaned toward him across the bar, locking her blue eyes with his.

Cold beer dripped from the bar onto his lap. Daphne moved her lips toward his ear and whispered to him in an American accent. "Not as much as you might think."

She didn't notice the man with graying red hair who watched her from across the room as she smiled and walked away.

~ * ~

We hope you enjoyed *Smile and Walk Away*. Visit Champagne Book Group (http://www.champagnebooks.com) and sign up for our newsletter to get advance notice of sales and special deals for newsletter subscribers, including chances to get advance copies of releases before the general reader public does.

About the Author

Danielle Riedel grew up just outside of Philadelphia. She attended Sarah Lawrence College in New York where she received a very diverse education.

Her studies included psychology, biology, philosophy, anthropology, and fiction writing. After graduating in 2004, she spent time as a bartender, a police cadet, a counselor, an actress, a waitress, and an author.

She currently resides in Phoenixville, Pennsylvania with her husband and two quirky orange cats. Her hobbies are classified.

Readers can find more about Danielle at:

Website: http://www.danielleriedel.com
Twitter: https://twitter.com/DanielleERiedel

Turn the page for a sneak peak at *Witch on Parole* by Kay Latour and available in August.

Witch on Parole
By Kay Latour

All Bryn ever wanted was to fit in, to be one of the respected professional thieves and never practice the magic that destroyed her mother. But her dreams crashed and cremated when she was captured on her first thieving mission. Incarcerated and paroled two months later, Bryn snatches at the chance of a new life.

But her corrupt parole officer won't let her. He has every intention of using her magic to suit his own dark plans. She finds herself wedged between a rock and a jail cell. Doing what he wants will cost her freedom and her newfound family. If she tells on him—no one will believe her. He's a respected supernatural corrections officer and she's—just a WITCH ON PAROLE.

Excerpt

Taking a deep breath, I tried to set the image in my mind as I had before, but the image was now fuzzy. I rotated my head attempting to crick my neck bones and get rid of that knot. Nothing. Not one crack. The knot stayed where it was as a throbbing reminder of my anxiety.

The stress I held ate at my pride. I had to conquer it. I had to. I focused harder on the image. This time I saw the molecules as little bits of sandpaper smoothing out lines. Yes. That it. I've got it. A clear solid image. *"Levo concedo ostendo."*

The potion turned a light lilac, just as Galeron's had. Awesome. Lilac is good. Then it turned purple. I held my breath as little tingles swirled around in my chest. But those tingles dropped to the floor when the mixture glowed a brownish red.

I stared at it. What happened? Did it work? The surface of the concoction moved. Yes. Moved. I couldn't tear my gaze away from it. I knew this was my first time doing this spell, but I was sure it wasn't supposed to move. Galeron's potion didn't move. Why was mine moving? The knot in my neck grew larger.

A bubble the size of a baseball rose out of the brownish red cream and popped, emitting a loud belch.

Did my potion burp? I was sure it wasn't supposed to burp either.

A pair of copper eyes attached to a russet-colored head pushed themselves out of the goo. The creature locked eyes with me. I blinked. It blinked back.

A split second later it let out a small roar. It flew out of the bowl, jumped up and latched onto me. Shocked, I didn't move. Didn't do anything. It rubbed my face with its flat paws.

"Ouch!" Damn. That hurts.

It's like it was sanding the skin right off my cheeks. I grabbed its small arms and forced it to stop. It was covered in gritty rust-colored sand. The whole time I was staring at it, it kept struggling to rub my face with its grainy paws. Sharp prickles of pain pulsed on my palms and fingers as its coarse dry skin wiggled under my grip. He was a strong little guy. He kept up his squirming and then managed to slip a sandy little paw past me and scratch my cheek again.

"Ow!" Geez.

Without thinking, I whipped him away from me. He soared through the air and landed on one of the loveseats in the sitting area of the kitchen. I watched, dumbfounded, as he picked himself up and rubbed the arm of the loveseat. He was going to town on it. He began shredding the upholstery. Bits and pieces of brown fabric sprinkled onto the wooden floor.

My heart pounded. I touched my throbbing cheek and came away with blood on my fingertips. It took me a moment to register what this meant, and it dawned on me. I created a sandpaper monster.

What am I going to do? What am I supposed to do? I stared at the blood on my hand. Not only was this little guy destructive, but he was also dangerous. Think, Bryn. Think.

The banishing spell.

That's it. I needed to banish his little sandpaper butt. I crept up on him slowly. I didn't want him to run away before I had the chance to say the spell. When I was about two feet away, I said, "*Pello pepulli pulsum.*"

The sandpaper dude kept on sanding. He didn't look up. Didn't even blink. By now he'd made a hole in the arm of the chair. The white stuffing and structural wood peeked through. Crap. Galeron's couch was wrecked, and it was my fault because I created this little guy. He shifted to the inside arm of the loveseat. His copper gaze darted between me and the part of the loveseat he was working on. Why hadn't he disappeared? I said the right spell words.

Running my hand over my ponytailed hair, I spotted the bowl of salt water. Oh man. I forgot to sprinkle him. I grabbed a cup from the right-hand side cupboard and dunked it into the salty water. I tiptoed toward him and flung the liquid.

But he was on to me now. He squeaked and dashed to the other end of the loveseat. The water rained onto the shredded arm of the couch. Nowhere near him. Wary of my intent, he kept his gaze on me as he continued to sand the other arm. If he was smart, he would have hidden. But I guess his need to scrub overpowered his need for safety. He stayed there. Sanding. Arms rotating in circular motions.

I grabbed another cup of salty water. He saw me coming, let out another squeak and scurried around the room. His need to survive kicked in. He shot under the round coffee table, skittered behind the other loveseat, and sailed around the triangle counter. I made tracks after him, sloshing some of the precious liquid onto the wooden floor as I ran.

He hightailed it toward the archway leading out of the kitchen. Panic stabbed at my heart as I bolted after him. I had to stop him before he escaped and sandpapered everything in town.

46495837R00126

Made in the USA
Middletown, DE
02 August 2017